1

Lotus Buds

by Amy Carmichael

Copyright © 7/15/2015
Jefferson Publication

ISBN-13: 978-1515090137

Printed in the United States of America

Contents

CHAPTER I

Lotus Buds

NEAR an ancient temple in Southern India is a large calm, beautiful pool, enclosed by stone walls, broken here and there by wide spaces fitted with steps leading down to the water's edge; and almost within reach of the hand of one standing on the lowest step are pink Lotus lilies floating serenely on the quiet water or standing up from it in a certain proud loveliness all their own.

We were travelling to the neighbouring town when we came upon this pool. We could not pass it with only a glance, so we stopped our bullock-carts and unpacked ourselves—we were four or five to a cart—and we climbed down the broken, time-worn steps and gazed and gazed till the beauty entered into us.

Who can describe that harmony of colour, a Lotus-pool in blossom in clear shining after rain! The grey old walls, the brown water, the dark green of the Lotus leaves, the delicate pink of the flowers; overhead, infinite crystalline blue; and beyond the old walls, palms.

With us was a young Indian friend. "I will gather some of the lilies for you," he said, with the quick Indian desire to give pleasure; but some one interposed: "They must not be gathered by us. The pool belongs to the Temple."

It was as if a stone had been flung straight at a mirror. There was a sense of crash and the shattering of some bright image. The Lotus-pool was a Temple pool; its flowers are Temple flowers. The little buds that float and open on the water, lifting young innocent faces up to the light as it smiles down upon them and fills them through with almost a tremor of joyousness, these Lotus buds are sacred things—sacred to whom?

For a single moment that thought had its way, but only for a moment. It flashed and was gone, for the thought was a false thought: it could not stand against this—"All souls are Mine."

All souls are His, all flowers. An alien power has possessed them, counted them his for so many generations, that we have almost acquiesced in the shameful confiscation. But neither souls nor flowers are his who did not make them. They were never truly his. They belong to the Lord of all the earth, the Creator, the Redeemer. The little Lotus buds are His—His and not another's. The children of the temples of South India are His—His and not another's.

So now we go forth with the Owner Himself to claim His own possession. There is hope in the thought, and confidence and the purest inspiration. And, stirred to the very depths, as we are and must be many a time when we see the tender Lotus buds gathered by a hand that has no right to them, and crushed underfoot; bewildered and sore troubled, as the heart cannot help being sometimes, when the mystery of the apparent victory of evil over good is overwhelming: even so there will be always a hush, a rest, a repose of spirit, as we stand by the Lotus-pools of life and seek in His Name to gather His flowers.

CHAPTER II

Opposites

BALA is nearly four. There are so many much younger things in the nursery, that Bala feels almost grown up: four will be quite grown up; it will be nice to be four. Bala takes life seriously, she has always done so; she thinks it would be monotonous to have too many frivolous babies. But Bala's eyes can sparkle as no other eyes ever do; and her mirth is something by itself, like a little hidden fountain in the heart of a wood, with the sweetness of surprise in it and very pure delight.

When Bala came to us first she was between one and two, an age when most babies have a good deal to say. Bala said nothing. She was like a book with all its leaves uncut; and some who saw her, forgetting that uncut books are sometimes interesting, concluded she was dull. "Quite a prosaic child," they said; but Bala did not care. There are some babies, like some grown-up people, who show all they have to show upon first acquaintance and to all. Others cover the depths within, and open only to their own. Bala is one of these; and even with her own she has seasons of reserve.

Her first remark, however, shown rather than said, was not romantic. She was too old for a bottle, and she seemed to feel sore over this. But she noted the time the infants were fed, and followed the nurses about while they were preparing the meal; and when they sat down to give it, each to her respective baby, Bala would choose the one of most uncertain appetite, and sit down beside it and wait. There was an expression on her face at such times which suggested a hymn, set it humming in one's head in fact, in spite of all efforts to escape it. More than once we have caught ourselves singing it, and pulled up sharply: "Even me! Even me! Let some droppings fall on me."

"God's Fire."
Taken on the bank of the Red Lake, near Dohnavur.

Most of our family remind us very early that they trace their descent to the mother of us all. Bala, on the contrary, was good: so we almost forgot she was human, and began to expect too much of her; but she got tired of this after a while, and one day suddenly sinned. The surprise acted like "hypo," and fixed the photograph.

The place was the old nursery, which has one uncomfortably dark corner in it. Something had offended Bala; she marched straight into that corner and stamped. We can see her—poor little girl—as she rumpled her curls with both her hands, and flashed on the world a withering glance. "Scorn to be scorned by those I scorn" was written large all over the indignant little face.

After this shock we were prepared for anything, but nothing special happened; only when the demands made upon her are unreasonable, then Bala retires into herself and turns upon all foolish insistence a face that is a blank. If this point is passed, the dark eyes can flash. But such revealings are rare.

When Bala was something under three, she was very tender-hearted. One evening, after the first rains had flooded the pools and revived the mosquitoes, the nursery wall was the scene of many executions; and Bala could not bear it. "Sittie, don't kill the poor pûchies!" she said pitifully; and Sittie, much touched, stopped to comfort and explain. The other babies were delighting in the slaughter, pointing out with glee each detested "pûchie"; but Bala is not like the other babies. Later, the ferocious instinct common to most young animals asserted itself in a relish for the horrible, which rather contradicted the mosquito incident. Bala visibly gloats over the gory head of Goliath, and intensely admires David as he operates upon it. Her favourite part of the story about his encounter with the lion is the suggestive sentence, "I caught him by the beard"; and Bala loves to show you exactly how he did it. But then that is different from seeing it done; and after all it is only a story, and it happened long ago.

God's Fire

I have told how the ignorant once called Bala prosaic. Bala knows nothing of poetry, but is full of the little seeds of that strange and wonderful plant; and the time to get to know her is when the evening sky is a golden blaze, or glows with that mystic glory which wakens something within us and makes it stir and speak.

"God has not lighted His fire to-night," she said wistfully one evening when the West was colourless; but when that fire is lighted she stands and gazes satisfied. "What does God do when His fire goes out?" was a question on one such evening, as the mountains darkened in the passing of the after-glow; and then: "Why does He not light it every night?"

"Amma! I have looked into Heaven!" she said suddenly to me after a long silence. "I have seen quite in, and I know what it is like." "What is it like? Can you tell me?" and the child's voice answered dreamily: "It was shining, very shining." Then with animation, in broken but vivid Tamil: "Oh, it was beautiful! all a garden like our garden, only bigger, and there were flowers and flowers and flowers!"—here words failed to describe the number, and a comprehensive sweep of the hand served instead. "And our dolls can walk there. They never can down here, poor things! And Jesus plays with our babies there" (the dear little sisters who have gone to the nursery out of sight, but are unforgotten by the children). "He plays with Indraneela—lovely games."

"What games, Bala?" I asked, wondering greatly what she would say. There was a long, thoughtful pause, and Bala looked at me with grave, contented eyes:—

"New games," she said simply.

Bala's opposite is Chellalu. We never made any mistake about her. We never thought her good. Not that she is impossibly bad. She was created for play and for laughter, and very happy babies are not often very wicked; but she is so irrepressible, so hopelessly given up to fun, that her kindergarten teacher, Rukma, smiles a rueful smile at the mention of her name. For to Chellalu the most unreasonable thing you can ask is implicit obedience, which unfortunately is preferred by us to any amount of fun. She will learn to obey, we are not afraid about that; but more than any of our children, her attitude towards this demand has been one of protest and surprise. She thinks it unfair of grown-up people to take advantage of their size in the arbitrary way they do. And when, disgusted with life's dispensations, she condescends to expostulate, her "Ba-a-a-a" is a thing to affright. But this is the wrong side of Chellalu, and not for ever in evidence. The right side is not so depressing.

7

It is a brilliant morning in late November. The world, all washed and cooled by the rains, has not had time to get hot and tired, and the air has that crystal quality which is the charm of this season in South India. Every wrinkle on the brown trunks of the trees in the compound, every twig and leaf, stands out with a special distinctness of its own, and the mountains in the distance glisten as if made of precious stones.

The Blameless Chellalu

Suddenly, all unconscious of affinity or contrast, a little person in scarlet comes dancing into the picture, which opens to receive her, for she belongs to it. Her hands are full of Gloriosa lilies, fiery red, terra-cotta, yellow, delicate old-rose and green—such a mingling of colour, but nothing discordant—and the child, waving her spoils above her head, sings at the top of her voice something intended to be the chorus of a kindergarten song:—

Oh, the delight of the glorious light!
The joy of the shining blue!
Beautiful flowers! wonderful flowers!
Oh, I should like to be you!

"But, Chellalu, where did you get them?" for the lilies in the garden are supposed to be safe from attack. Chellalu looks up with frank, brown eyes. "For you!" she says briefly in Tamil; but there is a wealth of forgiveness in the tone as she offers her armful of flowers. Chellalu wonders at grown-up hearts which can harbour unworthy suspicions about blameless little children. As if she would have picked them!

"But, Chellalu, where did you get them?" and still looking grieved and surprised and forgiving, Chellalu explains that yesterday evening the elder sisters went for a walk in the fields, and brought home so many lilies, that after all just claims were met there were still some over—an expressive gesture shows the heap—so Chellalu thought of her Ammal (mother) and went and picked out the best for her. Then by way of emphasis the story is attempted in English: "Very good? Yesh. Naughty? No. Kindergarten room want flowers? No. I" (patting herself approvingly) "very good; yesh." With Chellalu, speech is a mere adjunct to conversation, a sort of footnote to a page of illustration. The illustration is the thing that speaks. So now both Tamil and English are illuminated by vivid gesture of hands, feet, the whole body indeed; curls and even eyelashes play their part, and the final impression produced upon her questioner is one of complete contrition for ever having so misjudged a thing so virtuous.

"AIYO!"

(Fingers and toes curled in grieved surprise.)
"Did you think I would have done it?"

But Chellalu wastes no sympathy upon herself. She is accustomed to be believed; and perfectly happy in her mind, casts a keen glance round, for who knows what new delights may be somewhere within reach! "Ah!"—the deep-breathed sigh of content—is always a danger signal where this innocent child is concerned. I turn in time to avert disaster, and Chellalu, finding life dull with me, departs.

Then the little scarlet figure with its crown of careless curls scampers across the sunny space, and dives into the shadow of a tree. There it stays. Something arresting has happened—some skurry of squirrel up the trunk, or dart of lizard, or hurried scramble of insect, under cover out of reach of those terrible eyes. Or better still, something is "playing dead," and the child, fascinated, is waiting for it to resurrect. And then the song about the lilies begins again, only it is all a jumble this time; for Chellalu sings just as it comes, untrammelled by thoughts about sequence or sense, and when she forgets the words she calmly makes them up. And I cannot help thinking that Chellalu is very like

9

her song; here is an intelligible bit, a line or two in order, then a cheerful tumble up, and an irresponsible conclusion. The tune too seems in character—"Speed, bonnie boat, like a bird on the wing"; the swinging old Jacobite air had fitted itself to a nursery song about the brave fire-lilies, and something in its abandon to the happy mood of the moment seems to express the child.

It is not easy to express her. "If you had to describe Chellalu, how would you do it?" I asked my colleague this morning, hoping for illumination. "I would not attempt it! Who would?" she answered helpfully.

Only More So

"Chellalu! Oh, you need ten pairs of eyes and ten pairs of hands, and even then you could never be sure you had her"—this was her nurse's earliest description. She was six months old then, she is three and three-quarters now; but she is what she was, "only more so."

Before Chellalu had a single tooth she had developed mother-ways, and would comfort distressed babies by thrusting into their open mouths whatever was most convenient. At first this was her own small thumb, which she had once found good herself; but she soon discovered that infants can bite, and after that she offered rattle-handles. Later, she used to stagger from one hammock to another and swing them. And often, before she understood the perfect art of balance, she would find herself, to her surprise, on the floor, as the hammock in its rebound knocked her over. She felt this ungrateful of the baby inside; but she seemed to reflect that it was young and knew no better, for she never retaliated, but picked herself up and began again. These hammocks, which are our South Indian cradles, are long strips of white cotton hung from the roof, and they make delightful swings. Chellalu learned this early, and her nurse's life was a burden to her because of the discovery.

"She could walk before she could stand"—this is another nursery description, and truer than it sounds. Certainly no one ever saw Chellalu learning to walk. She was a baby one day, rapid in unexpected motion, but only on all fours; the next day—or so it seems, looking back—she was everywhere on her two feet. "Now there will be no place where she won't be!" groaned the family, the first time she was seen walking about with an air of having done it all her life. And appalling visions rose of Chellalu standing on the wall of the well looking down, or sitting in the bucket left by some careless water-drawer just on the edge of the wall, or trying to descend by the rope.

Before this date such diversions as the classic Pattycake had been much in favour. Chellalu's Attai (the word here and hereafter signifies Mrs. Walker, "Mother's elder sister") had taught it to her; and whenever and wherever Chellalu saw her Attai, she immediately began to perform "Prick it and nick it" with great enthusiasm. But after she could walk, Chellalu would have nothing more to do with such childish things. "Show us Edward Rajah!" the older children would say; and instead of standing up with a regal dignity and crowning her curls with the appropriate gesture, Chellalu would merely look surprised. They had forgotten. She was not a baby now. Such trifles are for babies.

CHAPTER III

The Scamp

"PAT-A-CAKE is a thing of the past, but the stage from the highest point of view is still distinctly attractive"; so decided Chellalu, and resolved to devote herself thenceforth to this new and engrossing pursuit. She chose the scene of her first public performance without consulting us. It was the open floor of the church, on a Sunday morning, in the midst of a large congregation. This was how it happened.

Chellalu's Attai, who in those days was unaware of all the painful surprises in store, had taken her to morning service, and allowed her to sit beside her on the mat at the back of the church. All through the first part of the service Chellalu was good; and as the sermon began, she was forgotten. In our church we sit on the floor, men on one side, women and children on the other. A broad aisle is left between, and the Iyer (Mr. Walker), refusing to be boxed up in the usual manner, walks up and down as he preaches. This interested Chellalu.

That morning the sermon was to children, and the subject was "Girdles." The East of this ancient India is the East to which the prophet spoke by parable and picture; and, following that time-worn path, the preacher pictured the parable of Jeremiah's linen girdle: the attention of the people was riveted upon him, and no one noticed what was happening on the mat at the end of the church. Only we, up at the front with all the other children, saw, without being able to stop it, the dreadful pantomime. For Chellalu, wholly absorbed and pleased with this unexpected delight, first stood on the mat and acted the girdle picture; then, growing bolder, advanced out into the open aisle, and, following the preacher's gestures, reproduced them all exactly. It was a moment of tension; but if ever a child had a good angel in attendance, Chellalu has, for something always stops her before the bitter end. I forget what stopped her then; something invisible, and so, doubtless, the angel. But we did not breathe freely till we had her safe at home.

CHELLALU, WATCHING THE PICTURE-CATCHER WITH SOME SUSPICION.
"Whatever is he doing with that black box?"

Chellalu's visible angel is the gentle Esli, a young convert-helper, of a meek and lowly disposition. At first sight nothing seems more unsuitable, for Chellalu needs a firm hand. But firmness without wisdom would have been disastrous; so as we had not the perfect combination, we chose the less dangerous virtue, and gave the nursery scamp to the gentlest of us all. Sometimes, to tell the whole unromantic truth, we have been afraid less Esli was spilling emotion in vain upon this graceless soul; and we have suggested an exchange of angels—but somehow it has never come to pass. Once we almost did it. For a noise past all bounds called us down to the nursery, and we found the cause of it in a huddled heap in the corner. "Chellalu! what is the matter?" Only the softest of soft sobs, heard in the silence that followed our advent, and one round shoulder heaved, and the curly head went down on the arm in an attitude of woe. Now this is not Chellalu's way at all. Soft sobbing is not in her line; and I turned to the twenty-nine children now prancing about in unholy glee, and they shouted the explanation: "Oh, she is Esli Accal! She was very exceedingly naughty. She would not come when Accal called; she raced round the room so fast that Accal could not catch her, and then she jumped out of her cumasu" (the single small garment worn), "and ran out into the garden! And Esli Accal sat down in a corner and cried. And Chellalu is Esli Accal!"

Their Real Use

But the pet opportunity in those glad days was when some freak of manner in friend or visitor suggested a new game. We used to wish, sometimes, that these kind people understood how much pleasure they were giving to the artless babe who was studying them with such interest, while they, all unconscious of their real use, imagined probably she was thinking of nothing more serious than sweets. After an hour in the bungalow, Chellalu would wander off, apparently because she was tired of us, but really because she was full of a new and original idea, and wanted an audience. Once she puzzled the nursery community who had not been visiting the bungalow, by mincing about on pointed toes, with shoulders shrugged like a dancing master in caricature. The babies thought this a very nice game, and for weeks they played it industriously.

Chellalu talked late—she has long ago made up for lost time—but she was never at a loss for an answer to a question which could be answered by action. "Who is in the nursery now?" we asked her one afternoon when she had escaped before the tea-bell, that trumpet of jubilee to the nursery, had rung. She smiled and sat down slowly, and then sighed. Another sigh, and she proceeded to perform her toilet. When the small hands went up to the head with an action of decorously swinging the back hair up and coiling it into a loose knot, and when a spasmodic shake suggested it must be done over again, there was no doubt as to who was in charge. No one but the excellent Pakium, one of our earlier workers, ever did things quite like this. No one else was so ponderous. No one sighed in that middle-aged manner, no one but Pakium. We never could blame Pakium for Chellalu's escape. As well blame a mature cat for the escapades of her kitten. Chellalu, watching for a clue as to her fate, would sigh again profoundly. It was never easy to return her.

"OH, IT'S A JOKE!"

We were not sorry when this phase passed into something safer for herself, though perhaps not so charming to the public. Chellalu at two and three-quarters had surgical ambitions. Medical work she considered slow. She liked operations. Her first, so far as we know, was performed upon the unwilling eye of a smaller and weaker sister. "Lie down!" she had commanded, and the patient had lain down. "Open your eyes!" At this point the victim realised what she was in for, and her howls brought deliverance; but not before Chellalu had the agitated baby's head in a firm grip between her knees, and holding the screwed-up eye wide open with one hand, was proceeding to drop in "medicine" with the other. Mercifully the medicine was water.

Thwarted in this direction, Chellalu applied herself to bandaging. She would persuade someone to lend her a finger or a toe; the owner was assured it was sore—very sore. She would then proceed to bandage it to the best of her ability. But all this was mere play. What Chellalu's soul yearned for was a real knife, or even only a needle, provided it would prick and cause red blood to flow. Oh to be allowed to operate properly, as grown-up people do! Chellalu had seen them do it—had seen thorns extracted from little bare feet, and small sores dressed; and it had deeply interested her. The difficulty was, no one would offer a limb. She walked up and down the nursery one morning with a bit of an old milk tin, very jagged and sharp and inviting, and secreted in her curls was a long, bright darning needle; but though she took so much trouble to prepare, no one would give her a chance to perform, and Chellalu was disgusted. Someone who did not know her suggested she should perform on herself. This disgusted her still more. Do doctors perform on themselves!

Yesh: No

Chellalu's latest phase introduces the kindergarten. For an educational comrade, perceiving our defects in this direction, furnished a kindergarten for us, and gave us a kind push-off into these pleasant waters; so the little boat sails gaily, and the children at least are content.

Chellalu has never been so keen about this institution as the other babies are. "Do you like the kindergarten?" some one asked her the other day; and she answered with her usual decision: "Yesh. No." We thought she was talking at random, and tested her by questions about things which we knew she liked or disliked. But she was never caught. "Well, then, don't you like the kindergarten?" "Yesh. No." It was evident she knew what she meant, and said it exactly. Bits of it she likes, other bits she thinks might be improved. The trouble is that she has an objection to sitting in the same place for more than a minute at longest. Other babies, steady, mature things of five, are already evolving quite orderly sentences in English—the language in which the kindergarten is partly taught—and we feel they are getting on. Chellalu never stops long enough to evolve anything, and yet she seems to be doing a little. From the first week she has talked all she knew in unabashed fashion. "Good morning very much" was an early production; and it was followed by many oddments forgotten now, but comical in effect at the time, which perhaps may explain the otherwise inexplicable fact that she sometimes learns something.

One only of those early dashes into the unexplored land is remembered, because it enriched us with a new synonym. It was at afternoon tea that a sympathetic Sittie (the word means "Mother's younger sister"), knowing that Chellalu had received something thoroughly well earned, asked her in English: "What did Ammal give you this morning?" Chellalu caught at the one familiar word in this sentence (for the babies learn the names of the flowers in the garden before they are troubled with lesser matters), and she answered brightly: "Morning-glory!" So Morning-glory has become to us an *alias* for smacks.

This same Morning-glory is the subject of one of the kindergarten songs. For after searching through two or three hundred pages of nursery rhymes, and interviewing many proper kindergarten songs, we found few that belonged to the Indian babies' world; and so we had to make them for ourselves. These songs are about the flowers and the birds and other simple things, and are twittered by the tiniest with at least some intelligence, which at present is as much as we can wish. All the babies sing to the flowers, but it is Chellalu who gives them surprises. One day we saw her standing under a bamboo arch, covered with her favourite Morning-glory. She had two smaller babies with her, one on either side. "Amma! *Look!*" she called; but italics are inadequate to express the emphasis. "Look, Morning—glory—kissing—'chother," and she pointed with eagerness to the nestling little clusters of lilac, growing, as their pretty manner is, close to each other. Then, seizing each of the babies in a fervent and somewhat embarrassing embrace, she hugged and kissed them both; and finally wheeling round on the flowers, addressed them impressively: "For—all—loving—little—Indian—children—want—to—be—like—you."

CHAPTER IV

The Photographs

"THAT THING AGAIN!" (*Page 28*.)

I DO not know how they will strike the critical public, but the photos are so much better than we dared to expect, that we are grateful and almost satisfied. Of course, they are insipid as compared with the lively originals; but the difficulty was to get them of any truthful sort whatsoever, for the babies regarded the photographer—the kindest and mildest of men—with the gravest suspicion: and the moment he appeared, little faces, all animation before, would stiffen into shyness, and the light would slip out of them, and the naturalness, so that all the camera saw, and therefore all it could show, was a succession of blanks.

Then, too, when our artist friend was with us we were in the grasp of an epidemic of cholera. Morning and evening, and sometimes into the night, we were tending the sick and dying in the village; and in the interval between we had little heart for photographs. But the visit of a real photographer is a rare event in Dohnavur, and we forced ourselves to try to take advantage of it. Remembering our difficulties, we wonder we got anything at all; and we hope that stranger eyes will be kind.

PYÂRIE AND VINEETHA.

"Do smile, you little Turk!"

Often when we looked at the pretty little reversed picture in the camera, with its delicate colouring and the grace of movement, we have wished that we could send it as we saw it, all living and true. The photos were taken in the open air; underfoot was soft terra-cotta-coloured sand; overhead, the cloudless blue. In such a setting the baby pictures look their brightest, something very different from these dull copies in sepia. An Oriental scene in print always looks sorry for itself, and quite apologetic. It knows it is almost a farce, and very flat and poor.

17

Then there were difficulties connected with character. Our photographer was more accustomed to the dignified ways of mountains than to the extremely restless habit of children; and he never could understand why they would not sit for him as the mountains sat, and let him focus them comfortably. The babies looked at things from an opposite point of view, and strongly objected to delays and leisureliness of every description. Sometimes when the focussing process promised to be much prolonged, we put a child we did not wish to photograph in the place of one upon whom we had designs, and then at the last moment exchanged her. But the baby thus beguiled seemed to divine our purpose; and, resenting such ensnarements, would promptly wriggle out of focus. It was like trying to observe some active animalculæ under a high power. The microscope is perfect, the creatures are entrapped in a drop of water on the slide; but the game is not won by any means. Sometimes, after spoiling more plates than was convenient, our artist almost gave up in despair; but he never quite gave up, and we owe what we have to his infinite patience.

The Bête Noir

Pyârie was the most troublesome of these small sitters, though she was old enough to know better. My mother was with us when she came to us, a tiny babe and very delicate. She had loved her and helped to nurse her, and so we wanted a happy photograph for her sake; but nothing was further from Pyârie's intentions, and instead of smiling, she scowled. Our first attempt was in the compound, where a bullock-bandy stood. Pyârie and Vineetha, a little girl of about the same age, were very pleased to climb over the pole and untwist the rope and play see-saw; but when the objectionable camera appeared, they stared at it with aversion, and no amount of coaxing would persuade Pyârie to smile. "Can't you do something to improve her expression?" inquired the photographer, emerging from his black hood; then someone said in desperation: "*Do* smile, you little Turk!" Vineetha, about whose expression we were not concerned, obediently smiled; but Pyârie looked thunderclouds, and turned her head away. She was caught before she turned, poor dear, so that photograph was a failure.

Once again our kind friend tried. This time he gave her a doll. Pyârie is most motherly. She is usually tender and loving with dolls, and we hoped for a sweet expression. But in this we were disappointed. She accepted the doll—a beautiful thing, with a good constitution and imperturbable temper; and she looked it straight in the face—a rag face painted—smiling as we wanted her to smile. Then she smote it, and she scolded it, and called for a stick and whacked it, and called for a bigger stick and repeated the performance. Finally she stopped, laid the doll upon the step, sat down on it, and smiled. But she was hopelessly out of focus by this time, and it was weary work getting her in. She smiled during the process in a perfectly exasperating manner, but the moment all was ready she suddenly wriggled out; and when invited to go in again, she shook her head decidedly, and pointing to the camera with its glaring glass eye, covered at that moment with its cloth, she remarked, "Naughty! Naughty!" and we had to give her up.

"DISGUSTING!" SHE REMARKED IN EXPLICIT YOUNG TAMIL, AND LOOKED DISGUSTED.

"Perhaps she would be happier in someone's arms," next suggested the long-suffering artist; and so one morning, just after her bath, she was caught up, sweet and smiling, and played with till the peals of merry laughter assured us of an easy victory. But the camera was no sooner seen stalking round to the nursery, than suspicions filled Pyârie's breast. That thing again! And the photograph taken under such circumstances is left to speak for itself. Why did it follow her everywhere? Life, haunted by a camera, was not worth living—in which sentiment some of us heartily concur.

I want a birthday

Once an attempt was made when Pyârie and two other little girls were busily playing on the doorstep. Pyârie soon perceived and expressed her opinion about the fraud—for the camera's stealthy approach could not be kept from the children. "Disgusting!" she remarked in explicit young Tamil, and looked disgusted. The photograph which resulted was perfect in detail of little rounded limb and curly head, but it was lamentable as regards expression; so once more our persevering friend tried to catch her unawares. He showed us the result at breakfast in the shape of a negative which we recognised as Pyârie. He seemed very pleased. "Look at the pose!" he said. There was pose certainly, but where was the smile? Pyârie's one idea had evidently been to ward off something or someone; and our artist explained it by saying that in despair of getting her quiet for one second, he had directed his servant to climb an almost overhanging tree, and the child apparently thought he was going to tumble on the top of her, and objected. "I got another of her smiling beautifully, but the plate is cracked," we were told, after the table had admired the pose. That is a way plates have. The one you most want cracks.

19

"'LOOK AT THE POSE!'
He said. There was pose, certainly, but where was the smile?" (_Page 28._)

Poor little Pyârie; we sometimes fear lest her "pose" should be too true of her. She takes life hardly, and often protests. "_I_ want a birthday!"—this was only yesterday, when everyone was rejoicing over a birthday jubilation. Pyârie alone was sorrowful. She stood by her poor little lonely self, with her head thrown back and her mouth wide open, and her tears ran into her open mouth as she wailed: "Aiyo! Aiyo! (Alas! Alas!) _I_ want a birthday!"

But she is such a loving child, so loyal to her own and so unselfish to all younger things, that we hope for her more than we fear. And yet underneath there is a fear; and we ask those who can understand to remember this little one sometimes, for the world is not always kind to its poor little foolish Pyâries.

I am writing in the afternoon, and two little people are playing on the floor. One has a picture-book, and the other is looking eagerly as she turns the pages and questions: "What is it? What is it?" I notice it is always Pyârie who asks the question, and Vineetha who answers it: "It is a cow. It is a cat." "Why don't you let Vineetha ask you what it is?" I suggest; but Pyârie continues as before: "What is it? What is it?" varied by "What colour is it? What shape is it? Who made it?" and the mischief in her eyes (would that our artist could have caught it!) explains the game. It is decidedly better to be teacher than scholar, because suitable questions can cover all ignorance. Pyârie has not been to the kindergarten of late, and has reason to fear Vineetha is somewhat ahead of her; so she ignores my proposals, and continues her safe questions. We sometimes think we shall one night be heard talking in our sleep, and the burden of our conversation will be always— "What is it? What colour is it? What shape is it? Who made it?"

CHAPTER V

Tara and Evu

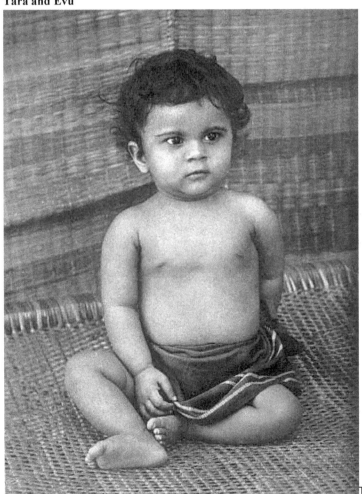

TARA.

OUR nurseries are full of contrasts, but perhaps the two who are most unlike are the little Tara and Evu, aged, at the hour of writing, three years and two and a half. I am hammering at my typewriter, when clear through its metallic monotony comes in distinct double treble, "Amma! Tala!" "Amma! Evu!" They always announce each other in this order, and with much emphasis. If it is impossible to stop, I give them a few toys, and they sit down on the mat exactly opposite my table and play contentedly. This lasts for a short five minutes; then a whimper from Tara makes me look up, and I see Evu, with a face of more mischief than malice, holding all the toys—Tara's share and her own—in a tight armful, while Tara points at her with a grieved expression which does not touch Evu in the least. A word, however, sets things right. Evu beams upon Tara, and pours the whole armful into her lap. Tara smiles forgivingly, and returns Evu's share. Evu repentantly thrusts them back. Tara's heart overflows, and she hugs Evu. Evu wriggles out of this embrace, and they play for another five minutes or so without further misadventure.

Only once I remember Evu sinned beyond forgiveness. The occasion was Pyârie's rag-doll of smiling countenance, which had been badly neglected by the family. But Tara felt for it and loved it. She was small at the time, and the doll was large, and Tara must have got tired of carrying it; but she would not tell it so, and for one whole morning she staggered about with the cumbersome beauty tilted over her shoulder, which gave her the appearance of an unbalanced but very affectionate parent.

This was too much for Evu, to whom the comic appeals much more than the sentimental. She watched her opportunity, and pounced upon the doll. Tara gave chase; but Evu's fat legs can carry her faster than one would suppose, and Tara's wails rose to a shriek when across half the garden's width she saw that ruthless sinner swing her treasure round by one arm and then deliberately jump on it. It was hours before Tara recovered.

Such a breach of the peace is happily rare; for the two are a pretty illustration of the mutual attraction of opposites. At this moment they are playing ball. This is the manner of the game: Tara sits in a high chair and throws the ball as far as she can. Evu dashes after it like an excited kitten, and kitten-wise badly wants to tumble over and worry it; for it is made of bits of wool, which, as every sensible baby knows, were only put in to be pulled out. She resists the temptation, however, and presents the ball to Tara with a somewhat inconsequent "Tankou!" "Tankou!" returns Tara politely, and tosses the ball again. This time Evu sits down with her back to Tara, and proceeds to investigate the ball. It is perfectly fascinating. The ends are all loose and quite easily pulled out. Evu forgets all about Tara in her keen desire to see to the far end of this delight. "Evu!" comes from the chair in accents of dignified surprise. "Tala!" exclaims Evu abashed, and hurries up with the ball. "Tankou!" she says as before, and Tara responds "Tankou!" This is an integral part of the game. If either forgets it, the other corrects her by remarking inquiringly, "Tankou?" whereupon the echo replies in a tone of apology, "Tankou!"

Devotions

Both these babies are devout, as most things Indian are. But Evu cannot sit still long enough to be promoted to go to church; and perhaps this is the reason why in religious matters Tara takes the lead, for she does go to church. In secularities it is always Evu who initiates, and Tara admiringly follows. The ball game was exceptional only because Evu prefers the *rôle* of kitten to that of queen.

This little characteristic is shown in common ways. The two are sitting on your knee entirely comfortable and content. The prayer-bell rings. Down struggles Tara. "To prayers I must go!" she says with decision in Tamil. "Evu too," urges Evu, also in Tamil. "Tum!" says Tara in superior English, and waits. Evu "tums," and they hastily depart.

Or it is the time for evening hymns and good-night kisses. We have sung through the chief favourites, ending always with, "Jesus, tender Shepherd." "Now sing, 'Oh, luvvly lily g'oing in our garden!'" This from Tara. Echo from Evu: "Yes; 'Oh, luvvly lily g'oing in our garden!'" You point out to the garden: "It is dark, there are no lovely lilies to be seen; besides, that is not exactly a hymn; shall we have 'Jesus, tender Shepherd,' again, and say good-night?" But this is not at all satisfactory. Tara looks a little hurt. "Tender Shepperd, *no!* Oh, luvvly lily!" Evu wonders if we are making excuses. Perhaps we have forgotten the tune, and she starts it:—

Oh, lovely lily,
Growing in our garden,
Who made a dress so fair
For you to wear?
Who made you straight and tall
To give pleasure to us all?
Oh, lovely lily,
Who did it all?

Oh, little children,
Playing in our garden,
God made this dress so fair
For us to wear.
God made us straight and tall
To give pleasure to you all.
Oh, little children,
God did it all.

Then Tara smiles all round, and you are given to understand you have earned your good-night kisses. Evidently to Tara at least there is a sense of incompleteness somewhere if the lovely lilies are excluded from the family devotions.

To Tara and to Evu, as to most babies, the garden is a pleasant place. But when they grow up and make gardens, they will not fill them with forbidden joys as we do. One of the temptations of life is furnished by inconsiderate ferns, which hold their curly infant fronds just within reach. Then there are crotons, with bright leaves aggressively yellow and delightful, and there are "tunflowers"; and the babies think us greedy in our attitude towards all these things. The croton was especially alluring; and one day Tara was found tiptoe on a low wall, reaching up with both hands, eagerly pulling bits of leaf off. She was brought to me to be judged; and I said: "Poor leaves! Shall we try to put them on again?" And hand in hand we went to the garden, and Tara tried. But the pulled-off bits would not fit on again; and Tara's face was full of serious thought, though she said nothing. Next day she was found on the same low wall, reaching up tiptoe in the same sinful way to the shining yellow leaves overhead. Quite suddenly she stopped, put her hands behind her back, and never again was she known to pick croton leaves to pieces.

The same plan prevailed with the ferns. The poor little crumples of silver and green moved her to pity, and she left them to uncurl in peace when once she had tried and sadly failed to help them. But the sunflowers' feelings did not affect her in quite the same way. The kind we have in abundance is that little dwarf variety with a thin stalk, and a cheerful face which smiles up at you even after you behead it, and does not seem to mind. Tara was convinced such treatment did not hurt them. They would stop smiling if it did. But one day she suddenly seemed to feel a pang of compunction, for she looked at the little useless heads and sighed. I had suggested their being fitted on again, as with the croton leaves and ferns. But this idea had failed; and what worked the change I know not, for Tara never told. But "tunflowers" now are left in peace so far as she is concerned; and she is learning to pick the free grasses and wild-flowers, which happily grow for everybody, and to make sure their stalks are long enough to go into water, which is the last thing untutored babies seem to think important.

Tara's Way

There is much to be done for all our children, but perhaps for Tara especially, if she is to grow up strong in soul to fight the battles of life. We felt this more than ever on the day of our last return from the hills, after nearly seven weeks' absence. On the evening when we left them, we had gone round the nurseries after the little ones had fallen asleep, and said goodbye to each of them without their knowing it; but when we came to Tara's mat, and kissed the little sleeping face, she stirred and said, "Amma!" in her sleep; and we stole away fearing she should wake and understand. Now in the early morning we were home again, and all the children who were up were on the verandah to welcome us, each in her own way. It was Tara's way which troubled us.

At first most of the babies were shy, for six weeks are like six years to the very young; but soon there was a general rush and a thoroughly cheerful chatter. Tara did not join in it. She stood outside the little dancing dazzle of delight—the confusion of little animated coloured dots is rather like the shake of a kaleidoscope—and she just looked and looked. Then, as we drew her close, the little hands felt and stroked one's face as if the evidence of eye and ear were not enough to make her sure beyond a doubt that her own had come back to her; and then, as the assurance broke, she clung with a little cry of joy, and suddenly burst into tears.

If only we could hold her safe and sheltered in our arms for ever! How the longing swept through one at that moment: for the winds of the world are cold. But it cannot be, it should not be, for such love would be weak indeed. Rather do we long to brace the gentle nature so that its very sensitiveness may change to a tender power, and the fountain of sweet waters refresh many a desert place. But who is sufficient for even this? Handle the little soul carelessly, harden rather than brace, misinterpret the broken expression, misunderstand the signs—and the sweet waters turn to bitterness. God save us from such mistake!

We covet prayer for our children. We want to know that around them all is thrown that mysterious veil of protection which is woven out of prayer. We need prayer, too, for ourselves, that our love may be brave and wise.

Kittenhood

Evu's disposition is different. It would not be easy to imagine Evu overcome by her feelings as Tara was at that hour of our return. One cannot imagine a kitten shedding tears of joy; and Evu is a kitten, a dear little Persian kitten, with nothing worse than mischief at present to account for. Of that there is no lack. "Oh, it is Evu!" we say, and everyone knows what to expect when "it is Evu." Evu's chief sentiment that morning, so far as she expressed it, was rather one of wonder at our ignorant audacity. "You vanished in the night when we were all asleep, and now you suddenly drop from the skies before we are properly awake, and expect us all to begin again exactly where we left off. How little you know of babies!" Doubtless this sentence was somewhat beyond her in language; but Evu is not dependent on language, and she conveyed the sense of it to us. She backed out of reach of kisses, and stood with a small finger upraised; much as a kitten might raise its paw in mock protest to its mother. She soon made friends, however, and proved herself an affectionate kitten, though wholly unemotional.

When Tara is naughty, as she is at times, like most people of only three, a reproachful look brings her spirits down to the lowest depths of distress. Evu is more inclined to hold up that funny little warning first finger, and shake it straight in your face. This, at two and a half, is terrible presumption; but the brown eyes are so innocent, you cannot be too shocked. Sometimes, however, the case is worse, and Evu tries to sulk. She sits down solemnly on the ground, and throws her four fat limbs about in a dreadful recklessness, supposed to strike the grown-up offender dumb with awe and penitence. Sometimes she even tries to put out her lower lip, but it was not made a suitable shape, for it smiles in spite of itself; and then there is a sudden spring; and two little arms are round your neck, and you are being told, if you know how to listen, what a very tiresome thing it is to feel obliged to sin. Then, with the comforting sense of irresponsible kittenhood fully restored, Evu discovers some new diversion, and you find yourself weakly wishing kittens need not grow into cats.

CHAPTER VI

Principalities, Powers, Rulers

IT may seem a quick transition from nursery to battle-field; but rightly to understand this story, it must be remembered that our nursery is set in the midst of the battle-field. It is a little sheltered place, where no sound of war disturbs the babies at their play, and the flowers bloom like the babies in happy unconsciousness of battles, and make a garden for us and fill it full of peace; but underlying the babies' caresses and the sweetness of the flowers there is always a sense of conflict just over, or soon coming on. We "let the elastic go" in the nursery. We are happy, light-hearted children with our children; sometimes we even wonder at ourselves; and then remember that the happiness of the moment is a pure, bright gift, not meant to be examined, but just enjoyed, and we enjoy it as if there were no battles in the world or any sadness any more.

And yet this book comes hot from the fight. It is not a retrospect written in the calm after-years, when the outline of things has grown indistinct and the sharpness of life is blurred. There is nothing mellowed about a battle-field. Even as I write these words, the post comes in and brings two letters. One tells of a child of twelve in whom the first faint desires have awakened to lead a different life. "She is a Temple girl. Pray that she may have grace to hold on; and that if she does, we may be guided through the difficult legal complications. Poor little girl! It makes one sick to think of her spoiled young life!" The other is a Tamil letter, about another child who is in earnest, so far as the writer can ascertain, to escape from the life planned out for her. She learned about Jesus at school, and responded in her simple way; but was suddenly taken from school, and shut up in the back part of the house and not allowed to learn any more. "Like a little dove fluttering in a cage, so she seemed to me. But she is a timid dove, and the house is full of wickedness. How will she hold out against it? By God's grace I was allowed to see her for one moment alone. I gave her a little Gospel. She kissed it with her eyes" (touched her eyes with it), "and hid it in her dress."

Only a little while ago we traced a bright young Brahman girl to a certain Temple house, and by means of one of our workers we made friends with her. The child, a little widow, was ill, and was sent to the municipal hospital for medicine. It was there our worker met her, and the child whispered her story in a few hurried words. She had been kidnapped (she had not time to tell how), and shut up in the Temple house, and told she must obey the rules of the house and it was useless to protest. "If we could help you," she was asked, "would you like to come to us?" The child hesitated—the very name "Christian" was abhorrent to her—but after a moment's doubt she nodded, and then slipped away. Our worker never saw her again. The conversation must have been noticed by the child's escort, and reported. She was sent off to another town, and all attempts to trace her failed.

"The Great"

And the god to whom these young child-lives are dedicated? In South India all the greater symbols of deity are secluded in the innermost shrine, the heart of the Temple. In our part of the country the approach to the shrine is always frequented by Brahman priests, who would never allow the foreigner near, even if he wished to go near. "Far, far! remove thyself far!" would be the immediate command, did any polluting presence presume to draw near the shrine. There are idols by the roadside, and these are open to all; but they are lesser creations. The Great, as the people call that which the Temple contains, is something apart. It is to these—The Great—that little children are dedicated; the whole Temple system is worked in their name.

"Have you ever seen the god to whom your little ones would have been given?" is a question we are often asked; and until a few days ago we always answered, "Never." But now we have seen it, seen it unexpectedly and unintentionally, as we waited for an opportunity to talk to the crowds of people who had assembled to see it being ceremonially bathed. We cannot account for our being allowed to see it, except by the fact that the Brahmans had withdrawn for the moment, and we being, as our custom is, in Indian dress, were not noticed in the crowd.

Near the place where the idol was being bathed, with much pomp by the priests, was a little rest-house, where we had waited till some child told us all was over. Then we came out and mingled with the throng, not fearing they would misunderstand our motive. While we talked with them, the Brahmans, who had been bathing in the river after the water had been sanctified by the god, began to stream up the steps and pass through the crowd, which opened respectfully and made a wide avenue within itself: for well the smallest child in that crowd understood that no touch might defile those Brahmans as they walked, wringing out their dripping garments and their long black hair.

How we searched the faces as they passed!—sensual, cynical, cold faces, faces of utter carelessness, faces full of pride and aloofness. But there were some so different—earnest faces, keen faces, faces sensitive and spiritual. Oh, the pathos of it all! How our hearts went out to these, whose eager wistfulness marked them out as truly religious and sincere! How we longed that they should hear the word, "Come unto Me, and I will give you rest"! They passed, men young and old, women and children, and very many widows; and then suddenly two palanquins which had been standing near were carried down to the awning where the idol had been bathed; and before we realised what was happening, they passed us. In the first was the disk, the symbol of the god; in the second, the god itself.

"We wrestle not against flesh and blood; but against principalities, against powers, against the rulers of the darkness of this world, against spiritual wickedness in high places"—this was the word that flashed through us then. That small, insignificant, painted, and bejewelled image, in its gaudy little palanquin, was not only that. It was the visible representative of Powers.

We thought of a merry child in our nursery who was dedicated at birth to this particular Power. By some glad chance that little girl was the first to run up to us in welcome upon our return home in the evening. We thought of her with thankfulness which cannot be expressed; but the sorrow of other children bound to this same god swept over us as we stood gazing after the palanquins, till they became a coloured blur in the shimmering sunshine. There was one such, a bright little child of eight, who was in attendance upon an old blind woman belonging to that Temple. "Yes," she had answered to our distressed questions, "she is my adopted daughter. Should I not have a daughter to wait upon me and succeed me? How can I serve the god, being blind?" We thought of another, only six, who was to be given to the service "when she was a suitable age." Her parents were half-proud and half-ashamed of their intention; and when they knew we were aware of it, they denied it, and we found it impossible to do anything.

"Only as Souls"

We turned to the people about us. They were laughing and chatting, and the women were showing each other the pretty glass bangles and necklets they had bought at the fair. Glorious sunshine filled the world, the whole bright scene sparkled with life and colour, and all about us was a "lucid paradise of air." But "only as souls we saw the folk thereunder," and our spirit was stirred within us. There is something very solemn in such a scene—something that must be experienced to be understood. The pitiful triviality, the sense of tremendous forces at work among these trivialities; the people, these crowds of people, absorbed in the interests of the moment—and Eternity so near; all this and much more presses hard upon the spirit till one understands the old Hebrew word: "The burden which the prophet did see."

Does this sound intolerant and narrow, as if no good existed outside our own little pale? Surely it is not so. We are not ignorant of the lofty and the noble contained in the ancient Hindu books; we are not of those who cannot recognise any truth or any beauty unless it is labelled with our label. We know God has not left Himself without witnesses anywhere. But we know—for the Spirit of Truth Himself has inspired the description—how desolate is the condition of those who are without Christ. We dare not water down the force of such a description till the words mean practically nothing. We form no hard, presumptuous creed as to how the God of all the earth will deal with these masses of mankind who have missed the knowledge of Him here; we know He will do right. But we know, with a knowledge which is burnt into us, how very many of the units live who compose these masses. We know what they are missing to-day, through not knowing our blessed Saviour as a personal, living Friend; and we know what it means to the thoughtful mind to face an unknown to-morrow.

A Hindu in a town in the northern part of our district lay dying. He knew that death was near, and he was in great distress. His friends tried to comfort him by reminding him of the gods, and by quoting stanzas from the sacred books; but all in vain. Nothing brought him any comfort, and he cried aloud in his anguish of soul.

Then to one of the watchers came the remembrance of how, as a little lad, he had seen a Christian die. In his desperation at the failure of all attempts to comfort the dying man, he thought of this one little, far-back memory; and though he could hardly dare to hope there would be much help in it, he told it to his friend. The Christian was Ragland, the missionary. He was living in a little house outside the town, when a sudden hæmorrhage surprised him, and he had no time to prepare for death. He just threw himself upon his bed, and looking up, exclaimed, "Jesus!" and passed in perfect peace. Outside the window was a little Hindu boy, unobserved by any in the house. He had climbed up to the window, and, leaning in, watched all that happened, heard the one word "Jesus," saw the quick and peaceful passing; and then slipped away unnoticed.

The dying Hindu listened as his friend described it to him. And this little faint ray was the only ray of comfort that lightened the dark way for him.

Compare that experience with this:—

"Oh for a Love——"

The missionary to whom this tale was told by the Hindu who had tried to console his dying friend, was himself smitten with dangerous illness, and lay in the dim borderland, unable to think or frame a prayer. Then like the melody of long familiar music, without effort, without strain, came the calming words of the old prayer: "Lighten our darkness, we beseech Thee, O Lord; and by Thy great mercy defend us from all perils and dangers of this night; for the love of Thine only Son, our Saviour, Jesus Christ."

Could any two scenes present a more moving contrast? Could any contrast contain a more persuasive call?

As we went in and out among the crowd, there were many who turned away uninterested; but some listened, and some sat down by the wayside to read aloud, in the sing-song chant of the East, the little booklets or Gospels we gave them. We, who are constantly among these people, feel our need of a fresh touch, as we speak with them and see them day by day. We need renewed compassions, renewed earnestness. It is easy to grow accustomed to things, easy to get cool. We pray not only for those at home, who as yet are not awake to feel the eloquence and the piteousness of the great "voiceless silence" of these lands, but we pray for ourselves with ever deepening intensity:—

Oh for a love, for a burning love, like the fervent flame of fire!
Oh for a love, for a yearning love, that will never, never tire!
Lord, in my need I appeal unto Thee;
Oh, give me my heart's desire!

CHAPTER VII

How the Children Come

THEY come in many ways through the help of many friends. We have told before how our first two babies came to us through two pastors, one in the north, the other in the south of our district. Since then many Indian pastors and workers, and several warm-hearted Christian apothecaries and nurses in Government service, have become interested; with the result that little children who must otherwise have perished have been saved.

One little babe, who has since become one of our very dearest, was redeemed from Temple life by the wife of a leading pastor, who was wonderfully brought to the very place where the little child was waiting for the arrival of the Temple people. We have seldom known a more definite leading. "I being in the way, the Lord led me," was surely true of that friend that day, and of other Indian sisters who helped her. Later, when she came to stay with us, she told us about it. "When first I heard of this new work, I was not in sympathy with it. I even talked against it to others. But when I saw that little babe, so innocent and helpless, and so beautiful too, then all my heart went out to it. And now——" Tears filled her eyes. She could not finish her sentence. Nor was there any need; the loving Indian heart had been won.

My mother was with us when this baby came; and she adopted her as her own from the first, and always had the little basket in which the baby slept put by her bedside. When the mosquitoes began to be troublesome, the basket was slipped under her own mosquito net, lest the little pink blossom should be disturbed. But the baby did not thrive at first; and the pink, instead of passing into buff, began to fade into something too near ivory for our peace of mind. It was then the friend who had saved the little one came to stay with us; and she proposed taking her and her nurse out to her country village, in hopes of getting a foster-mother for her there. So my mother, the pastor's wife, the baby, and her nurse, went out to the Good News Village, and stayed in the pastor's hospitable home. The hope which had drawn them there was not fulfilled; but the memory of that visit is fresh and fragrant. We read of alienation between Indian Christians and missionaries. We are told there cannot be much mutual affection and contact. We often wonder why it should be so, and are glad we know by experience so little of the difficulty, that we cannot understand it. We have found India friendly, and her Christians are our friends. In these matters each can only speak from personal experience. Ours has been happy. There may be unkindness and misunderstanding in India, as in England; but nowhere could there be warmer love, more tender affection.

All sorts of people help us in this work of saving the children. Once it was a convert-schoolboy who saw a widow with a baby in her arms. Noticing the bright large eyes, and what he described as the "blossoming countenance of the child," he got into conversation with the mother, and learned that she had been greatly tempted by Temple women in the town, who had admired the baby and wanted to get it. "If I give her to them, she will never be a widow," was the allurement there. The bitterness of widowhood had entered into her soul, and poisoned the very mother-love within her; and yet there was something of it left, for she did not want her babe to be a widow. The boy, with the leisureliness of the East, dropped the matter there; and only in a casual fashion, a week or so later, mentioned in a letter that he had seen this pretty child, and that probably, the mother would end in yielding to the temptation to give her to the Temple—"but it may be by the grace of God that you will be able to save her." We sent at once to try to find the mother; but she had wandered off, and no one knew her home. However, the boy was stirred to prayer, and we prayed here; and a search through towns and villages resulted at last in the mother being traced and the child being saved.

The Talk on the Verandah

Christian women have helped us. One such, sitting on her verandah after her morning's work, heard two women in the adjoining verandah discuss the case of a widow who had come from Travancore with a bright little baby-girl, whom she had vowed she would give to one of our largest temples. The Christian woman had heard of the Dohnavur nurseries, and at once she longed to save this little child, but hardly knew how to do it. She feared to tell the two women she had overheard their conversation, so in the simplicity of her heart she prayed that the widow might be detained and kept from offering her gift till our worker, old Dévai, could come; and she wrote to old Dévai.

Happily Dévai was at home when the letter reached her; otherwise days would have been lost, for her wanderings are many. She went at once, and found the mother most reasonable. Her idea had been to acquire merit for herself, and an assured future for her child, by giving it to the gods; but when the matter was opened to her, she was willing to give it to us instead. In her case, as in the other, our natural instinct would have been to try to make some provision by which the mothers could keep their babies; but it would not have been possible. The cruel law of widowhood had begun to do its work in them. The Temple people's inducements would have proved too much for them. The children would not have been safe.

Once it was a man-servant who saved a lovely child. He heard an aside in the market which put him on the track. The case was very usual. The parents were dead, and the grandmother was in difficulties. For the parents' sake she wanted to keep the dear little babe; but she was old, and had no relatives to whose care she could commit it. Mercifully we were the first to hear about this little one; for even as a baby she was so winning that Temple people would have done much to get her, and the old grandmother would almost certainly have been beguiled into giving her to them. How often it has been so! "She will be brought up carefully according to her caste. All that is beautiful will be hers, jewels and silk raiment." The hook concealed within the shining bait is forgotten. The old grandmother feels she is doing her best for the child, and the little life passes out of her world.

"It is a dear little thing, and the man (its grandfather) seemed really fond of it. He said he would not part with it; but its parents are both dead, and he did not know what might happen to it if he died." This from the letter of a fellow-missionary, who saved the little one and sent her out to us, is descriptive of many. "Not the measure of a rape-seed of sleep does she give me. I have done my best for her since her mother died, but her noise is most vexatious." This was a father's account of the matter only a week or two ago. "Have you no women relations?" we asked him. "Numerous are my womenfolk, but they are all cumbered with children: how can they help me?"

Not Waifs and Strays

Given these circumstances of difficulty, and the strong under-pull of Temple influence—is it wonderful that many an orphaned babe finds her way to the Temple house? For in the South the child of the kind we are seeking to save is never offered to us because there is no other place where she is wanted. Everywhere there are those who are searching for such children; and each little one saved represents a counter-search, and somewhere, earnest prayer. The mystery of our work, as we have said before, is the oftentimes apparent victory of wrong over right. We are silent before it. God reigns; God knows. But sometimes the interpositions are such that our hearts are cheered, and we go on in fresh courage and hope.

Among our earliest friends were some of the London Missionary Society workers of South Travancore. One of these friends interested her Biblewomen; and when, one morning, one of these Biblewomen passed a woman with a child in her arms on the road leading to a well-known Temple, she was ready to understand the leading, and made friends with the mother. She found that even then she was on her way to a Temple house. A few minutes later and she would not have passed her on the road.

There was something to account for this directness of leading. At that time we had our branch nursery at Neyoor, in South Travancore, ten miles from the place where the Biblewoman met the mother. On that same morning, Ponnamal, who was in charge there, felt impelled to go to the upper room to pray for a little child in danger. She remained in prayer till the assurance of the answer was given, and then returned to her work. That evening a bandy drove up to the nursery, and she saw the explanation of the pressure and the answer to the prayer. A little child was lifted out of the bandy, and laid in her arms. She stood with her nurses about her, and together they worshipped God.

This prayer-pressure has been often our experience when special help is needed to effect the salvation of some little unknown child. It was our Prayer-day, July 6, 1907. Three of us were burdened with a burden that could not be lightened till we met and prayed for a child in peril. We had no knowledge of any special child, though, of course, we knew of many in danger. When we prayed for the many, the impression came the more strongly that we were meant to concentrate upon one. Who, or where, we did not know.

Five days later, a letter reached us from a friend in the Wesleyan Mission, working in a city five hundred miles distant. The letter was written on the 8th:—

"On the morning of the 6th, a woman who knows our Biblewomen well, told them of a little Brahman baby in great danger; so J. and two others went at once and spent the greater part of the morning trying to save the child. It was in the house of a so-called Temple woman, who had adopted it, and she had taken every care of it. For some reason she wanted to go away, and could not take it with her. Two or three women of her own kind were there and wanted it. One had money in her hand for it. But J. had already got the baby into her arms, and reasoned and persuaded until the woman at last consented. They at once brought it here. Had the friendly woman not told J., the baby would now be in the hands of the second Temple woman. I visited the woman afterwards. She had two grown girls in the room with her, the elder such a sweet girl. She told me openly it was all according to custom, and that God had arranged their lives on those lines, and they could not do otherwise. It is terribly sad, and such houses abound."

"Father, we adore Thee"

Happenings of this sort—if the word "happen" is not irreverent in such a connection—have a curiously quieting effect upon us. We are very happy; but there is a feeling of awe which finds expression in words which, at first reading, may not sound appropriate; but we write for those who will understand:—

Oh, fix Thy chair of grace, that all my powers
May also fix their reverence ;. . .
Scatter, or bind, or bend them all to Thee!
Though elements change and Heaven move,
Let not Thy higher court remove,
But keep a standing Majesty in me.

FOOTNOTE:

"Overweights of Joy."

CHAPTER VIII

Others

STURDY AND STOLID, AND LITTLE VEERA

—whose story, however, is different.

WE have some children who were not in Temple danger, but who could not have grown up good if we had not taken them. "If peril to the soul is of importance," wrote the pastor who sent us two little girls, "then it is important you should take them": so we took them. These little ones were in "peril to the soul," because their nominal Christian mother had, after her husband's death, married a Hindu, against the rules of her religion and his. The children were under the worst influence; and both were winning little things, who might have drifted anywhere. We have found it impossible to refuse such little ones, even though danger of the Temple kind may not be probable.

Such a child, for example, is the little girl the Moslem is ready to adopt and convert to the faith. Our first redeemed from this captivity (literally slavery under the name of adoption) was a cheerful little person of six, with the sturdy air the camera caught, and a manner all her own. An American missionary in an adjoining district heard of her and her little sister, and wrote to know if we would take them if he could save them. We could not say No; so he tried, and succeeded in getting the elder child; the little one had been already "adopted," and he could not get her. "The whole affair was the most astonishing thing I have ever seen in India," he wrote when he sent the little girl. The child upon arrival made friends with another, and confided to her in a burst of confidence: "Ah, she was a jewel, my own little sister—not like me, not dark of skin, but 'fair' and tender; and the great man in the turban saw her and desired her, and he took her away; and she cried and cried and cried, because she was only such a very little girl."

"The business was being discussed out in the open street"—the writer was another missionary—"the pastor heard of it from a Christian who was passing, and saw the cluster of Muhammadans round the mother and her children. It was touch-and-go with the child." These two, Sturdy and Stolid, side by side in the photograph, are in all ways quite unlike the typical Temple child; but the danger from which they were delivered is as real, and perhaps in its way as grave.

We know what her Heart is Saying

One of the sweetest of our little girls, a child with a spiritual expression which strikes all who see her, came to us through a young catechist who heard of her and persuaded her people to let her come to Dohnavur. She is an orphan; and being "fair" and very gentle, needed a mother's care. Her nearest relatives had families of their own, and were not anxious for this addition to their already numerous daughters; and the little girl, feeling herself unwanted, was fretting sadly. Then an offer came to the relations—not made expressly in words, but implied—by which they would be relieved of the responsibility of the little niece's future. All would not have been straight for the child, however, and they hesitated. The temptation was great; and in the end it is probable they would have yielded, had not the catechist heard of it, and influenced them to turn from temptation. It was the evening of our Prayer-day when the little Pearl came; and when we saw the sweet little face, with the wistful, questioning eyes like the eyes of a little frightened dog taken away alone among strangers, and when we heard the story, and knew what the child's fate might have been, then we welcomed her as another Prayer-day gift. We do not look for gratitude in this work; who does? But sometimes it comes of itself; and the grateful love of a child, like the grateful love of a little affectionate animal lifted out of its terror and comforted, is something sweet and tender and very good to know. The Pearl says little; but her soft brown eyes look up into ours with a trustful expression of peaceful happiness; and as she slips her little hand into ours and gives it a tight squeeze, we know what her heart is saying, and we are content.

Two more of these "others" are the two in the photograph who are playing a pebble game. Their parents died leaving them in the care of an aunt, a perfectly heartless woman whose record was not of the best. She starved the children, though she was not poor; and then punished them severely when, faint with hunger, they took food from a kindly woman of another caste. Finally she gave them to a neighbour, telling her to dispose of them as she liked.

About this time our head worker, Ponnamal, was travelling in search of a child of whom we had heard in a town near Palamcottah. She could not find the child, and, tired and discouraged, turned into the large Church Missionary Society hall, where a meeting was being held to welcome our new Bishop. As Ponnamal was late, she sat at the back, and could not hear what was going on; so she gave herself up to prayer for the little child whom she had not found, and asked that her three days' journey might not be all in vain.

32

PEBBLES.

As she prayed in silence thus, another woman came in and sat down at the back near Ponnamal. When Ponnamal looked up, she saw it was a friend she had not met for years. She began to tell her about her search for the child; and this led on to telling about the children in general, and the work we were trying to do. The other had known nothing of it all before; but as she listened, a light broke on her face, and she eagerly told Ponnamal how that same morning she had come across a Hindu woman in charge of two little girls. The Tamils when they meet, however casually, have a useful habit of exchanging confidences. The woman had told Ponnamal's friend what her errand was. Ponnamal's talk about children in danger recalled the conversation of the morning. In a few hours more Ponnamal was upon the track of the Hindu woman and her two little charges. It ended in the two little girls being saved.

CHAPTER IX

Old Dévai

SHE has been called "Old Dévai" ever since we knew her, twelve years ago; and she is still active in mind and body. "As I was then, even so is my strength now for war, both to go out and to come in," she would tell you with a courageous toss of the old grey head. Her spirit at least is untired.

We knew her first as a woman of character. One Sunday, in our Tamil church, a sermon was preached upon the love of the Father as compared with the love of the world. That Sunday Dévai went home and acted upon the teaching in such fashion that she had to suffer from the scourge of the tongue in her own particular world. But she went on her way, unmoved by adverse criticism. Some years later, when we were in perplexity as to how to set about our search for children in danger of being given to temples, old Dévai offered to help. She was peculiarly suitable, both in age and in position, for this most delicate work; and we accepted her offer with thanksgiving. Since then she has travelled far, and followed many a clue discovered in strange ways and in strange company. Perhaps no one in South India knows as much as Dévai knows about the secret system by which the Temple altars are supplied with little living victims; but she has no idea of how to put her knowledge into shape and express it in paragraph form. We learn most from her when she least knows she is saying anything interesting.

When first we began the work, our great difficulty was, as it is still, to get upon the track of the children before the Temple women heard of them. Once they were known to be available, Temple scouts appeared mysteriously alert; and it is doubly difficult to get a little child after negotiations have been opened with the subtle Temple scout. How often old Dévai has come to us sick at heart after a long, fruitless search and effort to save some little child who, perhaps, only an hour before her arrival was carried off in triumph by the Temple people! "I pursued after the bandy, and I saw it in the distance; but swiftly went their bullocks, and I could not overtake it. At last they stopped to rest, and I came to where they were. But they smiled at me and said: 'Did you ever hear of such a thing as you ask in foolishness? Is it the custom to give up a child, once it is ours?'" Sometimes a new story is invented on the spot. "Did you not know it was my sister's child; and I, her only sister, having no child of my own, have adopted this one as my own? Would you ask me to give up my own child, the apple of my eye?" Oftener, however, the clue fails, and all Dévai knows is that the little one is nowhere to be found. Once she traced it straight to a Temple house, won her way in, and pleaded with tears, offering all compensation for expenses incurred (travelling and other) if only the Temple woman would let her take the child. But no: "If it dies, that matters little; but disgrace is not to be contemplated." When all else fails, we earnestly ask that the little one in danger may be taken quickly out of that polluted atmosphere up into purer air; and it is startling to note how solemnly the answer to that prayer has come in very many instances.

The Knock at Night

The clue for which we are always on the watch is often like a fine silk thread leading down into dark places where we cannot see it, can hardly feel it; it is so thin a thread. Sometimes, when we thought we held it securely, we have lost it in the dark.

Sometimes it seems as if the Evil One, whose interest in these little ones may be greater than we know, lays a false clue across our path, and bewilders us by causing us to spend time and strength in what appears to be a wholly useless fashion. Once old Dévai was lured far out of our own district in search of two children who did not even exist. She had taken all precautions to verify the information given, but a false address had baffled her; and we can only conclude that, for some reason unknown to us, but well known to those whom we oppose, they were permitted on that occasion to gain an advantage over us. We made it a rule, after that will-of-the-wisp experience, that any address out of our own district must be verified; and that the nearest missionary thereto, or responsible Indian Christian, must be approached, before further steps are taken. This rule has saved many a fruitless journey; but also we cannot help knowing it has sometimes occasioned delays which have had sad results. For distances are great in India. Dévai herself lives two days' journey from us, and her address is uncertain, as she sets off at a moment's notice for any place where she has reason to think a child in danger may be saved. Then, too, missionaries and responsible Indian Christians are not everywhere. So that sometimes it is a case of choosing the lesser of two evils, and choosing immediately.

LATHA
(FIREFLY) BLOWING BUBBLES.

Once in the night a knock came to Dévai's door. A man stood outside, a Hindu known to her. "A little girl has just been taken to the Temple of A., where the great festival is being held. If you go at once you may perhaps get her." The place named was out of our jurisdiction; but in such cases Dévai knows rules are only made to be broken. Off she went on foot, got a bandy *en route*, reached the town before the festival was over, found the house to which she had been directed—a little shut-up house, doors and windows all closed—managed, how we never knew, to get in, found a young woman, a Temple woman from Travancore, with a little child asleep on the mat beside her, persuaded her to slip out of the house with the child without wakening anyone, crept out of the town and fled away into the night, thankful for the blessed covering darkness. The child was being kept in that house till the Temple woman to whom she was to be given produced the stipulated "Joy-gift," after which she would become Temple property. Some delay in its being given had caused that night's retention in the little shut-up house. The child, a most lovable little girl, had been kidnapped and disguised; and the matter was so skilfully managed, that we have never been able to discover even the name of her own town. We only know she must have been well brought up, for she was from the first a refined little thing with very dainty ways. She and her little special friend are sitting on the steps looking at Latha (Firefly), who is blowing bubbles. The other little one has a similar but different history. Her father brought her to us himself, fearing lest she should be kidnapped by one related to her who much wanted to have her. "I, being a man, cannot be always with the child," he said, "and I fear for her."

"It"

On another occasion the clue was found through Dévai's happening to overhear the conversation of two men in a wood in the early morning. One said to the other something about someone having taken "It" somewhere; and Dévai, whose scent is keen where little "Its" are concerned, made friends with the men, and got the information she wanted from them. Careful work resulted in a little child's salvation; but Dévai hardly dared believe it safe until she reached Dohnavur. When that occurred we were all at church; for special services were being held in week-day evenings, and old Dévai had to possess her soul in patience till we came out of church. Then there was a rush round to the nursery, and an eager showing of the "It." I shall never forget the pang of disappointment and apprehension. Several little ones had been sent to us who could not possibly live; and the nurses had got overborne, and we dreaded another strain for them. It was a tiny thing, three pounds and three-quarters of pale brown skin and bone. Its face was a criss-cross of wrinkles, and it looked any age. But "Man looketh upon the outward appearance" would have been assuredly quoted to us, regardless of context, had we ventured upon a remark to old Dévai, who poured forth the story of its salvation in vivid sentences. Next evening the old grannie of the compound told us the baby could not live till morning. She laid it on a mat and regarded it critically, felt its pulses (both wrists), examined minutely its eyes and the bridge of its nose: "No, not till morning. Better have the grave prepared, for early morning will be an inconvenient hour for digging." Others confirmed her diagnosis, and sorrowfully the order was given and the grave was dug.

But the baby lived till morning; and though for two years it needed a nurse to itself, and over and over again all but left us, this baby has grown one of our healthiest; and now when old Dévai comes to see us she looks at it, and then to Heaven, and sighs with gratitude.

CHAPTER X

Failures?

BUT sometimes old Dévai brings us little ones who do not come to stay. Failures, the world would call them. Twice lately this has happened, and each time unexpectedly; for the babies had stories which seemed to imply a promise of future usefulness. Surely such a deliverance must have been wrought for something special, we say to ourselves, and refuse to fear.

One dear little fat "fair" baby was brought to us as a surprise, for we had not heard of her. It had seemed so improbable that Dévai could get her, that she had not written to us to ask us to pray her through the battle, as she usually does. The sound of the bullock-bells' jingle one moonlight night woke us to welcome the baby. She had travelled fifty miles in the shaky bullock-cart, and she was only a few days old; but she seemed healthy, and we had no fears. "Ah, the Lord our God gave her to me, or never could I have got her! Her mother had determined to give her to the Temple; and when I went to persuade her, she hid the baby in an earthen vessel lest my eyes should see her. But earthen pots cannot hide from the eyes of the Lord. And here she is!" The details, fished out of Dévai by dint of many questions, made it clear that in very truth the Lord, to whom all souls belong, had worked on behalf of this little one; moving even Hindu hearts, as His brave old servant pleaded, making it possible to break through caste and custom, those prison walls of most cruel convention, till even the Hindus said: "Let the Christian have the babe!" We do not know why she was taken. She never seemed to sicken, but just left us; perhaps she was needed somewhere else, and Dohnavur was the way there.

The other meant even more to us, for she was our first from Benares, the heart of this great Hinduism; and her very presence seemed such a splendid pledge of ultimate victory.

This little one was saved through a friend, a Wesleyan missionary, who had interested her Indian workers in the children. The baby's mother was a pilgrim from Benares, and her baby had been born in the South. A Temple woman had seen it and was eager to get it, for it was a child of promise. Our friend's worker heard of this, and interposed. The mother consented to give her baby to us. It was not a case in which we dare have persuaded her to keep it; for such babies are greatly coveted, and the mother was already predisposed to give her child to the gods.

When we heard of this little one, old Dévai was with us. She had only just arrived after a journey of two days with a little girl, but she knew the perils of delay too well to risk them now. "Let me go! I will have some coffee, and immediately start!" So off she went for five more days of wearisome bullock-cart and train. But her face beamed when she returned and laid a six-weeks-old baby in our arms—a baby fair to look upon. We gathered round her at once, and she lay and smiled at us all. Hardly ever have we had so sweet a babe. But the smiling little mouth was too pale a pink, and the beautiful eyes were too bright. She had only been with us a month when we were startled by the other-world look on the baby's face. We had seen it before; we recognised it, and our hearts sank within us. That evening, as she lay in her white cradle, the waxy hands folded in an unchildlike calm, she looked as if the angel of Death had passed her as she slept, and touched her as he passed.

Passion-flowers

She stayed with us for another month, and was nursed day and night till more and more she became endeared to us; and then once more we heard the word that cannot be refused, and we let her go. We laid passion-flowers about her as she lay asleep. The smile that had left her little face had come back now. "She came with a smile, and she went with a smile," said one who loved her dearly; and the flowers of mystery and glory spoke to us, as we stood and looked. "Who for the joy that was set before Him ;. . . endured." The scent of the violet passion-flower will always carry its message to us. "Let us be worthy of the grief God sends."

And oh that such experiences may make us more earnest, more self-less in our service for these little ones! Someone has expressed this thought very tenderly and simply:—

Because of one small low-laid head, all crowned
With golden hair,
For evermore all fair young brows to me
A halo wear.
I kiss them reverently. Alas, I know
The pain I bear!

Because of dear but close-shut holy eyes
Of heaven's own blue,
All little eyes do fill my own with tears,
Whate'er their hue.
And, motherly, I gaze their innocent,
Clear depths into.

Because of little pallid lips, which once
My name did call,
No childish voice in vain appeal upon
My ears doth fall.
I count it all my joy their joys to share,
And sorrows small.

Because of little dimpled hands
Which folded lie,
All little hands henceforth to me do have
A pleading cry.
I clasp them, as they were small wandering birds,
Lured home to fly.

Because of little death-cold feet, for earth's
Rough roads unmeet,
I'd journey leagues to save from sin and harm
Such little feet.
And count the lowliest service done for them
So sacred—sweet.

   "Until He find it"

  But grief is almost too poignant a word for what is so stingless as this. And yet God the Father, who gives the love, understands and knows how much may lie behind two words and two dates. "Given ;. . . Taken ;. . ." Only indeed we do bless Him when the cup holds no bitterness of fear or of regret. There is nothing ever to fear for the little folded lambs. If only the veil of blinding sense might drop from our eyes when the door opens to our cherished little children, should we have the heart to toil so hard to keep that bright door shut? Would it not seem almost selfish to try? But the case is different when the child is not lifted lovingly to fair lands out of sight, but snatched back, dragged back down into the darkness from which we had hoped it had escaped. This work for the children, which seems so strangely full of trial of its own (as it is surely still more full of its own particular joy), has held this bitterness for us, and yet the bitter has changed to sweet; and even now in our "twilight of short knowledge" we can understand a little, and where we cannot we are content to wait.

Four years ago, after much correspondence and effort, a little girl was saved from Temple service in connection with a famous Temple of the South from which few have ever been saved. She had been dedicated by her father, and her mother had consented. Dévai got a paper signed by them giving her up to us instead. But shortly after she left the town, the father regretted the step he had taken, and followed Dévai, unknown to her. Alas, the child had not been with us an hour before she was carried off.

For two years we heard nothing of her. Old Dévai, who was broken-hearted about the matter, tried to find what had been done with her, but it was kept secret. She almost gave up in despair.

At last information reached her that the child was in the same town; and that her father having died of cholera, the mother and another little daughter were in a certain house well known to her. She went immediately and found the older child had not been given to the gods. Something of her pleadings had lingered in the father's memory, and he had refused to give her up. But the mother was otherwise minded, and intended to give both children to the Temple. Dévai had been guided to go at the critical time of decision. The mother was persuaded, and Dévai returned with two sheaves instead of one—and even that one she had hardly dared to expect. Once more we were called to hold our gifts with light hands. The younger of the welcome little two was one of ten who died during an epidemic at Neyoor. The elder one is with us still—a bright, intelligent child.

The only other one whom we have been compelled to give up in this most hurting way was saved through friends on the hills, who, before they sent the little child to us, believed all safe as to claims upon her afterwards. She was a pretty child of five, and we grew to love her very much; for her ways were sweet and gentle and very affectionate. Lala, Lola, and Leela were a dear little trio, all about the same age, and all rather specially interesting children.

But the father gave trouble. He was not a good man, and we knew it was not love for his little daughter which prompted his action. He demanded her back, and our friends had to telegraph to us to send her home. It was not an easy thing to do; and we packed her little belongings feeling as if we were moving blindly in a grievous dream, out of which we must surely awaken.

There was some delay about a bandy, but at last it was ready and standing at the door. We lifted the little girl into it, put a doll and a packet of sweets in her hands, and gave our last charges to those who were taking her up to the hills, workers upon whom we could depend to do anything that could yet be done to win her back again. Then the bandy drove away.

But we went back to our room and asked for a great and good thing to be done. We thought of little Lala, with her gentle nature which had so soon responded to loving influence, and we knew her very gentleness would be her danger now; for how could such a little child, naturally so yielding in disposition, withstand the call that would come, and the pressure that had broken far stronger wills? So we asked that she might either be returned to us soon or taken away from the evil to come. A week passed and our workers returned without her; they evidently felt the case quite hopeless. But the next letter we had from our friends told us the child was safe.

Carried by the Angels

She had left us in perfect health, but pneumonia set in upon her return to the colder air of the hills. She had been only a few days ill, and died very suddenly—died without anyone near her to comfort her with soothing words about the One to whom she was going. Even in the gladness that she was safe now, there was the pitiful thought of her loneliness through the dark valley; and we seemed to see the little wistful face, and felt she would be so frightened and shy and bewildered; and we longed to know something about those last hours. But one of the heathen women who had been about her at the last told what she knew, and our friends wrote what they heard. "She said she was Jesus' child, and did not seem afraid. And she said that she saw three Shining Ones come into the room where she was lying, and she was comforted." Oh, need we ever fear? Little Lala had been with us for so short a time that we had not been able to teach her much; and so far as any of us know, she had heard nothing of the ministry of angels. We had hardly dared to hope she understood enough about our Lord Himself to rest her little heart upon Him. But we do not know everything. Little innocent child that she was, she was carried by the angels from the evil to come.

Old Dévai keeps a brave heart. When she comes to see us, she cheers herself by nursing the cheerful little people she brought to us, small and wailing and not very hopeful. She is full of reminiscences on these occasions. "Ah," she will say, addressing an astonished two-year-old, "the devil and all his imps fought for you, my child!" This is unfamiliar language to the baby; but Dévai knows nothing of our modern ideas of education, and considers crude fact advisable at any age. "Yes, he fought for you, my child. I was sitting on the verandah of the house wherein you lay, and I was preaching the Gospel of the grace of God to the women, when five devils appeared. Yea, five were they, one older and four younger. Men were they in outward shape, but within them were the devils. I had nearly persuaded the women to let me have you, my child; and till they fully consented, I was filling up the interval with speech, for no man shall shut my mouth. And the women listened well, and my heart burned within me—for it was life to me to see them listening—when lo! those devils came—yea, five, one older and four younger—sent by their master to confound me. And they rose up against me and turned me out, and told the women folk not to listen; and you—I should never get you, said they; and so it appeared, for with such is might, and their master waxes furious when he knows his time is short. But the Lord on high is mightier than a million million devils, and what are five to Him? He rose up for me against them and discomfited them"—Dévai does not go into secular particulars—"and so you were delivered from the mouth of the lion, my child!"

We are not anxious that our babies should know too much ancient history. Enough for them that they are in the fold—

I am Jesus' little lamb,
Happy all day long I am;
He will keep me safe from harm,
For I'm His lamb—

is enough theology for two-year-olds; but Dévai's visits are not so frequent as to make a deep impression, and the baby thus addressed, after a long and unsympathetic stare, usually scrambles off her knee and returns unscathed to her own world.

CHAPTER XI

God Heard: God Answered

OLD Dévai, with her vivid conversation about the one old devil and four younger, does not suggest a conciliatory attitude towards the people of her land. And it may be possible so to misinterpret the spirit of this book as to see in it only something unappreciative and therefore unkind. So it shall now be written down in sincerity and earnestness that nothing of the sort is intended. The thing we fight is not India or Indian, in essence or development. It is something alien to the old life of the people. It is not allowed in the Védas (ancient sacred books). It is like a parasite which has settled upon the bough of some noble forest-tree—on it, but not of it. The parasite has gripped the bough with strong and interlacing roots; but it is not the bough.

We think of the real India as we see it in the thinker—the seeker after the unknown God, with his wistful eyes. "The Lord beholding him loved him," and we cannot help loving as we look. And there is the Indian woman hidden away from the noise of crowds, patient in her motherhood, loyal to the light she has. We see the spirit of the old land there; and it wins us and holds us, and makes it a joy to be here to live for India.

The true India is sensitive and very gentle. There is a wisdom in its ways, none the less wise because it is not the wisdom of the West. This spirit which traffics in children is callous and fierce as a ravening beast; and its wisdom descendeth not from above, but is earthly, sensual, devilish. . . . And this spirit, alien to the land, has settled upon it, and made itself at home in it, and so become a part of it that nothing but the touch of God will ever get it out. We want that touch of God: "Touch the mountains, and they shall smoke." That is why we write.

For we write for those who believe in prayer—not in the emasculated modern sense, but in the old Hebrew sense, deep as the other is shallow. We believe there is some connection between knowing and caring and praying, and what happens afterwards. Otherwise we should leave the darkness to cover the things that belong to the dark. We should be for ever dumb about them, if it were not that we know an evil covered up is not an evil conquered. So we do the thing from which we shrink with strong recoil; we stand on the edge of the pit, and look down and tell what we have seen, urged by the longing within us that the Christians of England should pray.

"Only pray?" does someone ask? Prayer of the sort we mean never stops with praying. "Whatsoever He saith unto you, do it," is the prayer's solemn afterword; but the prayer we ask is no trifle. Lines from an American poet upon what it costs to make true poetry, come with suggestion here:—

Deem not the framing of a deathless lay
The pastime of a drowsy summer day.
But gather all thy powers, and wreck them on the verse
That thou dost weave. . . .
The secret wouldst thou know
To touch the heart or fire the blood at will?
Let thine eyes overflow,
Let thy lips quiver with the passionate thrill.

"And call. . . . So will I hear thee"

"Arise, cry out in the night; in the beginning of the night watches pour out thine heart like water before the Lord; lift up thine hands towards Him for the life of thy young children!"

The story of the children is the story of answered prayer. If any of us were tempted to doubt whether, after all, prayer is a genuine transaction, and answers to prayer no figment of the imagination—but something as real as the tangible things about us—we have only to look at some of our children. It would require more faith to believe that what we call the Answer came by chance or by the action of some unintelligible combination of controlling influences, than to accept the statement in its simplicity—God heard: God answered.

In October, 1908, we were told of two children whose mother had recently died. They were with their father in a town some distance from Dohnavur; but the source from which our information came was so unreliable that we hardly knew whether to believe it, and

41

we prayed rather a tentative prayer: "If the children exist, save them." For three months we heard nothing; then a rumour drifted across to us that the elder of the two had died in a Temple house. The younger, six months old, was still with her father. On Christmas Eve our informant arrived in the compound with his usual unexpectedness. The father was near, but would not come nearer because the following day being Friday (a day of ill-omen), he did not wish to discuss matters concerning the child; he would come on Saturday. On Saturday he came, carrying a dear little babe with brilliant eyes. She almost sprang from him into our arms, and we saw she was mad with thirst. She was fed and put to sleep, and hardly daring yet to rejoice (for the matter was not settled with the father), we took him aside and discussed the case with him. There were difficulties. A Temple woman had offered a large sum for the child, and had also promised to bequeath her property to her. He had heard, however, that we had little children who had all but been given to Temples, and he had come to reconnoitre rather than to decide.

"Though it tarry, wait for it . . .

The position was explained to him. But the Temple meant to him everything that was worshipful. How could anything that was wrong be sanctioned by the gods? The child's mother had been a devout Hindu; and as we went deeper and deeper into things with him, it was evident he became more and more reluctant to leave the little one with us. "Her mother would have felt it shame and eternal dishonour." We were in the little prayer-room, a flowery little summer-house in the garden, when this talk took place. On either side are the nurseries, and playing on the wide verandahs were happy, healthy babes; their merry shouts filled the spaces in the conversation. Sometimes a little toddling thing would find her way across to the prayer-room, and break in upon the talk with affectionate caresses. To our eyes everything looked so happy, so incomparably better than anything the Temple house could offer, that it was difficult to adjust one's mental vision so as to understand that of the Hindu beside us, to whose thought all the happiness was as nothing, because these babes would be brought up without caste. In the Temple house caste is kept most carefully. If a Temple woman breaks the rules of her community she is out-casted, excommunicated. "You do not keep caste! you do not keep caste!" the father repeated over and over again in utter dismay. It was nothing to him that the babes were well and strong, and as happy as the day was long; nothing to him that cleanliness reigned, so far as constant supervision could ensure it, through every corner of the compound. We did not profess to keep caste; we welcomed every little child in danger of being given to Temples, irrespective altogether of her caste. All castes were welcome to us, for all were dear to our Lord. This was beyond him; and he declared he would never have brought his child to us, had he understood it before. "Let her die rather! There is no disgrace in death." As he talked and expounded his views, he argued himself further and further away from us in spirit, until he became disgusted with himself for ever having considered giving the baby to us. All this time the baby lay asleep; and as we looked at the little face and noted the "mother-want," the appealing expression of pitiful weariness even in sleep, it was all we could do to turn away and face the almost inevitable result of the conversation. Once the father, a splendid looking man, tall and dignified, rose and stood erect in sudden indignation. "Where is the babe? I will take her away and do as I will with her. She is my child!" We persuaded him to wait awhile as she was asleep, and we went away to pray. Together we waited upon God, whose touch turns hard rocks into standing water, and flint-stone into a springing well, beseeching Him to deal with that father's heart, and make it melt and yield. And as we waited it seemed as if an answer of peace were distinctly given to us, and we rose from our knees at rest. But just at that moment the father went to where his baby slept in her cradle, and he took her up and walked away in a white heat of wrath.

The little one was in an exhausted condition, for she had not had suitable food for at least three days. It was the time of our land-winds, which are raw and cold to South Indian people; and it seemed that the answer of peace must mean peace after death of cold and starvation. It would soon be over, we knew; twenty-four hours, more or less, and those great wistful eyes would close, and the last cry would be cried. But even twenty-four hours seemed long to think of a child in distress, and her being so little did not make it easier to think of her dying like that. So on Sunday morning I shut myself up in my room asking for quick relief for her, or—but this seemed almost asking too much—that she might be given back to us. And as I prayed, a knock came at the door, and a voice called joyously, "Oh, Amma! Amma! Come! The father stands outside the church; he has brought the baby back!"

But the child was almost in collapse. Without a word he dropped the cold, limp little body into our arms, and prostrated himself till his forehead touched the dust. We had not time to think of him, we hardly noted his extraordinary submission, for all our thought was for the babe. There was no pulse to be felt, only those far too brilliant eyes looked alive. We worked with restoratives for hours, and at last the little limbs warmed and the pulse came back. But it was a bounding, unnatural pulse, and the restlessness which supervened confirmed the tale of the brilliant eyes—the little babe had been drugged.

From that day on till our Prayer-day, January 6th, it was one long, unremitting fight with death. We wrote to our medical comrade in Neyoor, and described the symptoms, which were all bad. He could give us little hope. Gradually the brilliance passed from the eyes, and they became what the Tamils call "dead." The film formed after which none of us had ever seen recovery. Then we gathered round the little cot in the room we call Tranquillity, and we gave the babe her Christian name Vimala, the Spotless One; for we thought that very soon she would be without spot and blameless, another little innocent in that happy band of innocents who see His Face.

On the evening of the 5th, friends of our own Mission who were with us seemed to lay hold for the life of the child with such fresh earnestness and faith, that we ourselves were strengthened. Next morning we believed we saw a change in the little deathlike face, and that evening we were sure the child's life was coming back to her.

". . .Because it will surely come"

It was not till then we thought of the father, who, after signing a paper made out for him by our pastor, who is always ready to help us, had returned to his own town. When we heard all that had occurred we saw how our God had worked for us. It was not fear of his baby's death that had moved the man to return to us. "What is the death of a babe? Let her die across my shoulders!" He was not afraid of the law. After all persuasions had failed, we had tried threats: the thing he purposed to do was illegal. The Collector (chief magistrate) would do justice. "What care I for your Collector? How can he find me if I choose to lose myself? How can you prove anything against me?" And in that he spoke the truth. There are ways by which the intention of the law concerning little children can be most easily and successfully circumvented. Our pleadings had not touched him. "Is she not my child? Was her mother not my wife? Who has the right to come between this child of mine and me her father?" And so saying he had departed without the slightest intention of coming back again. But a Power with which he did not reckon had him in sight; and a Hand was laid upon him, and it bent him like a reed. We hope some ray of a purer light than he had ever experienced found its way into his darkened soul, and revealed to him the sin of his intention. But we only know that he left his child and went back to his own town. God had heard: God had answered.

CHAPTER XII

To what Purpose?

AMONG the closest of our little children's friends is one whose name I may not give, lest her work should be hindered; for in this work of saving the little ones, though we have the sympathy of many, we naturally have to meet the covert opposition of very many more, and it is not well to give too explicit information as to the centres of supply. This dear friend's help has been invaluable. From the first she has stood by us, interesting her friends, Indian and English, in the children, and stirring them into practical co-operation. Then, when the babies have been saved and had to be cared for and sent off, she made nothing of the trouble, and above all she has never been discouraged. Sometimes things have been difficult. Some have doubted, and many have criticised, and even the kindest have lost heart. This friend has never lost heart.

For not all the chapters of the Temple children's story can be written down and printed for everyone to read. We think of the unwritten chapters, and remember how often when the pressure was greatest the thought of that undiscouraged comrade has been strength and inspiration. No one except those who, in weakness and inexperience, have tried to do something not attempted before can understand how the heart prizes sympathy just at the difficult times, and how such brave and steadfast comradeship is a thing that can never be forgotten.

Among the babies saved through this friend's influence was one with a short but typical story.

The little mite was seen first in her mother's arms, and the mother was standing by the wayside, as if waiting. Something in her attitude and appearance drew the attention of an Indian Christian, whom our friend had interested in the work, and she got into conversation with the mother, who told her that her husband had died a fortnight before the baby's birth, and she, being poor though of good caste, was much exercised about the little one's future. How could she marry her properly? She had come to the conclusion that her best plan would be to give her to the Temple. So she was even then waiting till someone from a Temple house would come and take her little girl.

The news that such a child is to be had soon becomes known to those who are on the watch, and it is improbable that the mother would have had long to wait. The Christian persuaded her to give up the idea, and the little babe was saved and sent to us. On the journey to Dohnavur a Temple woman chanced to get into the carriage where the little baby slept in its basket. There was nothing to tell who she was; and like the other women in the carriage, she was greatly interested in its story. But presently it became evident that her interest was more than superficial. She looked well at the baby and was quiet for a time; then she said to the Christian who was bringing it to us: "I see it is going to be an intelligent child. Let me have it; I will pay you." The Christian of course refused, and asked her how she knew it was going to be intelligent. "Look at its nose," said the Temple woman. "See, here is money!" and she offered it. "Let me have the baby! You can tell your Missie Ammal it died in the train!"

"He banged the door!"

Sometimes our babies have to run greater risks than this in their journeys south to us. The distances which have to be covered by train and bullock-cart are great, and the travelling tedious. And there are many delays and opportunities for difficulties to arise; so that when we know a baby is on its way to us we feel we want to wrap it round in prayer, so that, thus invisibly enveloped, it will be protected and carried safely all the way. Once a little child, travelling to us from a place as distant, counting by time, as Rome is from London, was observed by some Brahman men, who happened to be at the far end of the long third-class carriage. Our worker, who was alone with the child, noticed the whispering and glances toward her little charge, and wrapped it closer in its shawl, and, as she said, "looked out of the window as if she were not at all afraid, and prayed much in her heart." Presently a station was reached. The language spoken there was not her vernacular, but she understood enough to know something was being said about the baby. Then an official appeared, and there was a cry quite understandable to her: "A Brahman baby! That Christian there is kidnapping a Brahman baby!" The official stopped at the carriage door. She was pushed towards him amidst a confused chatter, a crowd gathered at the door in a moment, and someone shouted in Tamil, above the excited clamour on the platform: "Pull her out! A Christian with a Brahman baby!"

"Then did my heart tremble! I held the baby tight in my arms. The man in clothes said, 'Show it to me!' And he looked at its hands and he looked at its feet, and he said: 'This is no child of yours!' But as I began to explain to him, the train moved, and he banged the door; and I praised God!"

India is a land where strange things can be accomplished with the greatest ease. As all went well it is idle to imagine what might have been; but we knew enough to be thankful.

Among the unwritten chapters is one which touches a problem. There are some little children—often the most valuable to the Temple women—who cannot live with us, but can live with them, because the baby in the Temple house is nursed by a foster-mother for the sake of merit, and thus it is given its best chance of life; whereas with us it is impossible to get foster-mothers. Indian children of the castes approved for the service are not, as a class, as robust as others; the secluded lives of their mothers, and the rigid rules pertaining to widows (girl-children born after the mother becomes a widow are, as has been seen, in special danger), partly account for this; and in other cases there are other reasons. Whatever the cause, however, the effect is manifest. The baby is seldom the little bundle of content of our English nurseries. It may become so later on, if all goes well. Often it lives upon its birth-strength for four months, or less, and then slips away. We have often hesitated about taking such babies; and then we have found that by refusing one who is likely to die we have discouraged those who were willing to help us, and the next baby in danger has been taken straight to the house where its welcome was assured. So we have hardly ever dared to refuse, and we have taken little fragile things whose days we knew were numbered unless a foster-mother could be found, for it seemed to us that death with us was better than life with the Temple people; and also we have not dared to risk losing the next, who might be healthy. "One dies, one lives," say the Temple women in their wisdom, and take all who are suitable in caste and in appearance. "She will be 'fair,'" or, "She will be intelligent," settles the matter for them. They give the baby a chance: should we do less?

"To what Purpose?"

One night I woke suddenly with the feeling of someone near, and saw, standing beside my bed out on the verandah, the friend who has sent us so many little ones. She had something wrapped in a shawl in her arms, and as she moved the shawl a thin cry smote me with a fear, for a baby who has come to stay does not cry like that.

It was a dear little baby, one of the type the Temple women prize, and will take so much trouble to rear. The little head was finely formed, and the tiny face, in its minute perfection of feature, looked as if some fairy had shaped it out of a cream rose-petal. Alas, there was that look we know so well and fear so much—that look of not belonging to us, the elsewhere, other-world look. But we could not do this work at all, we would not have the heart to do it, if we did not hope. So we go on hoping.

The baby filled the next half-hour, for a thing so small can be hungry and say so; and together we heated the water and made the food, till, satisfied at length that her little charge was comfortable, our friend lay down to rest. "Jesus therefore being weary with His journey, sat thus on the well." There is something in the utter weariness after a long, hot journey, ending with seven hours in a bullock-cart over rough tracks by night, which always recalls that word of human tiredness. How I wished that the morning were not so near as I saw my friend asleep at last! A few hours later she was on her homeward way, and we were left with our hopes and our fears, and the baby.

For three weeks we hoped against fear, till there was no room left for any more hope, or for anything but prayer that the child might cease to suffer. And after a month of struggle for life, the tiny, tossing thing lay still.

"To what purpose is this waste?" Was it strange that the question came again to ourselves, and to others too? Our dear friend's toilsome travelling—a journey equal in expenditure of time to one from London to Vienna and back again, and very much more exhausting, the faithful nurse's patience, the little baby's pain! And all the love that had grown through the weeks, and all the efforts that had failed, the very train ticket and bandy fare—was it all as water spilt on the ground? Was it waste?

We knew in our hearts it was not. The dear little babe was safe; and it might be that our having taken her, though she was so very delicate, would result in another, a healthy child, being saved, who, if she had been refused, would never have been brought. This hope comforted us; and we prayed definitely for its fulfilment, and it was fulfilled. For shortly after that little seed had been sown in death, information came from the same source through which she had been saved, that another child was in danger of being adopted by Temple women; and this information would not have been given to our friend had the first child been refused. Nundinie we called this little gift: the name means Happiness.

Sometimes in moments of depression and disappointment we go for change of air and scene to the Prémalia nursery; and the baby Nundinie, otherwise Dimples, of whom more afterwards, comes running up to us with her welcoming smile and outstretched arms; while others, with stories as full of comfort, tumble about us, and cuddle, and nestle, and pat us into shape. Then we take courage again, and ask forgiveness for our fears. It is true our problems are not always solved, and perhaps more difficult days are before; but we will not be afraid. Sometimes a sudden light falls on the way, and we look up and still it shines: and what can we do but "follow the Gleam"?

CHAPTER XIII

A Story of Comfort

SEELA IS THE BABY IN THE MIDDLE.

She slipped into the picture at the last moment, and so was caught unawares. Mala is to the right; Nullinie to the left. (This little one's left hand and foot are partially paralyzed through drugging in infancy.)

AMONG the stories of comfort is one that belongs to our merry little Seela. She is bigger now than when the despairing photographer broke thirteen plates in the vain attempt to catch her; but she is still most elusive and alluring, a veritable baby, though over two years old. Some months ago, the Iyer measured her, and told her she was thirty-two inches of mischief. For weeks afterwards, when asked her name, she always replied with gravity, "Terty-two inses of mistef."

All who have to do with babies know how different they can be in disposition and habits. There is the shop-window baby, who shows all her innocent wares at once to everyone kind enough to look. She is a charming baby. And there is the little wild bird of the wood, who will answer your whistle politely, if you know how to whistle her note; but she will not trust herself near you till she is sure of you. Seela is that sort of baby. We have watched her when she has been approached by some unfamiliar presence, and seen her summon all her baby dignity to keep her from breaking into tears of overwhelming shyness. Give her time to observe you from under long, drooping lashes; give her time to make sure—then the mischief will sparkle out, and something of the real child. But only something, never all, till you become a relation; with those who are only acquaintances Seela, like Bala, has many reserves.

Seela's joy is to be considered old and allowed to go to the kindergarten. She takes her place with the bigger babies, and tries to do all she sees them do. Sometimes a visitor looks in, and then Seela, naturally, will do nothing; but if the visitor is wise and takes no notice, she will presently be rewarded by seeing the eager little face light up again, and the fat hands busily at work. Seela is not supposed to be learning very seriously; but she seems to know nearly as much as some of the older children, and her quaint attempts at English are much appreciated. Seela has her faults. She likes to have her own way, and once was observed to slap severely an offender almost twice her own size; but on the whole she is a peaceful little person, beloved by all the other babies, both senior and junior. Her great ambition is to follow Chellalu into all possible places of mischief. Anything Chellalu can do Seela will attempt; and as she is more brave than steady on her little feet, she has many a narrow escape. Her latest escapade was to follow her reckless leader in an attempt to walk round the top of the back of a large armchair, the cane rim of which is a slippery slant, two inches wide.

Table Manners

On the morning of her arrival, not liking to leave her even for a few minutes, I carried her to the early tea-table, when she saw the Iyer and smiled her first smile to him. From that day on she has been his loyal little friend. At first his various absences from home perplexed her. She would toddle off to his room and hunt everywhere for him, even under his desk and behind his waste-paper basket, and then she returned to the dining-room with a puzzled little face. "Iyer is not!" "Where is he, Seela?" "Gone to Heaven!" was her invariable reply. When he returned from that distant sphere she never displayed the least surprise. That is not our babies' way. She calmly accepted him as a returned possession; stood by his chair waiting for the invitation, "Climb up"; climbed up as if he had never been away—and settled down to bliss.

Part of this bliss consists in being supplied with morsels of toast and biscuit and occasional sips of tea. Sometimes there is that delicious luxury, a spoonful of the unmelted sugar at the bottom of the cup. For Seela is a baby after all, and does not profess to be like grown-up people who do not appreciate nice things to eat, being, of course, entirely superior to food; but, excitable little damsel as she is in all other matters, her table manners are most correct, and she shows her appreciation of kind attentions in characteristic fashion. A smile, so quick under the black lashes that only one on the look-out for it would see it, a sudden confiding little nestle closer to the giver—these are her only signs of pleasure; and if no notice is taken of her, she sits in silent patience. Sometimes, if politeness be mistaken for indifference, a shadow creeps into her eyes, a sort of pained surprise at the obtuseness of the great; but she rarely makes any remark, and never points or asks, as the irrepressible Chellalu does in spite of all our admonitions. If, however, Seela is being attended to and fed at judicious intervals, and she knows the intention is to feed her comfortably, then her attitude is different. She feels a reminder will be acceptable; and as soon as she has disposed of a piece of biscuit, she quietly holds up an empty little hand, and glances fearlessly up to the face that looks down with a smile upon her. This little silent, empty hand, held up so quietly, has often spoken to us of things unknown to our little girl; and as if to enforce the lesson, the other babies, to our amusement, apparently noticing the gratifying result of Seela's upturned hand, began to hold up their little hands with the same silent expectancy, till all round the table small hands were raised in perfect silence, by hopeful infants of observant habits and strong faith.

THE COTTAGE NURSERY.

Mala, the rather stolid-looking little girl to the right of the photograph, is Seela's elder sister. She is not so square-faced as the photograph shows her, and she is much more interesting. This little one seems to us to have in some special sense the grace of God upon her; for her nursery life is so happy and blameless and unselfish, that we rarely have to wish her different in anything. Her coming, with little Seela's, is one of the very gladdest of our Overweights of Joy.

We heard of the little sisters through a mission schoolmaster, who—knowing that they had been left motherless, and that a Hindu of good position had obtained something equivalent to powers of guardianship, and thus empowered had placed them with a Temple woman—was most anxious to save them, and wrote to us; and, as he expressed it, "also earnestly and importunately prayed the benign British Government to intervene."

"And he said. . . . But God said"

The Collector to whom the petition was sent was a friend of ours. He knew about the nursery work, and was ready to do all he could; but he did not want a disturbance with the Caste and Temple people, and so advised us to try to get the children privately. We sent our wisest woman-worker, Ponnamal, to the town, and she saw the principal people concerned; but they entirely refused to give up the children. The man who had adopted them had got his authority from the local Indian sub-magistrate; and contended that as the Government had given them to him, no one had any right to take them from him; "and even if the Government itself ordered me to give them up, I never will. I will never let them go." This in Tamil is even more explicit: "The hold by which I hold them I will never let go." Ponnamal returned, weary in mind and in body, after three days of travelling and effort; she had caught a glimpse of the baby, and the little face haunted her. The elder child was reported very miserable, and she had seen nothing of her. The guardian, of course, had not dealt with her direct; but she heard he had taken legal advice, and was sure of his position. There was nothing hopeful to report. Once again we tried, but in vain. By this time a new bond had been formed, for the guardian had become attached to little Seela, and spent his time, so we heard, in playing with her. He let it be known that nothing would ever make him give her up. "She is in my hand, and my hand will never let go."

49

Then suddenly news came that he was dead. The baby had sickened with cholera. He had nursed her and contracted the disease. In two days he had died. He had been compelled to let go.

Then the feeling of all concerned changed completely. It hardly needed the Collector's order, given with the utmost promptitude, to cause the Temple woman to give the children up. To the Indian mind, quick to see the finger of God in such an event, the thing was self-evident. An unseen Power was at work here. Who were they that they should withstand it? A telegram told us the children were safe, and next day we had them here.

The baby was happy at once; but the elder little one, then a child of about three and a half, was very sorrowful. She was so pitifully frightened, too, that at first we could do nothing with her; and there was a look in her eyes that alarmed us, it was so distraught and unchildlike. "My mother did her best for them," wrote the kind schoolmaster to whose house the children had been taken when the Temple woman gave them up; "but the elder one has fever. She is always muttering to herself, and can neither stand nor sit." She could stand and sit now, only there was the "muttering," and the terrible look of bewilderment worse than pain. For days it was a question with us as to whether she would ever recover perfectly. That first night we had to give her bromide, and she woke very miserable. Next day she stood by the door waiting for her mother, as it seemed; for under her breath she was constantly whispering, "Amma! Amma!" ("Mother! Mother!") She never cried aloud, only sobbed quietly every now and then. She would not let us touch her, but shrank away terrified if we tried to pet her. All through the third day she sat by the door. This was better than the weary standing, but pitiful enough. On the morning of the fourth day she sat down again for a long watch; but once when her little hand went up to brush away a tear, we saw there was a toy in it, and that gave us hope. That night she went to bed with a doll, an empty tin, and a ball in her arms; and the next day she let us play with her in a quiet, reserved fashion. Next morning she woke happy.

Teachers—unawares

The babies teach us much, and sometimes their unconscious lessons illuminate the deeper experiences of life. One such illumination is connected in my mind with the little trellised verandah, shown in the photograph, of the cottage used as a nursery when Mala and Seela came to us.

It was the hour between lights, and five babies under two years old were waiting for their supper—Seela, Tara, and Evu (always a hungry baby), Ruhinie, usually irrepressible, but now in very low spirits, and a tiny thing with a face like a pansy—all five thinking longingly of supper. These five had to wait till the fresh milk came in, as their food was special; that evening the cows had wandered home with more than their usual leisureliness from their pasture out in the jungle, and so the milk was late.

The babies, who do not understand the weary ways of cows, disapproved of having to wait, and were fractious. To add to their depression, the boy whose duty it was to light the lamps and lanterns had been detained, and the trellised verandah was dark. So the five fretful babies made remarks to each other, and threw their toys about in that exasperated fashion which tells you the limits of patience have been passed; and the most distressed began to whimper.

At this point a lantern was brought and set behind me, so that its light fell upon the discarded toys, miscellaneous but beloved—a china head long parted from its body, one whole new doll, a tin with little stones in it, a matchbox, and other sundries. If anything will comfort them, their toys will, I thought, as I directed their attention to the tin with its pleasant rattling pebbles, and the other scattered treasures on the mat. But the babies looked disgusted. Toys were a mockery at that moment. Evu seized the china head and flung it as far as ever she could. Tara sat stolid, with two fingers in her mouth. Seela turned away, evidently deeply hurt in her feelings, and the other two cried. Not one of them would find consolation in toys.

Then the pansy-faced baby, Prâsie, pointed out to the bushes, where something dangerous, she was quite sure, was moving; and she wailed a wail of such infectious misery that all the babies howled. And one rolled over near the lantern which was on the floor behind me, and for safety's sake I moved it, and its light fell on my face. In a moment all five babies were tumbling over me with little exclamations of delight, and they nestled on my lap, caressing and content.

Are there not evenings when our toys have no power to please or soothe? There is not any rest in them or any comfort. Then the One whom we love better than all His dearest gifts comes and moves the lantern for us, so that our toys are in the shadow but His face is in the light. And He makes His face to shine upon us and gives us peace.

"For Thou, O Lord my God, art above all things best; . . . Thou alone most sufficient and most full; Thou alone most sweet and most comfortable.

"Thou alone most fair and most loving; Thou alone most noble and most glorious above all things; in whom all things are at once and perfectly good, and ever have been and shall be.

"And therefore whatever Thou bestowest upon me beside Thyself, or whatever Thou revealest or promisest concerning Thyself, so long as I do not see or fully enjoy Thee, is too little, and fails to satisfy me.

"Because, indeed, my heart cannot truly rest nor be entirely contented unless it rest in Thee, and rise above all Thy gifts and all things created.

"When shall I fully recollect myself in Thee, that through the love of Thee I may not feel myself but Thee alone, above all feeling and measure in a manner not known to all?"

CHAPTER XIV

Pickles and Puck

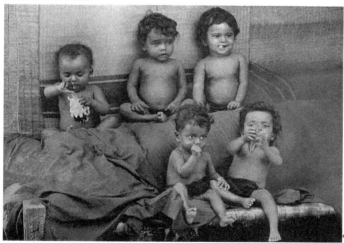

"PICKLES" AND HER FRIENDS.
"Pickles" sits with her thumb in her mouth, distrustful of photographers.

"AMMA! Amma!" then in baby Tamil, "Salala has come!" And one of the most enticing of the little interruptions to a steady hour's work scrambles over the raised doorstep, tripping and tumbling in her eagerness to get in. Now she is staggering happily about the room on fat, uncertain feet. Upsets are nothing to Sarala. She shakes herself, rubs a bumped head, smiles if you smile down at her, and picks herself up with a sturdy independence that promises something for her future. She has travelled to-day, stopping only to visit her Préma Sittie, a long way across the field all by herself. She has braved tumbles and captures, for her nurse may any minute discover her flight; and even now, safe in port, she keeps a wary eye on the door which opens on the nursery side of the compound. If she thinks I am about to suggest her departure, she immediately engages me in some interest of her own. She has ways and wiles unknown to any baby but herself; and if all seems likely to fail, she sits down on the floor, and first puts out her lower lip as far as it will go, and then springs up, climbs over you, clings with all four limbs at once, and buries her curly tangle deep into your neck. But if the case is hopeless, she sits down on the floor again and digs her small fists into her eyes, in silent indignation and despair. Then comes a howl impossible to smother, and at last such bitter bursts of woe as nothing short of dire necessity can force you to provoke. This is Sarala, one of the most affectionate, most wilful, most winsome of all the babies. She is truthful. She has just this moment pulled a drawing-pin out of its place, which happened to be within reach, and her solemn "Aiyo!" (Alas!) "Look, Amma!" shows she feels she has sinned, but wants to confess. Life will have many a battle for this baby; but surely if she is truthful and loving, and we are loving and wise, the Lord who has redeemed her will carry her through.

Her first great battle royal was with the new Sittie, who immediately upon arrival loved the babies. The battle was about Sarala's evening meal, which she refused to take from the new Sittie because she had offended her small majesty a few minutes before by allowing another baby to share the lap of which Sarala wished to have complete possession; and the baby had crawled off disgusted with the ways of such a Sittie.

As a rule we avoid collisions at bedtime. The day should end peacefully for babies; but the contest once begun had to be carried through, for Sarala is not a baby to whom it is wise to give in where a conflict of wills is concerned. Next morning it was evident she remembered all about it. When the new Sittie (now called Préma Sittie by the children) came to the nursery, Sarala hurried off and would have nothing to do with her. From the distance of the garden she would catch sight of her advancing form, and retreat round a corner. Sometimes if Préma Sittie sat down on the floor and fondled another baby, Sarala would crawl up from behind, put her arms round her neck, and even begin to sit down on her knee; but if her Sittie made the first advance, she was instantly repelled. This continued for a fortnight; and as Sarala was only a year and eight months old at the time, a fortnight's memory rather astonished us. In the end she forgot, and now there are no more devoted friends than Préma Sittie and Sarala.

Twins

But it was the other Sittie, Piria Sittie by name, who first made Sarala's acquaintance. She and I went to Neyoor together when the branch nursery was there; and as the new nursery was almost ready for the babies, we lightened the immense undertaking of removal by carting off whatever we could of furniture and infants. Sarala has eyes which can smile bewitchingly, and a voice which can coo with delicious affection; but those sweet eyes can look stormy, and cooing is a sound remote from Sarala's powers in opposite directions; so we wondered, as we packed her into the bandy, what would happen that night. If we had known Sarala better we should not have wondered. All this child wants to make her good is someone to hold on to. She woke frequently during the night, for we were not entirely comfortable, wedged sideways and close as herrings in a barrel. But all she did when she awoke was to push a soft little arm round either one or other of us, and cuddle as close as she possibly could; the least movement on our part, however, she deeply resented and feared. A limpet on a rock is nothing to this baby. Her very toes can cling.

Sarala's private name is Pickles. Her twin in mischief is Puck, and she, too, is fond of paying visits to the bungalow. But she always comes as a surprise; she never announces herself. You are busy with your back to the door when that curious feeling, a sense of not being quite alone, comes over you, and you turn and see an elfish thing, very still and small and shy, but with eyes so comical that Puck is the only possible name by which she could be called. Seen unexpectedly, playing among the flowers in a fragment of green garment washed to the softness of a tulip leaf, you feel she only needs a pair of small wings and a wand to be entirely in character.

Puck has none of Pickles' faults, and a good many of her virtues. She is a most good-tempered little person, loving to be loved, but equally delighted that others should share the petting. She gives up to everybody, and smiles her way through life; such a comical little mouth it is, to match the comical eyes. All she ever asks with insistence is somewhere to play. Bereft of room to play, Puck might become disagreeable, though a disagreeable Puck is something unimaginable. Yesterday it was needful to keep her in the shade; and as a special policeman-nurse could not be told off to keep watch over her, she was tied by a long string to the nursery door. At first she was sorely distressed; but presently the comic side struck her, and she sat down and began to tie herself up more securely. If they do such things at all they should do them better, she seemed to think. And this is Puck all through. She will find the laugh hidden in things, if she can. Sometimes in her eagerness to make everybody as happy as she is herself she gets into serious trouble. She was hardly able to walk when she was discovered comforting a crying infant by taking a bottle of milk from an older babe (who, according to her thinking, had had enough) and giving it to the younger one who seemed to need it more. What the older baby said is not recorded.

Disgraced Dohnavur

Puck in trouble is a pitiful sight. She tries not to give in to feelings of depression. She screws her smiling lips tight, twists her face into a pucker, and shuts her eyes till you only see two slits marked by the curly eyelashes. But if her emotions are too much for her she gives herself up to them thoroughly. There is no whining or whimpering or sulking; she wails with a wail that rivals Pickles' howl. "What an awful child!" remarked a visitor one morning, in a very shocked tone, as she went the round of the nurseries and came upon Puck on the floor abandoned to grief. We wondered if our friend knew how much more awful most babies are, and we wished the usually charming Puck had chosen some other moment to disgrace herself and us. But no, there she sat, her two small fists crushed over her mouth—for we insist that when the babes feel obliged to cry, they shall smother the sound thereof as much as may be—and the visitor retired, feeling, doubtless, thankful the awful child was not hers. But Puck's griefs are of short duration. Ten minutes later she was climbing the chain from which the swing hangs, trying to fit her little toes into the links, and laughing, with the tears still wet on her cheeks, because the chain shook so that she could not climb it properly, though she tried it valiantly, hand over head, like a dancing bear on a pole. Puck's Guardian Angel, like Chellalu's, must be ever in attendance.

FOOTNOTES:

Miss Lucy Ross.

"Préma" means *Beloved.*

Miss Mabel Wade, who joined us November 15, 1907. "Piria," like "Préma," means *Beloved.*

CHAPTER XV

The Howler

PICKLES and Puck at their worst and both together are nothing to the Howler in her separate capacity. We called her the Howler because she howled.

We heard of her first through our good Pakium, who, during a pilgrimage round the district, paid a visit to the family of which she was the youngest member. "She lay in her cradle asleep"—Pakium kindled over it—"like an innocent little flower, and she once opened her eyes—such eyes!—and smiled up in my face. Oh, like a flower is the babe!" And much speech followed, till we pictured a tender, flower-like baby, all sweetness and smiles.

Her story was such as to suggest fears, though on the surface things looked safe. Her grandfather, a fine old man, head of the house, was sheltering the baby and her mother and three other children; for the son-in-law had "gone to Colombo," which in this case meant he desired to be free from the responsibilities of wife and family. He had left no address, and had not written after his departure. So the old man had the five on his hands. A Temple woman belonging to a famous South-country Temple, knowing the circumstances, had made a flattering offer for the baby, then just three months old. The grandfather had refused; but the grandmother was religious, and she felt the pinch of the extra five, and secretly influenced her daughter, so that it was probable the Temple woman would win if she waited long enough. And Temple women know how to wait.

THE DOHNAVUR COUNTRY IN FLOOD.

A year passed quietly. We had friends on the watch, and they kept us informed of what was going on. The idea of dedication was becoming gradually familiar to the grandfather, and he was ill and times were hard. But still we could do nothing, for to himself and his whole clan adoption by Christians was a far more unpleasant alternative than Temple-dedication. After all, the Temple people never break caste.

Once a message reached us: "Send at once, for the Temple women are about to get the baby"; and we sent, but in vain. A few weeks later a similar message reached us; and again the long journey was made, and again there was the disappointing return empty-handed. It seemed useless to try any more.

About that time a comrade in North Africa, Miss Lilias Trotter, sent us her new little booklet, "The Glory of the Impossible." As we read the first few paragraphs and roughly translated them for our Tamil fellow-workers, such a hope was created within us that we laid hold with fresh faith and a sort of quiet, confident joy. And yet, when we wrote to our friends who were watching, their answer was most discouraging. The only bright word in the letter was the word "Impossible."

"Far up in the Alpine hollows, year by year, God works one of His marvels. The snow-patches lie there, frozen into ice at their edges from the strife of sunny days and frosty nights; and through that ice-crust come, unscathed, flowers in full bloom.

The Glory of the Impossible

"Back in the days of the bygone summer the little soldanella plant spread its leaves wide and flat on the ground to drink in the sun-rays; and it kept them stored in the root through the winter. Then spring came and stirred its pulses even below the snow-shroud. And as it sprouted, warmth was given out in such strange measure that it thawed a little dome of the snow above its head. Higher and higher it grew, and always above it rose the bell of air till the flower-bud formed safely within it; and at last the icy covering of the air-bell gave way and let the blossom through into the sunshine, the crystalline texture of its mauve petals sparkling like the snow itself, as if it bore the traces of the fight through which it had come.

"And the fragile things ring an echo in our hearts that none of the jewel-like flowers nestled in the warm turf on the slopes below could waken. We love to see the impossible done, and so does God."

These were the sentences which we read together. To the South Indian imagination Alpine snow is something quite inconceivable; but the picture on the cover and snow-scene photographs helped, and the Indian mind is ever quick to apprehend the spiritual, so the booklet did its work.

We have two seasons here, the wet and the dry. The dry is subdivided into hot, hotter, and hottest; but the wet stands alone. It is a time when the country round Dohnavur is swamp or lake according to the level of the ground; and we do not expect visitors—the heavy bullock-carts sink in the mud and make the way too difficult. If a letter had come just then asking us to send for the baby, we should certainly have tried to go; but no letter came, and it was then, when everything said, "Impossible," that suddenly all resistance gave way and the grandfather said: "Let her go to the Christians."

PAKIUM AND NAVEENA.

We were sitting round the dinner-table one wet evening, thinking of nothing more exciting than the flying and creeping creatures which insisted upon drowning themselves in our soup, when the jingle of bullock-bells made us look at each other incredulously; and then, without waiting to wonder who it was, we all ran out and met Rukma running in from the wet darkness. "It's it! it's it!" she cried, and danced into the dining-room, decorum thrown to the pools in the compound. "Look at it!" and we saw a bundle in her arms. And it howled.

From that day on for nearly a week it continued consistently to howl. We called the little thing Naveena, for the name means "new"; and it was our nearest approach to Soldanella, which we should have called her if we did not keep to Indian names for our babies. New and fresh as that little flower of joy, so was our new little gift to us, a new token for good. But flowers and howlers—the words draw their little skirts aside and refuse to touch each other. From certain points of view, in this case as so often, the sublime and the ridiculous were much too close together. The very crows made remarks about the baby when she wakened the morning with her howls. Mercifully for the family's nerves she fell asleep at noon; but as soon as she woke she began again, and went on till both she and we were exhausted. There were no tears, the big dark eyes were only entirely defiant; and the baby stood straight up with her hands behind her back and her mouth open—that was all. But we knew it meant pure misery, though expressed so very aggressively; and we coaxed and petted when she would allow us, and won her confidence at last, and then she stopped.

Friends

It took months to tame the little thing. She had been allowed to do exactly as she liked; for she was her grandfather's pet, and no one might cross her will. We had to go very gently; but eventually she understood and became a dear little girl, reserved but very affectionate, and scampish to such a degree that Chellalu, discerning a congenial spirit, decided to adopt her as "her friend."

This fact was announced to us at the babies' Bible-class, when the word "friend," which was new to the babies, was being explained. It has four syllables in Tamil, and the babies love four-syllabled words. They were rolling this juicy morsel under their tongues with sounds of appreciation, when Chellalu pointed across to Naveena, and with an air of possession remarked, "*She* is my friend." The other babies nodded their heads, "Yes, Naveena is Chellalu's friend!" Naveena looked flattered and very pleased.

These friends in a kindergarten class are rather terrible. They are always separated—as the Tamil would say, if one sits north the other sits south—but even so there are means of communication. This morning, passing the door of the kindergarten room, I looked in and saw something not included in the time-table. We have a little yellow bellflower here which grows in great profusion; and some vandal taught the babies to blow it up like a little balloon, and then snap it on the forehead. The crack it makes is delightful. We do not like this game, and try to teach the babies to respect the pretty flowers; but there are so many sins in the world, that we do not make another by actually forbidding it; we trust to time and sense and good feeling to help us. So it comes to pass that the worst scamps indulge in this game without feeling too guilty; and now I saw Chellalu with a handful of the flowers, cracking them at intervals, to the distraction of the teacher and the delight of all the class. One other was cracking flowers too. It was Naveena, and there was a method in her cracks. When Rukma turned to Chellalu, Naveena cracked her flower. When she turned to Naveena, then Chellalu cracked hers. How they had eluded the search which precedes admission to the kindergarten nobody knew; but there they were, each with a goodly handful of bells. At a word from Rukma, however, they handed them over to her with an indulgent smile, and even offered to search the other babies in case they had secreted any; and as I left the room the lesson continued as before, but the friends' intention was evident: they had hoped to be turned out together.

CHAPTER XVI

The Neyoor Nursery

"The roads are rugged, the precipices steep; there may be feelings of dizziness on the heights, gusts of wind, peals of thunder, nights of awful gloom. Fear them not!

"There are also the joys of sunlight, flowers such as are not in the plain, the purest of air, restful nooks, and the stars smile thence like the eyes of God."—Père Didon (*translated by Rev. Arthur G. Nash*).

ON THE ROAD TO NEYOOR.

AND now for a chapter of history. We had not been long at the new work before we discovered difficulties unimagined before, and impossible to describe in detail. Some of these concerned the health of the younger children; and eventually it seemed best to move the infants' nursery to within reach of medical help, and keep the bigger babies and elder children, whose protection was another grave anxiety, with us at Dohnavur.

Shortly before that time we had been brought into touch with the medical missionaries at Neyoor, in South Travancore. The senior missionary, Dr. Fells, was about to retire; but his successor, Dr. Bentall, cordially agreed to let us rent a little house in the village and fill it with babies, though he knew such a houseful might materially add to the fulness of his already overflowing day. He, and afterwards Dr. Davidson (now the only survivor at Neyoor of that kind trio of doctors), seemed to think nothing a trouble if only it helped a friend. So the little house was taken and the babies installed.

ON THE OUTSKIRTS OF NAGERCOIL, WHERE WE STOPPED TO REST.

The first day, September 25, 1905, is a day to be remembered. I had gone on before to prepare the house, and for a day and a half waited in uncertainty as to what had happened to the little party which was to have followed close behind. I had left one baby ill. She was the first child sent to us from the Canarese country; and I thought of the friends who had sent her, newly interested and stirred to seek these little ones, and of what it would mean of discouragement to them if she were taken, and my heart held on for her.

At last the carts appeared in sight. It was the windy season, and six carts had been overturned on the road, so they had travelled slowly. Then a wheel came off one of their carts and an accident was narrowly averted. This had caused the delay. The baby about whom I had feared had recovered in time to be sent on. She was soon quite well, and has continued well from that day to this.

The Welcome

How familiar the road between Dohnavur and Neyoor became to us, as the months passed and frequent journeys were made with little new babies! Sometimes those journeys were very wearisome. There was great heat, or a dust-laden wind filled the bandy to suffocation and blew out the spirit-lamp when we stopped to prepare the babies' food. How glad we used to be when, in the early evening, the white gleam of the stretch of water outside Nagercoil appeared in sight! We used to stop and bathe the babies, and feed them under some convenient trees, and then go on to our friends with whom we were to spend the night, trusting that the soothing effect of the bathe and food would not pass off until after our arrival. Those friends, our comrades of the L.M.S., like the Medicals at Neyoor, seemed made of kindness. How often their welcome has rested us after the long day!

Next morning we tried to start early, so as to arrive at Neyoor before the sun shone in fever-threatening strength straight in through the open end of the cart. This plan, however, proved too difficult, so we found it better to travel slowly straight on from Dohnavur to Neyoor. In this way we missed the blazing sun; but we also missed the refreshment of our friends at Nagercoil, and arrived more or less tired out, after a journey which, because of slow progress and frequent stops, was equal in time to one from London to Marseilles. But the welcome at the nursery made up for everything.

How vividly the photograph recalls it! The house opened upon the main street of the village, and there was nearly always a watcher on the look-out for us. Sometimes it was Isaac, our good man-of-all-work, who never failed Ponnamal through the two years he was with us. Then we would hear a call, and Ponnamal (we used to call her the Princess, but dignity gives place to something more human at such moments) would come flying down the path with a face which made words superfluous. Then there was the scramble out of the bandy, and the handing down of babies and exclamations about them; and all the nurses seemed to be kissing us at once and making their amazed babies kiss us, and everything was for one happy moment bewilderingly delightful.

Then there was the run round the cradles in which smaller babies were sleeping, and an eager comparing of notes as to the improvement of each. And if there were no improvement, how well one remembers the smothered sense of disappointment—smothered in public at least, lest the nurses should be discouraged. Then came a cup of tea on the mat in the little front room, where four white hammock-cradles hung, one in each corner; while Ponnamal sat beside me with three babies on her knee and two or three more somewhere near her. The babies used to study me in their wise and serious fashion, and then make careful advances. And so we would make friends.

Ponnamal had always much to tell about the exhaustless kindness of the doctors and their wives and the lady superintendent of the hospital. And the chief Tamil medical Evangelist had been true to his name, which means Blessedness. Once, in much distress of mind, we sent a little babe to the nursery, hardly daring to hope for her. When she arrived, the doctors were both away on tour, and the medical Evangelist was in charge. He attended to her at once, and by God's grace upon his work was able to relieve the little child, who has prospered ever since.

But I must leave unrecorded many acts of helpfulness. In those early days of doubt and difficulty, almost forgotten by us now, we beckoned to our "partners which were in the other ship," and their Master and ours will not forget how they held out willing hands and helped us.

It was not always plain sailing, even at Neyoor. "You are fighting Satan at a point upon which he is very sensitive; he will not leave you long in peace," wrote an experienced friend. On Palm Sunday, 1907, our first little band of young girls, fruit of this special work, confessed Christ in baptism, and we stood by the shining reach of water, and tasted of a joy so pure and thrilling that nothing of earth may be likened to it. A fortnight later we were ordered to the hills, and then the trouble came.

The immediate cause was overcrowding. Why did we overcrowd?

Could we Refuse?

Friends at home to whom the facts about Temple service were new, were stirred to earnest prayer. Out here fellow-missionaries helped us to save the children. God heard the prayer and blessed the work, and children began to come. Soon our one little room became too full. We had babies in the bungalow and on our verandah, babies everywhere. Then money came to build two more rooms, but they were soon too full. At Neyoor the pressure was worse, for we could only rent two small houses; and though we put up mat shelters, and the children lived as much as possible in the open air, it was difficult to manage. But how could we refuse the little children? The Temple women were ready to take them if we had refused. Their houses are never too full. There was no other nursery to which they could be sent. Little children who had passed the troublesome infant stage could sometimes find a home elsewhere; but only the Temple houses were open at all times to babies. Could we have written to the friend who had saved a little child: "Hand her back to the Temple. It is the will of our Father that this little one should perish"? Should we have done it? We dare not do it. We prayed that help would be sent to build new nurseries, and we went on and did our best; but it was difficult.

We had just reached the hills in early April, and were forbidden to return, when news reached us of a fatal epidemic of dysentery which had broken out in the Neyoor nursery. Unseasonable rains had fallen and driven the babies indoors; this increased the overcrowding. The doctors were away. Letters telling us about the disaster had been lost—how, we never knew—so that the second which reached us, taking it for granted we had the first, gave no details, only the names of the smitten babes—nineteen of them, and five dead. Then trouble followed trouble. "While he was yet speaking, there came also another." Some evil men who had sought to injure us before, caused us infinite anxiety. And for a time that cannot be counted in days or in weeks it was like living through a nightmare, when everything happens in painful confusion and the sense of oppression is complete.

THE NEYOOR NURSERY.

Out of the maelstrom came a letter from Ponnamal. "We are being comforted," she wrote. "You will be longing to come to us, but oh, do not come! If you were here all your strength would be given to fighting this battle with death, and you would have no strength left for prayer. God wanted to have one of us free to pray; and so He has taken you up to the mountain, as He took Moses when the people were fighting down in the plain." This was the true inward meaning of it all, and I knew it. But Ponnamal is far from strong, and I feared for her; and to stay away with the babies ill—it was the very hardest thing I had ever been asked to do.

When the trouble passed there were ten in heaven. One, a little child of two, had been saved so wonderfully from Temple dedication that we had looked forward to a future of special blessing for her; and another was a very lovely babe, dear to the missionary who, after much toil and many disappointments, had been comforted by saving her. Each of the ten had cost someone much. But this is an earthly point of view. They had cost Him most who had taken them, and he is only an owner in name who has no right to do as he will with his own.

The other side, the purely human side, pressed heavily just then. The doctors had most kindly at once ordered a mission room, vacated at that season, to be lent to the nursery, and another little house was taken for the month. How Ponnamal kept all four houses going in an orderly fashion, how she kept her nurses together through that time of almost panic, and how she herself, frail and delicate as she is, kept up till all was over, we cannot understand from any point of view but the Divine. She only broke down once. It was when her dearest child, our merry, beautiful little Heart's Joy, who, having more strength than most, had battled longer and almost recovered, suddenly sank. The visible cause was that a special nutrient, which, being costly, we stocked in small quantities, ran short, and the fresh supply reached the nursery just too late. "If only it had come yesterday!" moaned Ponnamal, and we with her when we heard of the series of contretemps which had delayed its arrival. The torture of second causes is as the blackness of darkness, but the Lord gave deliverance from it; for just as she had to part with all that was left her of our little Heart's Joy, a letter came from Dr. Davidson which was God's own blessed

61

comfort to a heart almost broken. She never refers to that letter without the quick tears starting. "I could let my little treasure go after I read that letter. It strengthened me."

"The Lord sat as King at the Flood"

While all this was going on in Neyoor, Chellalu, then just two years old, was very ill in Dohnavur. Mr. and Mrs. Walker were still there, and they nursed her night and day; but at last a letter came, evidently meant to prepare me for fresh sorrow. "Every little lamb belongs to the Good Shepherd, not to us," the letter said, and told of a temperature 106° and rising. The child, all spirit and frolic, had little reserve strength, and there was not much cause for hope. But we were spared this parting. Chellalu is with us still.

The sky was clearing again and we were beginning to breathe freely, when the worst that had ever touched us in all our years of work came suddenly upon us. How small things that affect the body appear when the point of attack wheels round to the soul! The death of all the babies seemed as nothing compared with the falling away of one soul. But God is the God of the waves and the billows, and they are still His when they come over us; and again and again we have proved that the overwhelming thing does not overwhelm. Once more by His interposition deliverance came. We were cast down, but not destroyed.

A time of calm succeeded this storm. Money came to build nurseries at Dohnavur, and buy more of the special nutrients we so much required. The Neyoor remnant picked up, and the nurses took heart again. I went out to them as soon as I could after our return from the hills, and found those who were left well and strong. "They shall see His face" had been the text in *Daily Light*, the evening the news reached me of the little procession heavenwards. I looked at the ten names written in the margin of my book; and, recalling the story of each, could be glad they have seen the face of the One who loves them best. Lower down on the page come the words, "We shall be satisfied." We thought of our babies satisfied so soon; and then we knelt together and said, "Even so, Father: for so it seemeth good in Thy sight."

Pretty pictures all in colours and bright sunshine tempt one to linger over that visit. I can see the white hammocks slung from the trees in the nursery compound, and happy baby-faces looking out of them. And another shows me one who had been like a sister to Ponnamal, lightening her load whenever she could; sitting with two dear babies in her arms, and another clinging round her neck. "She comes and helps us often in the mornings when we are very busy," said Ponnamal about the doctor's wife, as I noticed the babies' affection for her and her sweet, kind ways with them. "Sometimes when I am feeling down and home-sick, she comes in like this and plays with the babies, and cheers us all up." The Indian woman is very home-loving. Only devotion to the children could have kept the nurses and Ponnamal so long in exile for their sake; and there were times when even Ponnamal's brave heart sank. Then these love-touches helped.

Goodbye to Neyoor

When the time came for the nursery party to leave Neyoor and return to Dohnavur, after two and a half years in that hospitable mission, we were sorry to part. Days like the days we had passed through test the stuff of which souls are made, and they prove what we call friendship. After the fire has spent itself, the fine gold shines out purified, and there is something solemn in its light. We had grown close to our friends in Neyoor; but the cloud had moved, so far as we could read the sign, and it seemed right to return. The missionaries were away when the day came, but the Christians surrounded Ponnamal with tokens of goodwill. "The nursery has been like a little light in our midst," they said; and this word cheered her more than all other words. And so farewelled, they arrived home, all glad and warm with the glow that comes when hearts meet each other and each finds the other kind.

CHAPTER XVII

In the Compound and Near it

THE OLD NURSERY. THE "ROOM OF JOY."

"NOW I know why God put you in Dohnavur when He wanted this work done. He hid you from the eyes of the world for the little children's sake. He knew this work could never have been done by the road-side, so He hid you."

The speaker was a Christian friend from Palamcottah, an Indian lawyer who, for the first time, had come out to see us. He had found our approaches appalling, and had wondered at first why we lived in such an out-of-the-way place, three or four miles from the nearest road, and twenty-four from civilisation. When he saw the children he understood. Later, he helped us in an attempt to save two little ones in danger, and insisted not only upon paying his own and our worker's expenses, but in sending us a gift for the nurseries. With the gift came a letter full of loving, Indian sympathy; and again he added as before: "The Lord hid you in that quiet place for the little children's sake." Sometimes when the inconveniences of jungle life press upon us, we remember our friend's words: "This work could never have been done by the road-side, so He hid you."

We have children with us who would not have been safe for a day had we lived near a large town or near a railway. The stretch of open country between us and Palamcottah (the Church Missionary Society centre of the Tinnevelly district), to cover which, by bullock-cart, takes as long as to travel from London to Brussels, is not considered very safe for solitary Indian travellers, as the robber clan frequent it, and this is an added protection for the children. Several times, to our knowledge, unwelcome visitors have been deterred from making a raid upon us, by the rumour of the robbers on the road. We are also most mercifully quite out of the beat of the ordinary exploiter of missions; few except the really keen care for such a journey; so that we get on with our work uninterrupted by anything but the occasional arrival of welcome friends and comrades. These, when they visit us for the first time, are usually much astonished to find something almost civilised out in the wilds, and they walk round with an air of surprise, and quite inspiring appreciation, being kindly pleased with little, because they had looked for less.

THE COURTYARD.

The compound in which the nurseries are built is a field, bounded on three sides by fields, and on the fourth by the bungalow compound. The Western Ghauts with their foothills make it a beautiful place.

Coming-days

The buildings are not beautiful. With us, as elsewhere, doubtless, even the break of a gable in the straight, barn-like roof makes a difference in the estimate, and we have never had a margin for luxuries. But the walls are coloured a soft terra-cotta, the roofs are a dull red; while the porches (hidden by the palm trunks in the photograph) are a mass of greenery and bloom; and the garden at the moment of writing is rejoicing in over a hundred lilies, brilliant yellow and flame colour, each head with its many flowers rising separate and radiant in the sunshine. Then we have oleanders, crimson and pink and white, and little young hibiscus trees, crimson and rose and cream. The arches in the new nursery garden are covered with the lilac of morning-glory; and the Prayer-room in the middle of the garden is a mass of violet passion-flower, the pretty pink antigone, and starry jessamine. The very hedges at this season are out in yellow flower, and a trellis round the nursery kitchen is a delight of colour; so though our buildings are simple, we think the lines have fallen unto us in pleasant places.

The first picture shows the old nursery, used now for the kindergarten. It opens off the courtyard shown in the second photo. This courtyard serves as an open-air room, a bright little place which is filled with merrier children than the sober photograph shows. Tamils old and young move when they laugh or even smile; in fact they wriggle. Being still, with them, meant being seriously subdued; and so, where time-exposures were required, we had to choose between solemn photos, or no photos at all.

Opening off the courtyard on the opposite side to the kindergarten is a room used as a store-room and Bible-class room combined. It was so very uncomfortable that last Christmas, as a surprise for the children, we divided the room into two halves with a curtain between. Their half is made pretty with pictures and texts, painted in blue on pale brown wood. The children call this part of the room the Tabernacle. The part beyond the curtain is the court of the Gentiles.

The Coming-Day Feasts are a feature of Dohnavur life. Now that there are so many feasts to celebrate, we find it more convenient to combine; and the photograph overleaf shows as much as it can of one such happy feast. The children who are being fêted are distinguished from the others by having flowers in their hair. No Indian feast is complete without flowers. Jessamine is the favourite, but the prettiest wreaths are made of pink oleander; and sometimes a girl will surprise us with a new and lovely combination, as of brown flowering grasses and yellow Tecoma bells.

COMING-DAY FEAST.

Opposite the kindergarten room is the first of the two new nurseries—the lively Parrot-house. This nursery, really the Taraha (Star, called after its English giver, whose name means "star") is the abode of the middle-aged babies, aged between two years and four. Most of these attend the kindergarten, and are very proud of the fact.

The Prémalia nursery (Abode of Love), given by two friends in memory of a mother translated, lies beyond the Taraha. Here the tiny infants live, and we call it the Menagerie. This nursery, like the other, looks out on the glorious mountains. If beautiful things can make babies good, ours should be very good.

On the eastern side of the field we have lately built two small sick-rooms, used oftener as overflow nurseries. These little rooms have names meaning "peace" and "tranquillity"; and those of us who have lived in them with our babies, sick or well, find the names appropriate. In the foreground there is a garden, in the background the mountain; and to give purpose to it all, the foreground is full of life. A new nursery now being built is a welcome gift from Australia; and a new field with a noble tree, in whose shade a hundred children could play, is the gift of a friend who stayed with us for one bright week last year.

All this is a later development, unthought of when our artist friend was with us. We have often wished for him since the nurseries filled. When he was with us our choice of subject was very limited: now, wherever we look we see pictures, which to be properly caught ask for colour photography.

The story of these buildings is the story of the Ravens, so old and yet so new. When first the work began, we had only one mud-floored room for nursery, kitchen, bedroom, and everything else that was needed. We hardly knew ourselves whereunto things would grow, and feared to run before the Lord by even a prayer for buildings. And yet we could not go on as we were. The birds were soon too many for the nest, and we needed more nests. No one knew of our need; for visitors at that time were few at Dohnavur, and we told no one. But money began to come. We ventured on a single room without a verandah

65

or even foundations—built of sun-dried bricks as inexpensively as possible. But it was a palace to us. While we were building it, more little children came. We felt we should need more room, but had not more money; so we told the builders to wait for a day while we gave ourselves to prayer about the matter. Was the work going to grow much more? We were fearful of making mistakes. Were we right to incur fresh responsibility?—for buildings need to be kept in condition, and the cheaper they are the more care they need. No one at home was responsible for us. No one had authorised this new work. It would not be fair to saddle those on whom the burden might eventually fall with responsibilities for which they were not responsible. And yet surely the work of saving these little children had been given to us to do? Someone was responsible. Surely, unless we were utterly wrong and had mistaken the Shepherd's Voice, surely He was responsible! He could not mean us to search for the lambs for whom only the wolves had been searching, and then leave them out in the open, found but unfolded, or packed so close in the little fold that they could not grow as little lambs should?

The Registered Letter

We rolled the burden off that day as to the ultimate responsibility, and we asked definitely for all that was needed to build another room.

Three days later a registered letter came from a bank in Madras. It contained an anonymous gift of one hundred rupees, and was marked, "For a new nursery." The date showed that it had been posted in Madras on the day of our waiting upon God for guidance as to His wishes. A few days later, the same amount, with the same direction as to its use, was sent to us from the same bank. The giver, as we knew long afterwards, was a fellow-missionary in Tinnevelly, whose order to send these sums to us was given before even we ourselves had fully understood the meaning of the leading. The second room was built on to the first, and the children called it the Room of Joy.

THE RED LAKE.
Water Palms, with Mountains in the background.

There are no secrets in India. The Hindu masons were amazed at what they at once recognised as the hand of the Lord upon the work, and they spread the story everywhere. Later, when they built the nursery where poor little Mala stood and mourned, they understood why they had to stop before the verandah was built. Only enough was in hand to build the bare room; but to their eyes, as to ours, a verandah was much needed, and they were content to wait till what was required for one came. In this land of blazing sunshine and drenching monsoon a house without a verandah is hardly habitable, and a small square room without one has a Manx-cat appearance.

"These are Thy wonders, Lord"

The story of the rooms has been repeated in the story of the work ever since. "Do not thank us. It is only a belated tenth," wrote a fellow-missionary not long ago, as she sent a gift for the nurseries. Belated tenths have reached us sometimes when they have been like visible ravens flying straight from the blue above. All the long journeys in search of the children, all the expenses connected with their salvation, all that has been required to provide nurses and food (including the special nourishment without which the more delicate could not live at all), all that is now being needed for their education—all has come and is coming as the ravens came to Elijah. The work has been a revelation of how many hearts are sensitive and obedient to the touch of the Spirit; for sometimes help has reached us in such a way and in such form that we could not but stand and worship, awestruck by the token of the nearness of our God. There is many a spot marked in garden or in field or in the busy nursery or our own quiet room, where, with the open letter in our hand—the letter of relief from a pressure unknown even to the nearest fellow-worker—we have knelt in spirit with Jacob and said: "Surely the Lord is in this place!" and almost added, so dense are we in unilluminated moments, "and I knew it not."

Framed between red roofs and foliage, there are far blue glimpses of mountains shown in this lakeside photograph. We do not see the water from the compound. It lies on the other side of the boundary fields and hedges; but we see the mountains with perfect distinctness of outline, scarped with bare crags, which in the early morning are sometimes pink, and in the evening, purple. But the time to see the mountains in their glory is when the south-west monsoon is flinging its masses of cloud across to us. Then the mountains, waking from the lazy sleep of the long, hot months, catch the clouds on their pointed fangs, toss them back and harry them, wrap themselves up in robes of them, and go to sleep again.

The road that skirts the Red Lake leads through two ancient Hindu towns, from both of which we have children saved, in each case as by a miracle. In the first of these old towns there is a Temple surrounded by a mighty wall.

There are two large gates and one small side door in the wall; and, passing in through the small side door, one sees another wall almost as strong as the first, and realises something of the power that built it. The Temple is in the centre of the large enclosure. It is a single tower opening off the inner court. In the outer court a pillared hall is used as stable for the Temple elephant, and two camels lounge in the roughly kept garden in front. This Temple, with its double walls, its massive, splendidly-carved doors and expensive animal life, is somewhat of a surprise to the visitor, who hardly expects to see so much in a little old country town on the borders of the wilds. But Hinduism has not lost hold of this old remote India yet. There are some who think that the country town is the place to see it in strength.

AT THE DOOR OF THE TEMPLE.

It was early in August, three years ago, that we heard of a baby girl in that town, devoted from birth to the god. We set wheels in motion, and waited. A month passed and nothing was done. We could not go ourselves and attempt to persuade the mother to change the vow she had made, as any movement on our part would only have riveted the links that fettered the child to the god. We had to be quiet and wait. At last, one evening in September, a Hindu arrived in the town with whom our friends who were on the watch had intimate connection. He, too, knew about the child; and he knew a way unknown to our friends by which the mother might be influenced, and he consented to try. His arrival just at that juncture appeared to us, who were waiting in daily expectation of an answer of deliverance, as the evident beginning of that answer; thus our faith was quickened and we waited in keen hope. Two days later, after dark, there was a rush from the nursery to the bungalow. "The baby has come!" Another moment, and we were in the nursery. A woman—one of our friends—was standing with what looked like a parcel wrapped in a cloth hidden under her arm. Even then, though all was safe, she was trembling; and outside, two men, her relations, stood on guard. She opened the white cloth, and inside was the baby.

Her Choice

The men assured us that all was right. The mother had been convinced of the wrongness of dedicating the little babe, and would give us no trouble. But a day or two later, she came and demanded it back. She could not stand the derision of her friends, who told her she had sinned far more in giving her child to those who would break its caste than she ever could have done had she given it to the Temple. We pacified her with difficulty, and were thankful when the little thing was safe in the Neyoor nursery. For in those days, before we learned how best to protect our children, we were often glad to have some place even more out of reach than Dohnavur.

The second of these old towns is famous for its rock, and its Temple built into the rock. Looking down from above one can see inside the courtyard as into an open well. Connected with this Temple, some years ago, there was a beautiful young Temple woman, who had been given as a child—as all Temple women must be—to the service of the gods. She had no choice as regarded herself—probably the idea of choice never entered her mind—but for her babe she determined to choose; and yet she knew of no way of deliverance.

But there was a way of deliverance, and if it had only been for this one child's sake, and for the sake of the relief it must have been to that fear-haunted mother, we are glad with a gladness too deep for words that the nursery was here. For the mother heard of it. There were lions in the path. She quietly avoided them, and through others who were willing to help she sent her child to us. She herself would not come. She waited a mile or so from the bungalow till the matter was concluded, then returned to her home alone.

A week later she appeared suddenly at the bungalow. It was only to make sure the little one was safe and well, and in order to sign a paper saying she was wholly given to us. This done she disappeared again, refusing speech with anyone, and for months we heard nothing of her. Then cholera swept our countryside, and we heard she had taken it and died. We leave her to God her Creator, who alone knows all the story of her life: we only know enough to make us very silent. And through the quiet we hear as it were a voice that chants a fragment from an old hymn: "We believe that **THOU** shalt come to be our Judge."

CHAPTER XVIII

From the Temple of the Rock

ANOTHER little girl who came from that same Temple of the Rock has a story very different from the other, and far more typical.

It was on a blazing day in June, when the very air, tired of being hot, leaned heavily upon us, and we felt unequal to contest, that a cough outside my open door announced a visitor. "Come in!" Another cough, and I looked out and saw a shuffling form disappear round the corner of the house. I called again, and the figure turned. It was a man who had helped us before, but about whose *bonâ-fides* we had doubts; so we asked without much hopefulness what he had to tell us. He said he had reason to believe a certain Temple woman known to him had a child she meant to dedicate to the god of a Temple a day's journey distant. Then he paused. "Do you know where she is now?" "She is on her way to the Temple." "It would be well if she came here instead." "If that is the Animal's desire it may be possible to bring her." "Has she gone far? Could you overtake her?" "She is waiting outside your gate."

At such a moment it is wise to show no surprise and no anxiety. All the burning eagerness must be covered up with coolness. But in the hour that intervened before the woman "at the gate" could be persuaded to come further, we quieted ourselves in the Lord our God and held on for the little child.

At last the shuffling step and the sound of voices told us they had come—two women, the man, and a child. The child was a baby of something under two, a sad-looking little thing, with great, dark, pathetic eyes looking out from under limp brown curls. She was very pale and fragile; and when the woman who carried her set her down upon the floor and propped her against the wall, she leaned against it listlessly, with her little chin in her tiny hand, in a sorrowful, grown-up fashion. I longed to take her and nestle her comfortably; but, of course, took no notice of her. Any sign of pity or sympathy would have been misunderstood by the women. All through the interminable talk upon which her fate depended, that child sat wearily patient, making no demands upon anyone; only the little head drooped, and the mouth grew pitiful in its complete despondency.

The ways of the East are devious. The fact that the child had been brought to us did not indicate a decision to give her to us instead of to the Temple. The woman and the man who had persuaded them to come had much to say to one another, and there was much we had to explain. A child given to Temple service is not in all cases entirely cut off from her people. If the Temple woman's hold on her is sure, her relations are sometimes allowed to visit her; so far as friendly intercourse goes she is not lost to them. But with us things are different. For the child's own sake we have to refuse all intercourse whatever. Once given to us, she is lost to them as if they had never had her. We adopt the little one altogether or not at all.

Till the Battle is Won

It is a delicate thing to explain all this so clearly that there can be no misunderstanding about it, without so infuriating the relations that they will have nothing more to do with us. Naturally their view-point is entirely different from ours, and they cannot appreciate our reasons. At such a time we lean upon the Invisible, and count upon that supernatural help which alone is sufficient for us; we count also upon the prayers of those who know what it is to pray through all opposing forces, till the battle is won by faith which is the victory.

It was strange to watch the women as the talk went on. The *woman* within them had died, there was nothing of it left to which we could appeal; everything about them was perverted, unnatural. I looked at the insensitive faces and then at the sensitive face of the child, and entered deeper than ever into the mercifulness of God's denunciations of sin.

Once towards the close of what had been a time of some tension, the leader of the two women suddenly sprang up, snatched at the tired baby, and flung out of the room with her. She had been gradually hardening; and I had felt rather than seen the shutting down of the prison-house gates upon that little soul, and had, as a last resource, appealed to the sense, not wholly atrophied, the sense that recognises the supernatural. God is, I told them briefly; God takes cognisance of what we are and do: God will repay: some time, somewhere, God will punish sin. The arrow struck through to the mark. Startled, indignant, overwhelmed by the sweep of an awful conviction, with a passionate cry she rushed away; and we lived through one breathless moment, but the next saw the child dropped into our arms, safe at last.

Facts about any matter of importance are usually other than at first stated; but we have reason to believe that in this instance our shuffling friend spoke the truth. The women were really on their way to the Temple when he waylaid them. The wonder was that they allowed themselves to be persuaded by him to come to us. But if nothing happened except what we might naturally expect would happen in this work, we might as well give it up at once. If we did not expect our Jericho walls to fall down flat, it would be foolish indeed to continue marching round them.

It was a relief when the women left the compound, after signing a paper committing the child to us. There is defilement in the mere thought of evil, but such close contact with it is a thing by itself. The sense of contamination lasted for days; and yet would that we could go through it every day if the result might be the same! For the child woke up to a new life, and became what a child should be. At first it was very pitiful. She would sit hour after hour as she had sat through that first hour, with her chin in hand, her eyes cast down, and the little mouth pathetic. We found that, in accordance with a custom prevailing in the coterie of Temple women belonging to the Temple of the Rock, she had been lent by her mother to another woman when she was an infant, the other lending her baby in exchange. This exchange had worked sadly; for the little one had asked for something which had not been given her, and her two years had left her starved of love and experienced in loneliness. But when she came to us everything changed; for love and happiness took her hands and led her back to baby ways, and taught her how to laugh and play: and now there is nothing left to remind us of those two first years but a certain droop of the little mouth when she feels for the moment desolate, or wants some extra petting.

CHAPTER XIX

Yosépu

THE WATER CARRIERS.

NO description of the compound would be complete without mention of Yosépu, friend of the babies.

This photograph shows the Indian equivalent of pumps and water-pipes. We have neither; so all the water required for a family of about a hundred has to be drawn from the well and carried to the kitchens and nurseries. The elder girls, who would otherwise help

71

with the work, according to South Indian custom, are already fully employed with the babies. So at present the men do it all. They also buy the grain and other food-stuffs, look after the cows and vegetable garden—a necessity for those who dwell far from markets—and in all other possible masculine ways are of service to the family.

Chief of these men is Yosépu, whose seamed and wrinkled and most expressive face I wish we had photographed, instead of this not very interesting string of solemnities.

Yosépu is not like a man, he is more like a dear dog. He has the ways of our dog-friends, their patience and fidelity, their gratefulness for pats.

He came to us in a wrecked condition, thin and weak and rather queer. He had been beaten by his Hindu brother for becoming a Christian, and it had been too much for him. The first time we saw him, a few minutes after his arrival, he was standing leaning against a post with folded hands and upturned eyes and a general expression of resignation which went to our hearts. We found afterwards he was not feeling resigned so much as hungry, and he was better after food.

For a week he slept, ate, and meditated. Sometimes he would hover round us, if such a verb is admissible for his seriousness of gait. He would wait till we noticed him, then sigh and extend his hand. He wanted us to feel his pulse—both pulses. This ceremony always refreshed him, and he would return to his corner of the verandah and meditate till his next meal came.

Sometimes, however, more attention was required. He would linger after his pulses were felt, and we knew he was not satisfied. One day a happy thought struck us. The Tamil loves scent. The very babies sniff our hands if we happen to be using scented soap, and tell each other rapturously what they think about that "chope." Scent is the one thing they cannot resist. A tin of sweets on our table may be untouched for days, few babies being wicked enough to venture upon it in our absence; but a bottle of scent is irresistible, and scented "chope" on our washing-stands has a way of growing thin. The baby will emerge from our bathrooms rubbing suspiciously clean hands, and in her innocence will invite us to smell them. Then we know why our "chope" disappears. So now that Yosépu needed something to lift him over the trials of life, we remembered the gift of a good Scottish friend, and tried the effect of eau-de-Cologne. It worked most wonderfully. Yosépu held out his two hands joined close lest a single drop should spill, and then he stood and sniffed. It would have made a perfect advertisement—the big brown man with his hands folded over his nose, and an expression of absolute bliss upon every visible feature. Now, when Yosépu is down-hearted, we always try eau-de-Cologne.

Blessed be Drudgery

His first move towards being of use was when some of our children had small-pox and were put up in a half-finished room which was being built. "It has walls and it has a roof, therefore it is suitable," was Yosépu's opinion; and he offered to nurse the children. One evening we heard a terrible noise; it was like three cracked violins gone mad, all playing different tunes at the same time. It was only Yosépu singing hymns to the children. "For spiritual instruction is a thing to be desired, and there is nothing so edifying as music."

After this he announced his intention of becoming a water-carrier. "Water is a pure thing and a necessity. The young children demand much water if their bodies are to be"—here followed Scriptural quotations meant in deepest reverence. "I will be responsible for the baths of all the babes." And from that time Yosépu has been responsible. Solemnly from dawn to dusk, with breathing spaces for meals and meditation, he stalks across from nurseries to well and from well to nurseries. He is a man of few smiles; but he is the cause of many, and we all feel grateful to Yosépu for his goodness to us. Often on melancholy days he comes and comforts us.

It was so one anxious day before we went to the hills, when we were trying to plan for the safety of our family. We can only take a limited number of converts with us, and no babies; the difficulty is then which to take, which to hide, and which to leave in the nurseries. We were in the midst of this perplexity when Yosépu arrived. He stood in silence, and then sighed, as his cheerful custom is. We made the usual inquiries as to his health, physical and spiritual. Both soul and body (his invariable order, never body and soul) were well, he said; his pulse did not need to be felt to-day: no, there was something weightier upon his mind. There are times when it is like extracting a tooth to get a straight answer from Yosépu, for he resents directness in speech; he thinks it barbarous. At last it came. "Aiyo! Aiyo!" (Alas! Alas!) "My sun has set; but who am I, that I should complain or assault the decrees of Providence? But Amma! remember the word of truth: 'Then shall ye bring down my grey hairs with sorrow to the grave.'" And he slowly unwound his wisp of a turban, held it in his folded hands, and shook down his lanky, jet-black locks with a pathos that was almost sublime.

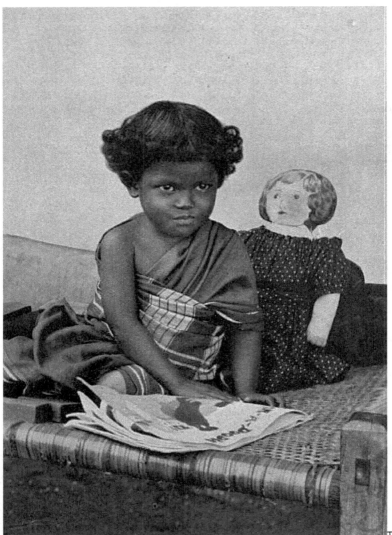

THE BELOVED TINGALU.

It took time to pierce to the meaning of it: the children were being scattered—the reason must be that we felt the bath-water carrying too much for his powers through the hot weeks. It was not so! He was strong to draw and to bear. The babies should never be deprived of their baths! But to-day as he went to the well he had heard what broke his heart; and he laid his hand upon the injured organ, and sighed with a sigh that assured us his lungs at least were sound. "*Tingalu* is to go away! The apple of my eye! that golden child who smiles upon me, and says, 'Oh, elder brother, good morning!' You are not going to leave her with me! Therefore spake I the word of truth concerning my grey hairs." Then quoting the text again, he turned and walked away.

Once the beloved Tingalu was slightly indisposed. She has not often the privilege of being ill, and so, when the opportunity offers, she does the invalid thoroughly; it would be a pity, Tingalu thinks, to be anything but correct. But Yosépu was much concerned. He appeared in the early morning with his usual cough and sigh. "Amma! Tingalu is ill!" "She will soon be better, Yosépu; she is having medicine." "What sort of medicine, Amma?" and Yosépu mentioned the kind he thought suitable. "That is exactly what she has had; you will see her playing about to-morrow." "But no smile is on her face to-day; I fear for the babe." (Tingalu never smiles when ill. Invalids should not smile.) Yosépu suggested another medicine to supplement the first, and departed.

I will pay for it

Next morning he came again, anxious and cast down in countenance. I had to keep him waiting; and when I came out, he was standing beside my verandah steps, head on one side, eyes shut, hands folded as if in prayer. "Well, Yosépu, what is it?" "Amma! the light of your eyes revives me!" "Well, tell me the trouble." "All yesterday I saw you not; it was a starless night to me!" This is merely the preface. "But, Yosépu, what is wrong?" "Tingalu, that golden child with a voice like a bird, she lies on her mat. I am concerned about the babe," (Tingalu, turned four, is as hardy as a gipsy), "I fear for her delicate interior. Those ignorant children" (the convert nurses would have been pleased if they had heard him) "know nothing at all. It may be they will feed her with curry and rice this morning. That would be dangerous. Amma! Let her have bread and milk, *and I will pay for it!*"

Yosépu came a few days ago with a request for a doll. "Who for?" "For myself." "But are you going to play with it?" Yosépu acknowledged he was, and he wished it to have genuine hair, a pink silk frock, and eyes that would open and shut. We had not anything so elaborate to give him, and he had to be contented with a black china head and painted eyes; but he was pleased, and took it away carefully rolled up in his turban, which serves conveniently for head-gear, towel, scarf, and duster. When and where he plays with the doll no one knows, but he assures us he does; and we have mentally reserved the first pink silk, with eyes that will open and shut, that a benevolent public sends to us, for Yosépu. . . . The words were hardly written when a shadow fell across the paper, and the unconscious subject of this chapter remarked as I looked up: "1 Corinthians vii. 31." "Do you want anything, Yosépu?" "Amma! 1 Corinthians vii. 31." "Well, Yosépu?" "As it is written in that chapter, and that verse: 'The fashion of this world passeth away.' Amma, if within the next two months a visitor comes to Dohnavur carrying a picture-catching box, I desire that you arrange for the catching of my picture. This, Amma, is my desire."

The Western mind is very dense; and for a moment I could not see the connection between the text and the photograph. Yosépu is never impatient. He squatted down beside me, dropped his turban round his neck, held his left foot with his left hand, and emphasised his explanation with his right.

"Amma, the wise know that life is uncertain. I am a frail mortal. You, who are as mother and as father to this unworthy worm, would feel an emptiness within you if I were to depart." "But, Yosépu, I hope you are not going to depart." This was exactly what Yosépu had anticipated. He smiled, then he sighed. "Amma! did I not say it before? 1 Corinthians vii. 31: 'The fashion of this world passeth away.' Therefore I said, Let me have my picture caught, so that when I depart you may hang it on your wall and still remember me."

Within me pulled the Strings of Love

Yosépu's latest freak has been to take a holiday. "My internal arrangements are disturbed; composure of mind will only be obtained by a month's respite from secularities." Yosépu had once announced his intention of offering himself to the

National Missionary Society, and we thought he now referred to becoming an ascetic for a month and wandering round the country, begging-bowl in hand; for he solemnly declared as he stroked his bony frame: "The Lord will provide." But his intention was a real holiday. He would go and see the brother who had beaten him, and forgive him. We suggested the brother might beat him again. He smiled at our want of faith, and went for his holiday. A month was the time agreed upon, but within three days he was back. He could not stay away, he explained, with a shame-faced air of affection. "Within me pulled the strings of love; pulled, yea, pulled till I returned." Faithful, quaint, and wholly original Yosépu! He calls himself our servant, but we think of him as our friend.

CHAPTER XX

The Menagerie

Fate which foresaw
How frivolous a baby man would be—

TWO VIEWS OF LIFE.

THE event of the week, from a Tamil point of view, is the midday Sunday service; so we take care of the nurseries during that hour, and send all grown-up life to church. In the Prémalia nursery the babies range from a few days old to eighteen months, and sometimes two years. There is a baby for every mood, as one beloved of the babies says; and the babies seem to know it. We have a lively time there on Sundays; for by noon the morning sleep is over, and nineteen or twenty babies are waking up one after the other or all together. And most of them want something, and want it at once.

These babies are of various dispositions and colour—nut-brown, biscuit, and buff; and there are two who, taken together, suggest chocolate-cream. Chocolate is a dear child, very good-tempered and easy to manage. Cream is a scamp. We see in her another Chellalu, and watch with mingled feelings her vigorous development.

Chocolate has another name. It is Beetle. This does not sound appreciative, but Beetle is beloved. The name was discovered by her affectionate Piria Sittie, who came upon her one morning lying on her back in the swinging cot, kicking her four limbs in the air in the agitated manner of that insect unexpectedly upset. But no beetle ever smiled as ours does.

Cream, whose real name is Nundinie, oftener called Dimples, because she dimples so when she laughs, is a baby of character. She early discovered her way to the bungalow, and scorning assistance or superintendence found her way over as soon as she could walk. Afternoon tea is never a sombre meal, for the middle-aged babies attend it in relays of four or five; and Dimples and her special chum, Lulla, like to arrive in good time for the full enjoyment of the function. Dimples sits down properly in a high chair close beside her Attai, who, according to her view of matters, was created to help her to sugar. Lulla, so as to be even nearer that exhaustless delight, insists upon her Attai's knee; and tapping her face with her very small fingers, immediately points to the sugar bowl.

Diversions

These preliminaries over, Dimples sets herself to pay for her seat. She smiles upon her Attai first, then upon all the company. If the Iyer is present, she notices him kindly: there is nothing in all nature so patronising as a baby. If in the mood, she will imitate her friends like her predecessor Scamp No. 1; or folding her fat arms will regard us all with a quizzical expression more comical than play. Her latest invention is drill. She stands straight up in her chair, and goes through certain actions intended to represent as much as she knows of that interesting exercise. We are kept anxious lest she should overbalance; but she is a wary babe, and always suddenly sits down when she gets to the edge of a tumble. Sometimes, however, when these diversions are in progress, we have wished that the family could see how very much more entertaining she is in her own nursery. There, from the beginning of the day till the sad moment when it ends, she seems to be engaged in entertaining somebody. Sometimes it is one of the Accals, those good elder sisters to whom the babies owe so much. Dimples thinks she looks tired. Tired people must be cheered, so Dimples devotes herself to her. Sometimes it is another baby who is dull. Dull babies are anomalies. Dimples feels responsible till the dull baby revives. Or it is just her own happy little self who is being entertained. If ever a baby enjoyed a game for its own sweet sake, it is Dimples.

But one thing she does not enjoy, and that is being put to bed at night. Our babies are anointed with oil, according to the custom of the East, before being put to sleep; but the moment Dimples sees the oil-bottle in her nurse's hand, she knows her fate is sealed and protests with all her might. Once she contrived to seize the bottle, pull out the cork, and spill the oil before she was discovered. She seemed to argue that as she was invariably oiled before being put to bed, the best way to avoid ever being put to bed would be to get rid of the oil. Another evening she succeeded in diverting her nurse into a long search for the cork, thereby delaying the fatal last moment; it was finally found in her mouth. When, in spite of all efforts to wriggle out of reach, she is captured, anointed, and put in her hammock, Dimples knows she must not get out; but her wails are so lamentable that it is difficult to restrain ourselves from throwing discipline to the winds, and if by any chance we do, her smiles are simply ravishing. But we hear about it afterwards.

If Dimples is asleep when we take charge of the nursery, we find things fairly quiet and almost flat. But she usually wakens early, and always in a good temper. It is instructive to see the way she scrambles out of her hammock before she is quite awake, and her sleepy stagger across the room is often interrupted by a tumble. Dimples does not mind tumbles. If her curly head has been rather badly knocked, she looks reproachfully at the floor, rubs her head, and gets up again. By the time she reaches us she is wide awake and most engaging.

In C. F. Holder's *Life of Agassiz* we are told that the great scientist "could not bear with superficial study: a man should give his whole life to the object he had undertaken to investigate. He felt that desultory, isolated, spasmodic working avails nothing, but curses with narrowness and mediocrity." This is exactly the view of one of our babies, already introduced, the little wise Lulla, who always knows her own mind and sticks to her intentions, unbeguiled by any blandishments.

This baby is a tiny thing, with a round, small head, covered with soft, small curls; and this head is very full of thoughts. Her face, which she rarely shows to a stranger, is like a doll in its delicate daintiness; but the mouth is very resolute, and the eyes very grave. Her hands and feet are sea-shell things of a pretty pinky brown, and her ways are the ways of a sea-anemone in a pool among the rocks.

Lulla, because of her anemone ways, is sometimes unkindly called "Huffs." She does not understand that there are days when those who love her most have little time to give to her. Lulla naturally argues that where there is a will there is a way, and desultory, isolated, spasmodic affection is worth little; so next time her friend appears, she explains all this to her by means of a single gesture: she draws her tentacles in.

Agassiz

But it is when Lulla has undertaken to investigate a tin of sweets that she most suggests Agassiz. The tin has a lid which fits tightly, and Lulla's fingers are very small and not very strong. The tin, moreover, is on the window-sill just out of reach, though she stands on tip-toe and stretches a little eager hand as far as it will go. Then it is you see persistence. Lulla finds another baby, leads her to the window and points up to the tin. The other baby tries. They both try together; if this fails, Lulla finds a taller one, and at last successful, sits down with the tin held tightly in both hands, and turns it over and shakes it. This process seems to inspire fresh hope and energy; for she sets to work round the lid, which is one of the fitting-in sort, and carefully presses and pulls. Naturally this does nothing, and she shakes the tin again. The joyful sound of rattling sweets stimulates to fresh attempts upon the lid. She tugs and pulls, and thumps the refractory thing on the floor. By this time the other babies, attracted by the hopeful rattle, have gathered round and are watching operations; some offer to help, but all such offers are declined. This oyster is Lulla's. She has undertaken to force it. Agassiz and his fishes are on her side. She will not give it up. But she is not getting on; and she sits still for a moment, knitting her brow, and frowning a little puzzled frown at the refractory tin.

Suddenly her forehead smooths, the anxious brown eyes smile, Lulla has thought a new good thought. The babies struggle up and offer to help Lulla up, but she shakes her head. She seems to feel if she herself unaided, of her own free will, hands her problem over to her Ammal or her Sittie, only so she may achieve her purpose without loss of self-respect.

Lulla's beloved nurse is a motherly woman, older than most of our workers. Her name is Annamai. When the nurses return from church, each makes straight for her baby; and the babies always respond with a cordial and pretty affection. But Lulla welcoming Annamai is something more than pretty. The big white-robed figure no sooner appears in the garden than the tiny Lulla is all a-quiver with excitement. But it is a quiet excitement; and if you take any notice, the tentacles suddenly draw in, and the little face is as wax. If no one seems to notice, then Lulla lets herself go. She all but dances in her eagerness, while Annamai is slowly sailing up the walk; and when she reaches the verandah, Lulla can wait no longer; one spring and she is in her arms, nestling, cuddling, burying her curls in her neck; then looking up confidentially, little Lulla begins to talk; everything we have done and said is being whispered into Annamai's ear. It does not matter that Lulla cannot yet speak any language known to men; she can make Annamai understand, and that is all she cares. Once we remember watching her, as she took the remnant of a sweet we had given her, out of her mouth and poked it into Annamai's. Could love do more?

Dimples and Lulla are quite inseparable. Lulla is to Dimples what Tara is to Evu. She immensely admires her vigorous little junior, and tries to copy her whenever possible. One delicious game seems to have been suggested by the arches in the garden. Dimples and Lulla stand on all fours close together. Then they lean over till their heads touch the ground, and look through the arch. If you are on the babies' level (that is on the floor), you will enjoy this game.

Another Sunday morning entertainment is kissing. Dimples advances upon Lulla. Lulla falls upon Dimples. Then Dimples hugs Lulla, nearly chokes her, almost certainly overturns her. The two roll over and over like kittens. Dimples seizes Lulla by her curls and vehemently kisses face, neck, and anything else she can get at; and then backs off, propelling herself on two feet and one hand, in which position she looks like a puppy on three paws. Lulla smooths her ruffled curls and person generally, regards Dimples with gravity, and, if in an affectionate humour herself, leads the attack upon Dimples, and the programme is repeated.

But the joy of the hour is to spin in the hammocks. These contrivances being hung from the roof swing freely, and the special excitement is to hold on with both hands, and run round so that the hammock twists into a knot and spins when released, with the baby inside it, in a giddy waltz till the coil untwists itself. This looks dangerous, and when the game was first invented we rather demurred. But we are wiser now, and we let them spin. Lulla especially enjoys this madness. It is startling to see the tiny thing whirl like a reckless young teetotum. But if you weakly interfere, Lulla thinks you want to learn the art, and goes at it with even madder zest, till her very curls are dizzy.

"Daren't laugh and wouldn't cry

Dimples and Lulla in disgrace are a piteous spectacle. Dimples opens her mouth till it is almost square, and the most plaintive wail proceeds from it for about a minute and a half. Then she stops, looks sadly on the world, surprised and hurt at its unkindness to her, and then suddenly she discovers something interesting to do; and hastily rubbing her knuckles into her eyes to clear them as quickly as maybe of tears, she scrambles on to her feet, and forgets her injuries. Once she had been very naughty, and had to be smacked. It is never easy to smack Dimples, and fortunately she seldom requires it; but hard things have to be done, so that morning the fat little hands, to their surprise, knew the feel of chastening pats. "She daren't laugh, and she wouldn't cry"; this description, her Piria Sittie's, is the best I can offer of that baby's attitude. The thing could not possibly be a joke, but if meant otherwise, it was an indignity far past tears.

Lulla is quite different. She drops on the floor, if admonished, as if her limbs had suddenly become paralysed, and takes absolutely no notice of the offending disciplinarian. She simply ignores her, and gazes mutely beyond her. The offence is not one for explanation, and if invited to repent, her aloofness of demeanour is perfectly withering. But take her up in your arms, and she buries her curls in your neck, and coos her apologies (or is it forgiveness?) in your ear, and loves you all the better for the momentary breach.

Our babies are often parables. Lulla stands for the Single Eye. How often we have watched her and learned the lesson from her! She sees someone to whom she wants to go at what must seem to her an immense distance. And the distance is filled with obstacles, some of them quite enormous. But Lulla never stops to consider possibilities. Difficulties are simply things to be climbed over. She looks at the goal and makes straight for it. Her only care is to reach it. Sometimes at afternoon tea, when she is sitting on someone's lap, facing an empty, uninteresting plate, she sees another plate three chairs distant, and upon that plate there is a biscuit or some other sweet attraction. Upon such occasions Lulla all but plunges into space between the chairs, in her singleness of purpose. Having reached the lap nearest that plate, she turns and smiles at her late entertainer just to make sure she is not offended. But even if she knew she would be, Lulla would not hesitate. Curly head foremost, eyes on the goal: that is Lulla.

Mixed pickles

We have a custom at Dohnavur which perplexes the sober-minded. We call most of our possessions by names other than their own. These names are entirely private. We have to keep to this rule of privacy, otherwise we get shocks. "O Lord, look upon our beloved Puppy, and make her tooth come through; and bless Alice (in Wonderland), whose inside has gone wrong," was the petition offered in all seriousness, which finally moved us to prudence. We do not feel responsible for these names, for they come of themselves, and we see them when they come. That is all we have to do with them. Besides the Beetle and the Sea-anemone we have a dear Cockatoo, who screws her nose and her whole face up into a delightful pucker when she either laughs or cries, and then suddenly unscrews it in the middle of either emotion and looks entirely demure. This is the little Vimala, who, under God, owes her life to her Piria Sittie's splendid nursing. This baby has always got a private little secret of joy hidden away somewhere inside. We surprise her sometimes, sitting alone on the floor talking to herself about it; and then she tells us bits of it—as much as she thinks we can understand. But most of it is still hidden away, her own private little secret. And there is an Owlet, a Coney, a Froglet, and a Cheshire Cat, a Teddy-bear, a Spider, a Ratlet, and a Rosebud. We are aware that this list is rather mixed; but to be too critical would end in being nothing, so we are a Menagerie.

The Rosebud is like her name, small and sweet. When she wants to kiss her friends, which is whenever she sees them, her mouth is like the pink point of a moss-rose bud just coming through the moss. George Macdonald, perfect interpreter of babies, must have had our Preethie's double in his mind when he wrote:—

Whence that three-cornered smile of bliss?
Three angels gave me at once a kiss.
How did you come to us, you dear?
God thought of you, and so I am here.

The Owlet is twin to that quaint little bird, so its name flew to her and stayed. This babe has round eyes with long curling lashes. When she is good, these round eyes beam, and every one forgets that anything so fascinating can ever be other than good. When she is naughty the case is exactly reversed. This baby's proper name is Lullitha, which means Playfulness, and illustrates a side of her character undiscovered by the visitor who only sees the Owlet sitting on her perch with serious, watchful, unblinking eyes, regarding the intruder. But most babies are complex characters, and are not known in an hour.

The Teddy-bear is a fine child with perfect lungs, a benevolent smile, and an appetite. Her ruling passion at present is devotion to her food. She feels unjustly treated because we do not see our way to feed her lavishly at her own five meal-times and also at the meal-times of all the other babies in the nursery.

Teddy

On Sunday morning, when we are in charge, we hear her views upon this subject expressed in a manner wholly her own. She has just drained her own bottle, and is indignantly explaining that it is not nearly enough, when another bottle arrives for another baby, and this is too much for Teddy's equanimity. We all know how hard it is to keep up under the shock of adversity. Teddy does not attempt to keep up; she invariably topples over. But the way she does this is instructive. She sits stiff and straight for one brief moment, her milky mouth wide open, her hands outstretched in despairing appeal; then she clasps her head with her hands in a tragic fashion, absurd in a very fat infant, sways backwards and forwards two or three times till the desperate rock ends suddenly, as the poor Teddy-bear overbalances and bursts with a mighty burst. But the storm is too furious to last, and she soon subsides with a gusty sob and a short snort.

Poor little injured Teddy-bear! If it were not for her splendid health we might believe her oft-repeated tale of private starvation. "They only feed me when you are here to see! Other times they give me nothing at all!" She tells us this frequently in her own particular language, but the sturdy limbs belie it. This babe in matters of affection and mischief is as strenuous and original as she is about the one supreme affair pertaining to her elastic receptacle—to quote a Tamil friend's polite reference to the cavity within us—and many more edifying scenes might have been shown from her eventful life. But undoubtedly the predominating note at the present hour is her insatiable hunger, and when her name is mentioned in the nursery there is a smile and a new tale about her amazing appetite.

CHAPTER XXI

More Animals

MORE ANIMALS: DEPRESSED.
Nurses: Karuna to left (the Duckling of "Things as They Are"); and Annamai, to right, Lulla's beloved.

IN full contrast to Teddy-bear is that floppy child, the Coney. In Hart's *Animals of the Bible*, there is a picture of this baby, only the fore-paws should be raised in piteous appeal to be taken up. The Coney is really a pretty child with pathetic eyes and a grateful smile; but she was long in learning to walk, and felt aggrieved when we remonstrated. Her feet, she considered, were created to be ornamental rather than useful, and no amount of coaxing backed up with massage could persuade her otherwise. So she was left behind in the march; and when her contemporaries departed for the middle-aged babies' nursery, she stayed behind with the infants. And the infants had no pity. They regarded her as a sort of hassock, large and soft and good to jump on. More than once we have come into the nursery and found the big, meek child of three kneeling resignedly under a window upon which an adventurous eighteen-months wished to climb; and often we have found her prostrate and patient under the dancing feet of Dimples.

However, the Coney can walk now. This triumph was effected with the help of an Indianised go-cart, which did what all our persuasions had entirely failed to do. But the process was not pleasant. The poor Coney would stand mournfully holding the handle of her instrument of torture, longing with a yearning unspeakable to sit down and give it up for ever. Someone would pass, and hope would rise in her heart. She would be carried now, carried out of sight of that detested go-cart. But no, the callous-hearted only urged her to proceed. She would howl then with a howl that told of bitter disappointment. Sometimes she would sit down flat and regard the thing with a blighting glance, the hatred of a gentle nature roused to unwonted vehemence. Always her wails accompanied the rumbling of its wheels.

"The Conies are but a feeble folk, yet they make their houses in the rocks." One day in deep depression of spirits the Coney arrived at the kindergarten. She sat down before the threshold, which is three inches high, and climbed carefully over it. She found herself in a new world, where babies were doing wonderful things and enjoying all they did. The Coney decided to join a class, and was offered beads to thread. Life with beautiful beads to thread became worth living, and it may be in the course of time that the tortoise will overtake the hare. In any case we find much cheer in the conclusion of the verse, for if our Coney builds in the Rock her being rather feeble will not matter very much.

Those who possess that friend of our youth, *Alice*, as illustrated by Sir John Tenniel, may find the photograph twice reproduced of our fat Cheshire Cat. This baby is remarkable for two things: she smiles and she vanishes. The time to see the vanishing conducted with more celerity than Alice ever saw it, is when the babies' warning call is sounded across the verandah and a visitor appears in the too near horizon. This baby then vanishes round the nearest corner. There is nothing left of her, not even a smile. In fact, the chief contrast between her and the cat among the foliage is that with our Cat the smile goes first.

"Beetle! Open your mouth!"

Sunday morning, to return to the beginning, is full of possible misadventure. Sometimes the babies seem to agree among themselves that it would be well to be good. Then their admiring Sittie and Ammal have nothing to do but enjoy them. But sometimes it is otherwise. First one baby pulls her sister's hair, and the other retaliates, till the two get entangled in each other's curls. Piria Sittie flies to the rescue, disentangles the combatants and persuades them to make friends. Meanwhile three restless spirits in bodies to match have crept out through the open door (it is too hot if we shut the doors), and we find them comfortably ensconced in forbidden places. The Beetle is a quiet child. She retires to a corner and looks devout. Presently a sound as of scraping draws our attention to her. "Beetle! Open your mouth!" Beetle opens her mouth. It is packed with whitewash off the wall. Then a scared cry rings through the nursery, and all the babies, imagining awful things imminent, tumble one on top of the other in a wild rush into refuge. It is only a large grasshopper which has startled the Cheshire Cat, whose great eyes are always on the look-out for possible causes of panic. The grasshopper is banished to the garden and the Cheshire Cat smiles all over her face. Peace restored, Dimples and the Owlet remember a dead lizard they found in a corner of the verandah, and set off to recover it. These two walk exactly like mechanical toys; and as they strut along hand in hand, or one after the other, they look like something wound up and going, in a Christmas shop window. Presently they return with the lizard. Its tail is loose, and they sit down to pull it off. This is not a nice game, and something else is suggested. Dimple's mouth grows suddenly square; she wants that lizard's tail.

Then a dear little child called Muff (because she ought to be called Huff if the name had not been already appropriated), who has been solemnly munching a watch, decides it is time to demand more individual attention. She objects to the presence of another baby on her Sittie's lap. Why should two babies share one lap? The thing is self-evidently wrong. One lap, one baby, should be the rule in all properly conducted nurseries. Muff broods over this in silence, then slides off the crowded lap and sits down disconsolate, alone. Tears come, big sad tears, as Muff meditates; and it takes time to explain matters and comfort, without giving in to the one-lap-one-baby theory.

TUBBING.

We have several helpful babies. Dimples has been discovered paying required attentions to things smaller than herself; and the Wax Doll pats the Rosebud if she thinks it will reassure her, when (as rarely happens) that pet of the family is left stranded on a mat. But Puck is the most inventive. It was one happy Sunday morning that we came upon her feeding the Ratlet on her own account. The Ratlet was making ungrateful remarks; and we hurried across to her and saw that Puck, under the impression doubtless that any hole would do, was pouring the milk in a steady stream down the poor infant's nose. Puck smiled up peacefully. She was sure we would be pleased with her. But the Ratlet continued eloquent for very many minutes.

The Spider and the Cod-fish

Sometimes (but this is an old story now) our difficulties were increased by the Spider's habit of whimpering, which had a depressing effect upon the family. This poor baby was a weak little bag of bones when first she came to us. The bag was made of shrivelled skin of a dusty brown colour. Her hair was the colour of her skin, and hung about her head like tattered shreds of a spider's web. She sat in a bunch and never smiled. Something about her suggested a spider. Her Tamil name is Chrysanthemum, which by the change of one letter becomes Spider. So we called her Spider.

At first we were not anxious about her; for such little children pick up quickly if they are healthy to begin with, as we believed she was. But she did not respond to the good food and care, and only grew thinner and more miserable as the weeks passed, till she looked like the first picture in a series of advertisements of some marvellous patent food, and we wondered if she would ever grow like the fat and flourishing last baby of the series. For two months this state of things continued; she grew more wizened every day; and the uncanny spider-limbs and attitude gave her the air of not being a human baby at all, but a terrible little specimen which ought not to be on view but should be hidden safely away in some private medical place—on a shelf in a bottle of spirits of wine.

We are asked sometimes if such tiny things can suffer other than physically. We have reason to think they can. As all else failed, we took a little girl from school for whom the Spider had an affection, and let her love her all day long; and almost at once there was a change in the sad little face of the Spider. She had been cared for by an old grandfather after her mother's death, and it seemed as if she had fretted for him and needed someone all to herself to make up for what she was missing.

This little girl, the Cod-fish by name, was devoted to the Spider. She nestled her and played with her—or attempted to, I should say, for at first the Spider almost resented any attempts to play. "She doesn't know how to smile!" said the Cod-fish disconsolately after a week's petting and loving had resulted only in fewer whimpers, but not as yet in smiles. A few days later she came to us, and announced with much emotion: "She has smiled three times!" Next day the record rose to seven; after that we left off counting.

The Spider is fat and bonnie now. Her skin is a clear and creamy brown, and her hair has lost its dustiness; but she still likes to sit crumpled up, and a small alcove in the kitchen is her favourite haven when tired of the world. Seen unexpectedly in there, bunched in a tight knot, her dark, keen little eyes peering out of the light-coloured little face, she still suggests a spider. But it is a cheerful Spider, which makes all the difference.

CHAPTER XXII

The Parrot House

RED LAKE AND HILL.
As seen (without the water) from the Taraha Nursery.

THE time to see the Taraha nursery at its best is between late evening and early morning, and again about noon. It is perfectly peaceful then. Thirty mats are spread upon the floor. Thirty babies are strewn upon the mats. All the thirty are asleep. A sleeping baby is good. Thirty babies all good at once is something we cannot promise at any other hour.

Shading your lantern, and walking carefully so as not to tread on more scattered limbs than may be, you wander round the nursery and meditate upon the beautiful ways of childhood. There is something so touching in sleeping innocence, and you are touched. Here two chubby babies are lying locked in each other's arms. You have to look twice before you see which limbs belong to which. There another is hugging a doll minus its head. Next to her a baby sleeps pillowed on another, and the other does not mind. In the middle of the floor, far from her mat, a sturdy three-year-old sprawls content. You pick her up gently and lay her on her mat. With an expression of determined resolution the baby rolls off again; and if you attempt another remove, an ominous pucker of the forehead warns you to desist. You wonder if the babies are quite as good as they seem. One of the dear, fat, devoted little pair you noticed at first, stirs, disentangles herself from her neighbour, and gives her a slight kick. There is a smothered, sleepy howl, and the kick is returned. "Water!" wails the first fat baby. "Water!" wails the second. You get water, give it, pat both fat babies till they go to sleep, and then cautiously retire. It would be a pity if all the babies were to waken thirsty and kick each other. At the door you turn and look back. Graceful babies, clumsy babies, babies who lie extended like young pokers, babies curled like kittens. All sorts of babies, good, bad, and middling, but all blessedly asleep.

Sleep, baby, sleep!
Thy father guards his sheep,
Thy mother shakes the dreamland-tree
Down fall the little dreams for thee,
Sleep, baby, sleep!

Sleep, baby, sleep!
Our Saviour loves His sheep.
He is the Lamb of God on high,
Who for our sakes came down to die.
Sleep, baby, sleep!

The pretty German lullaby rises unbidden, and is pushed away by the quick, sad thoughts that will not listen to it. For under all the laughter and nursery frolic and happiness, we cannot but remember why these little ones are here. Round about the compound in a great triangle there are three Temple towers. They are out of sight though near us, but we cannot forget they are there. They stand for that which deprives these children of their birthright. Oh for the day when those Temple towers will fall and the reign of righteousness begin! There was a time when it seemed impossible to desire that the fire should be allowed to touch the stately and beautiful things of the world. Now there is something that satisfies as nothing else could in the vision of that purifying fire; and the promise that stands out like a light in the darkness is that which tells that the Son of Man shall send forth His angels, and they shall gather out of His kingdom, all things that offend.

Higher Critics

In the tiny babies' nursery many a crooning Indian lullaby is sung to the babies in their swinging white cradles; but in the Taraha nursery we sing sweet old hymns, in Tamil and English, and then all sensible people are supposed to go to sleep. But one evening after the singing, two little tots settled down for a talk. Said one lying comfortably on her back with her two hands clasped behind her head: "Who takes care of us at night when we all go to sleep?" Said the other in a mixture of Tamil and English: "Jesus-tender-Shepherd takes care of us—Jesus-loves-me-this-I-know." The first baby rolled over upon her small sister with a crow of derision. "It is not! It is Accal! I woke one night and saw her!" The other baby insisted she was making a mistake. "Accal sleeps, all people sleep; they lie down like us and go to sleep. Only Jesus stays awake, and never, never goes to sleep." "Never, never?" questioned the first, and was quiet for a minute considering the matter; then with a sceptical little laugh, "Did you ever wake up and see Him?"

If the babies were always in a state of calm repose, the Taraha's pet name, Parrot-house, would be inappropriate: but for nearly ten hours of the day they are awake and talkative. Talk, however, is a mild word by which to describe their powers of conversation. Sometimes we wonder if they never tire of chattering, and then we remember they have only lately learned to talk. They have not had time to tire.

CHILDREN WADING

Once we listened, hoping that the trailing clouds of glory so recently departed had left some trace of illumination in this their first expression in earth's language of their feelings and emotions. But we found them very mundane. Most of the conversation concerned their "saman," a comprehensive Indian word used by people with limited vocabularies to express all manner of things to play with. Their "saman" was various. Dolls, of course, and the remnants of dolls; tins and the lids thereof; bits of everything which could break; corks, stones, seeds, half cocoa-nut shells; rags of many ages and colours; scraped down morsels of brick; withered flowers and leaves; sticks of all sorts and sizes; English Christmas cards, sometimes with much domestic information on the back; unauthorised sundries from the kindergarten—delivered up with a smile intended to assure you that they were only being kept for Sittie; and pûchies. Pûchies are insects. We have one baby who collects pûchies. "Look!" she said, one morning before prayers, "Deah little five pûchies!" and she opened her hand and five red and black beetles crawled slowly out, to the delight of the devout, who scrambled up from their orderly rows with shrieks of appreciation.

But if the babies' conversation was unenlightening, their chosen avocations are not uninteresting. They are always busy about something, and, from their point of view, something important. There are, of course, some among the thirty who are unimaginative and unenterprising. These sit in the sand and play. Others have more to do. Life to them is full of the unknown. The unknown is full of possibilities. The great thing is to experiment. Nothing is too insignificant to explore, and all five senses are useful to the thoroughly competent baby.

"Watching a Miracle"

They knew, of course, all the flowers, and the discovery of anything fresh was always followed by a scene which suggested a colony of small and active ants hauling some large object to their nest; for the nearest grown-up person was invariably hailed, and pulled, and pushed, and hurried along till the "new flower" was reached. Then, if the object was incautious enough to stoop down to examine it, the ants, ant-wise, would envelope it, climbing, swarming all over it, till there was nothing to be seen but ants.

CHILDREN WADING.

They knew the habits of caterpillars, and especially they had knowledge about the wonderful silver chrysalis which pins itself to the pointed leaves of the oleander. They knew what was packed up inside, and some with wide-open eyes had watched the miracle slowly evolving as the butterfly unpacked itself, and sunned its crumpled velvet wings, till the crumples smoothed, and the wings dried, and the butterfly fluttered away. They knew, too, the less approachable ways of the wild bees, and where they hive, and what happens if they are disturbed; and they knew the private feelings of calves, and which likes to be treated as a brother and which resents such liberties. Crows they knew intimately, and squirrels a little; for infants fallen from their nests have often been taken care of, much against their foolish wills, until old enough to look after themselves. Their namesakes, the parrots, they knew very well; and the dainty little sunbirds that flash from flower to flower like little living jewels in the sunlight; and the clever tailor-bird, which sews its own nest, knotting its thread like a grown-up human being; and the wise leaf-insect that can hardly be found till it moves; and the great, green, frisky grasshopper that seems to invite a chase.

We found they knew, alas, too much about the misuse of everything growing in the field! The tamarind fruit makes condiment, but eaten raw it gives fever; and the babies think we are wrong here, and they are fond of forgetting our rules. Many kinds of grasses are very good to eat; and here again we are mistaken, for we know not the flavour of grasses. Seeds may be useful to plant; but those who think their use ends there, are short-sighted and ignorant people. Upon these and other matters the babies feel we have much to learn.

ESLI AND
LITTLE KOHILA.
Taken a year earlier.

One weird joy has been theirs, and they never will forget it. For one whole blissful afternoon they followed the snake-charmer about at a respectful distance; and they cannot understand why we are not anxious they should dance as he danced, and pipe as he piped, round the hopeful holes they discover in the red mud walls.

Other things they had learned to do, not wholly innocent. They must have made friends with the masons who built their new nursery, and persuaded them to do their work in a sympathetic spirit; for they knew the weak points hidden from our eyes, and how pleasant it is to scoop mortar out of cracks between the bricks of the floor. They had learned how most of their toys were made, and how a doll could be most easily dissected, and the particular taste of its inside. They knew, too, the lusciousness of divers sorts of sand— this last, however, being a mixture of crime and disease, and treated as such, is not a popular sin. Finally, to our lasting disgrace, they had learned, after a series of thoughtful experiments, how best to obey a command and yet elude its intention; thus on a wet day, when they were commanded not to go out, their Sittie found them lying full length in a long row on the edge of the verandah, their heads protruding so as to catch the lovely drip from the roof. And all these things they had carefully learned in spite of a certain amount of supervision; and, being entirely unsuspicious, they will take you into their confidence and let you share the forbidden fruit, if you are so inclined.

The Kindness of the Babies

But, after all, perfection of goodness would make us more anxious than even these enormities; we should fear our babies were growing too good—a fear not pressing at present. The Parrot-house only overwhelms when the birds begin to sing. Then indeed all who can, flee far away, for the babies once started are difficult to stop. They are sure you like it as much as they do, and are anxious to oblige you when you visit their world. So they sing with the greatest earnestness, and as they invariably hang on to every available part of you, and punctuate their melodies with kisses and embraces, escape is not always practicable.

The Taraha nursery was our first substantial building. It is built upon foundations raised well off the ground, and has a wide verandah. When first it was opened and the children were invited to take possession, they did so most completely. One quaint little person of barely three, called Kohila, whose small, repressed face in the photograph gives no hint of character, used to stalk up and down the verandah with an air of proprietorship which left no doubt in any mind as to her opinion on the subject. Another (sharing the swinging cot with Kohila in the photo) sat on the top step and smiled encouragingly to visitors. It was nice to be smiled at, but there was something very condescending in the smile. Another stood guard over the plants, which grew in pots much bigger than herself all the way down the verandah. If any presumed to touch them, she would dart out upon them with an indignant chirrup. For days after the great event—the opening of the Taraha—small parties waited on visitors, formed in procession before and behind, and escorted them round, explaining all mysteries, and insisting upon due admiration. Everything had to be interviewed, from teaspoons to pots of fern. This concluded, the guests were politely dismissed, and departed, let us hope, properly penetrated with a sense of the kindness of the babies.

There have always been some who object to visitors. One of these showed her objection, not by crying and running away, as undignified babies do, but by sitting exactly where she was when she first caught sight of the intruder, and staring straight into space with a very stony stare. A sensitive visitor could hardly have had the temerity to pass her, but normal visitors are not sensitive. Sometimes they attempted to make friends. This was too much. One fat arm would be slowly raised till it covered the baby's eyes, and in this position she would sit like a small petrifaction, till the horror had withdrawn.

PREETHA

AWARE OF A FOE.
Tara on the left: the Coney on the right.

This baby, Preetha by name, has in most matters a way of her own. One of her little peculiarities is a strong preference for solo music as compared with concert. She listens attentively to others' performances, then disappears. If followed, she will be found alone in a corner, with her face to the wall and her back to the world; and if she thinks herself unobserved, you will be regaled with a solo. This experience is interesting to the musical. It is never twice alike. Sometimes it is a succession of sounds, like a tune that has lost its way; sometimes, a recognisable version of the chorus lately learned. At other times she delivers her soul in a series of short groans and grunts, beating time with her podgy hands. If she perceives through the back of her head that someone is looking or listening, she stops at once; and no persuasions can ever produce that special rehearsal again. Of late this baby, being now nearly three, has awakened to a sense of life's responsibilities, and she evidently wishes to prepare to meet them suitably. Yesterday evening she came to me with an exceedingly serious face, pointed in the direction of the kindergarten room, and then tapping herself, remarked: "Amma! I kindergarten." No more was said; but we know we shall soon see her solemnly waddling into the schoolroom, and we wonder what will happen. Will she continue to insist upon a corner to herself?

CHAPTER XXIII

The Bear Garden

JULLANIE AMONG THE GRASSES.

"THE fruit of the lotus—a capsule—ripens below the surface of the water. When the seeds are ripe and leave the berry, a small bubble of air attached to them brings them to the surface, and the seeds are carried wherever the wind and waves take them until the bubble bursts; when the seed, being heavier than water, sinks to the bottom, and then begins to grow to form a new plant, which may be at some distance from the parent one. In this simple way the lotus plant is enabled to spread." So says our botany book; and the thought of the lotus seed in its little air-boat floating away over the water to be sown, perhaps, far from the parent plant, is full of suggestion, and leads us straight to the Bear-garden.

A lotus-pool, a bear-garden—the connection is not obvious. *Alice* in her wanderings never wandered into bewilderment more profound than such a mixture of ideas. But this is the way we get to it: We have called these little children Lotus-buds—for such they are in their youngness and innocence; and the underlying thought runs deeper, as those who have read the first chapter know—but the Lotus-buds must grow into flowers and must be sown as living seeds, perhaps far away from the happy place they knew when they were buds. The little air-boat will come for them. The breath of the Spirit that bloweth where it listeth will carry them where it will, and we want them to be ready to be sown wherever the pools of the world are barren of lotus flowers. And this brings us straight to the newest of our beginnings in Dohnavur—the Kindergarten.

An ideal kindergarten is a place where the teachers train the scholars, and we hope to have that in time; at present the case is opposite, and that is why it has its name, the name that conflicts with the lotus-pool—the Bear-garden.

In this peaceful room Classes B, C, and D have taken their young teachers in hand— Rukma, Preena, and Sanda. Of these Rukma (Radiance) has the clearest ideas about discipline; Preena (the Elf) knows best how to coax; and Sanda, excellent Mouse that she is, has the gift of patience. These three (who after all are only school-girls, continuing their own education with their Préma Sittie) are attempting to instruct the babies on the lines of organised play; but the babies feel they have much to teach their teachers, and this is how they do it:—

Préma Sittie goes into the room when the kindergarten is in progress, and from three classes at once babies come springing towards her with squeals of joy, and they clasp her knees and look up with eyes full of affection and confidence in their welcome. "Go back to your place!" she says, and tries to look severe; with a chuckle the children obey, and she looks round and takes notes.

Chellalu is lying full-length on the bench, with a look of supreme content on her face, and her two feet against the wall. Pyârie has turned her back to the picture that is being shown, and is tying a handkerchief round her head. Ruhinie, an India-rubber-ball sort of baby, has suddenly bounced up from her seat, and is starting a chorus, of which she is fond, at the top of her not very gentle voice; and Komala, a perfect sprite, is tickling the child who sits next to her. "Sittie!" exclaims the distracted teacher, "they won't learn anything!" Or if she happens to be the Mouse, she is calmly engaged with the one good child in her class.

Babel

The next group is stringing beads on pieces of wire. "Look, look!" and an eager babe holds out her wire for admiration, and probably spills her beads in her effort to secure attention. If she does, there is a general scramble, beads rolling loose on the floor being quite irresistible. One wicked baby sits by herself and strings her beads on her curls.

A few minutes later it is mat-plaiting; and the agile little fingers are diligently weaving pieces of blue and yellow material, bits over from their elder sisters' garments, beautifully unconscious that they are supposed to be working the colours alternately. Sometimes in the gayest way they exclaim: "Sittie! It's wrong! it's wrong!" Occasionally there is a howl from a child who has been pinched by another, or whose neighbour has helped herself to her beads. Sittie crosses the room hurriedly. "What's the matter?" With tears rolling down her cheeks the victim points to her oppressor. "May you do that?" is the invariable English question. It is answered by a shake of the head, the tiniest baby understanding that particular remark. The injured baby smiles. A reproof, or at worst a pat on the fat arm next to hers, satisfies her sense of justice, and she is content.

When an English lesson begins, those afflicted with delicate nerves are happier elsewhere. One class has a toy farmyard, another a set of tea-things, the third a doll which every member of the class is aching to embrace. The teachers and children alike are inclined to talk with emphasis; and if you stand between the three classes you hear queer answers to queerer questions, and wonder if the babies at Babel were anything like so bewildering.

But this vision of the kindergarten is hardly a fortnight old; for Classes B, C, and D are of recent development, and are made up of some heedless characters, as Chellalu and Pyârie, who could not keep up with class A, and a few more young things from the nursery who were wilder than wild rabbits from the wood when we began. Also it should be stated that from the babies' point of view white people are only playthings. "They were very good before you came!" is the unflattering remark frequently addressed to us; and as we discreetly retire, the babies do seem to become suddenly beautifully docile. But even so they might be better, as an unconscious comedy over-seen this morning proves. I was in the porch outside the door, when Rukma, pointing to a blackboard on which were written sundry words, told Chellalu to show her "cat," and I looked in interested to know if Chellalu really knew anything of reading. Chellalu brandished the pointer, then turned to Rukma with a confidential smile, "Cat? Where is it, Accal? Is it at the top or at the bottom?" Rukma, who has a keen sense of the comic, seemed to find it difficult to look as she felt she ought. Chellalu caught the twinkle in her eye, and throwing herself heartily into the spirit of the game, which was evidently intended to be a kindergarten version of Hunt the Mouse through the Wood, she searched the blackboard for cat. Then to Rukma: "Accal! dear Accal! Tell *me*, and I'll tell *you!*"

There is nothing that helps us so much to be good as to be believed in and thought better than we are; and the converse is true, so we do not want to be always suspecting Chellalu of sin; but this last was entirely too artless, and this was apparently Rukma's view, for she sent Chellalu back to her seat and called up another baby, who, fairly radiating virtue, immediately found the cat.

Compassions of the Wise

The next room—which Class A (the first to be formed) has to itself—is a haven of peace after the Bear-garden. It is a pleasant room like the other, pretty with pictures and with flowers. And the little bright faces make it a happy place, for this class, though serious-minded, is exceedingly cheerful. There is the demure little Tingalu, the good child of the kindergarten, its hope and stay in troublous hours, and the quaint little trio, Jeya, Jullanie, and Sella—this last is called Cock-robin by the family, for she has eyes and manners which remind us of the bird, and she hardly ever walks, she hops. Mala and Bala are in the class, and a lively scamp called Puvai.

The kindergarten is worked in English, helped out with Tamil when occasion requires. This plan, adopted for reasons pertaining to the future of the children, is resulting in something so comical that we shall be sorry when the first six months are over and the babies grow correct. At present they talk with delightful abandon impossible to reproduce, but very entertaining to those who know both languages. They tack Tamil terminations to English verbs, and English nouns make subjects for Tamil predicates. They turn their sentences upside down and inside out, and any way in fact which occurs to them at the moment, only insisting upon one thing: you must be made to understand. They apply everything they learn as immediately as possible, and woe to the unwary flounderer in the realm of natural science who offers an explanation of any phenomena of nature other than that taught in the kindergarten. The learned baby regards you with a tender sort of pity. Poor thing, you are very ignorant; but you will know better in time—if only you will come to the kindergarten, the source of the fountain of knowledge.

The ease and the quickness with which a new word is appropriated constantly surprises us. As for example: one morning two babies wandered round the Prayer-room, and, discovering passion-flowers within reach, eagerly begged for them in Tamil. One of the two pushed the other aside and wanted all the flowers. "Greedy! greedy!" I said reprovingly, in English. "Greedy *mine!*" was the immediate rejoinder, and the little hand was held out with more certainty than ever now that the name of the flower was known. "Greedy *my* flower! *Mine!*"

But some of the quaintest experiences are when the eloquent baby, determined to express herself in English, falls back upon scraps of kindergarten rhyme and delivers it in all seriousness. On the evening before my birthday I was banished from my room, and the children decorated it exactly as they pleased. When I returned I was implored not to look at anything, as it was not intended to be seen till next morning. Next morning the babies came in procession with their elders, and while I was occupied with them out on the verandah, Chellalu and her friend Naveena, discovering something unusual in my room, escaped from the ranks and went off to examine the mystery. I found them a moment later gazing in astonished joy at the glories there revealed. "Who did it all?" gasped Chellalu, whose intention, let us hope, was perfectly reverent. "God did it all!"

The one kindergarten class taught entirely in Tamil is the Scripture lesson, illustrated whenever possible by pictures; and being always taught about sacred things in Tamil, the babies have no doubt about the language in use in Bible days. But sometimes a little mind is puzzled, as an instructive aside revealed a day or two ago. For their teacher had told them in English, not as a Scripture lesson, but just as a story, about Peter and John and the lame man. The picture was before them, and they understood and followed keenly; but one little girl whispered to another, who happened to be the well-informed Cock-robin: "Did Peter and John talk English or Tamil?" "Tamil, of course!" returned Cock-robin, without a moment's hesitation.

The Scripture lessons are usually given by Arulai, whose delight is Bible teaching. "So that as much as lieth in you you will apply yourself wholly to this one thing, and draw all your cares and studies this way," is a word that always comes to mind when one thinks of Arulai and her Bible. She much enjoys taking the babies, believing that the impressions created upon the mind of a little child are practically indelible.

Practical Politics

Sometimes these impressions are expressed in vigorous fashion. Once the subject of the class was the Good Samaritan. The babies were greatly exercised over the scandalous behaviour of the priest and the Levite. "Punish them! Let them have whippings!" they demanded. Arulai explained further. But one baby got up from her seat and walked solemnly to the picture. "Take care what you are doing!" she remarked impressively in Tamil, shaking her finger at the two retreating backs. "Naughty! naughty!"—this was in English—"take care!"

One of the favourite pictures shows Abraham and Isaac on the way to the mount of sacrifice. This story was told one morning with much reverence and feeling, and the babies were impressed. There were tears in Bala's eyes as she gazed at the picture, but she brushed them away hurriedly and hoped no one had noticed. Only Chellalu appeared perfectly unconcerned. She had business of her own on hand, and the story, it seemed, had not touched her. The babies are searched before they come to school, and all toys, bits of string, old tins, and sundries are removed from their persons. But there are ways of evading inquisitors. Chellalu knows these ways. She now produced a long wisp of red tape from somewhere—she did not tell us where—and proceeded to tie her feet together. This accomplished, she curled herself up on the bench like a caterpillar on a leaf, and to all appearances went to sleep. Why was she not awakened and compelled to behave properly? asks the reader, duly shocked. Perhaps because on that rather special morning the teacher preferred her asleep.

ARULA

I AND RUKMA, WITH NAVEENA.

The story finished, the children were questioned, and they answered with unwonted gravity. "What did Isaac say to his father as they walked alone together?" An awed little voice had begun the required answer, when Chellalu suddenly uncurled, sat up, and said in clear, decided Tamil: "He said, 'Father! do not kill me!' *Yesh!* that was what he said."

When first the babies heard about Heaven, they all wanted to go at once, and with difficulty were restrained from praying to be taken there immediately. There was one naughty child who, when she was given medicine, invariably announced, "I will not stay in this village: I am going to Heaven! I am going now!" But they soon grew wiser. It was our excitable, merry little Jullanie who summed up all desires with most simplicity: "Lord Jesus, please take me there or anywhere anytime; only wherever I am, please stay

95

there too!" Some of the babies are carnal: "When I go to that village (Heaven), I shall go for a ride on the cherubim's wings. I will make them take me to all sorts of places, just wherever I want to go."

The Way to Heaven

The latest pronouncement, however, was for the moment the most perplexing. "Come-anda-look-ata-well!" said Chellalu yesterday evening, the sentence in a single long word. The well is being dug in the Menagerie garden and is surrounded by a trellis, beyond which the babies may not pass, unless taken by one of ourselves. As we drew near to the well, Chellalu pointed to it and said: "Amma! That is the way to Heaven!" This speech, which was in Tamil, considerably surprised me, as naturally we think of Heaven above the bright blue sky. The yawning gulf of the unfinished well suggested something different.

But Chellalu was positive. "It is the way to Heaven. *I* may not go there, but *you* may! Yesh! *you* may go to Heaven, Amma, but *I* may not!" She had nothing more to say; and we wondered how she could possibly have arrived at so extraordinary a conclusion, till we remembered that it had been explained to the babies that any baby falling in would probably be drowned and die, and so until it was finished and made safe no baby must go near it. Chellalu had evidently argued that as to die meant going to Heaven, the well must be the way to Heaven; and as only grown-up people might go near it, they, and they alone apparently, were allowed to go to Heaven.

These babies are nothing if not practical. Arulai had been teaching the story of the Unmerciful Servant; and to bring it down to nursery life, supposed the case of a baby who snatched at other babies' toys, and was unfair and selfish. Such a baby, if not reformed, would grow up and be like the Unmerciful Servant. The babies looked upon the back of the offender as shown in the picture. "Bad man! Nasty man!" they said to each other, pointing to him with aversion. And Arulai closed the class with a short prayer that none of the babies might ever be like the Unmerciful Servant.

The prayer over, the babies rushed to the table where their toys were put during the Scripture lesson. Pyârie got there first, and, gathering all she could reach, she swept them into her lap and was darting off with them, when a word from Arulai recalled her. For a moment there was a struggle. Then she ran up to Tingalu, the child she had chiefly defrauded, poured all her treasures into her lap, and then sprang into Arulai's arms with the eager question: "Acca! Acca! Am I not a *Merciful* Servant?"

CHAPTER XXIV

The Accals

"This sacred work demands not lukewarm, selfish, slack souls, but hearts more finely tempered than steel, wills purer and harder than the diamond."—Père Didon.

PONNAMAL, WITH PREETHA ON HER KNEE, AND TARA BESIDE HER.

THE Accals, without whom this work in all its various branches could not be undertaken, are a band of Indian sisters (the word Accal means older sister) who live for the service of the children. First among the Accals is Ponnamal (Golden). With the quick affection of the East the children find another word for Gold and call her doubly Golden Sister.

Sometimes we are asked if we ever find an Indian fellow-worker whom we can thoroughly trust. The ungenerous question would make us as indignant as it would if it were asked about our own relations, were it not that we know it is asked in ignorance by those who have never had the opportunity of experiencing, or have missed the happiness of enjoying, true friendship with the people of this land. Those who have known that happiness, know the limitless loyalty and the tender, wonderful love that is lavished on the one who feels so unworthy of it all. If there is distance and want of sympathy between those who are called to be workers together with the great Master, is not something wrong? Simple, effortless intimacy, that closeness of touch which is friendship indeed, is surely possible. But rather we would put it otherwise, and say that without it service together, of the only sort we would care to know, is perfectly impossible.

SELLAMUTTU AND SUSEELA.

In our work all along we have had this joy to the full. God in His goodness gave us from the first those who responded at once to the confidence we offered them. In India the ideal of a consecrated life is a life with no reserves—which seeks for nothing, understands nothing, cares for nothing but to be poured forth upon the sacrifice and service. Pierce through the various incrustations which have over-laid this pure ideal, give no heed to the effect of Western influence and example, and you come upon this feeling, however expressed or unexpressed, at the very back of all—the instinct that recognises and responds to the call to sacrifice, and does not understand its absence in the lives of those who profess to follow the Crucified. Who, to whom this ideal is indeed "The Gleam," that draws and ever draws the soul to passionate allegiance, can fail to find in the Indian nature at its truest and finest that kinship of spirit which knits hearts together? "And it came to pass when he had made an end of speaking, that the soul of Jonathan was knit with the soul of David, and Jonathan loved him as his own soul": this tells it all. The spring of heart to heart that we call affinity, the knitting no hand can ever afterward unravel—these experiences have been granted to us all through our work together, and we thank God for it.

Pure Justice

Ponnamal's work lies chiefly among the convert-nurses and the babies. She has charge of the nurseries and of the food arrangements, so intricate and difficult to the mere lay mind; she trains her workers to thoroughness and earnestness, and by force of example seems to create an atmosphere of cheerful unselfishness that is very inspiring. How often we have sent a young convert, tempted to self-centredness and depression, to Ponnamal, and seen her return to her ordinary work braced and bright and sensible. We are all faulty and weak at times, and every nursery, like every life, has its occasional lapses; but on the whole it is not too much to say that the nurseries are happy places, and Ponnamal's influence goes through them all like a fresh wind. And this in spite of very poor health. For Ponnamal, who was the leader of our itinerating band, broke down hopelessly, and thought her use in life had passed—till the babies came and brought her back to activity again. And the joy of the Lord, we have often proved, is strength for body as well as soul.

Sellamuttu, who comes next to Ponnamal, is the "Pearl" of previous records, and she has been a pearl to us through all our years together. She is special Accal to the household of children above the baby-age—a healthy, high-spirited crow of most diverse dispositions; and she is loved by one and all with a love which is tempered with great respect, for she is "all pure justice," as a little girl remarked feelingly not long ago, after being rather sharply reproved for exceeding naughtiness: "within my heart wrath burned like a fire; but my mouth could not open to reply, for inside me a voice said, 'It is true, entirely true; Accal is perfectly just.'"

This Accal, however, is most tender in her affections, and among the babies she has some particular specials. One of these is the solemn-faced morsel of the photograph, to save whom she travelled, counting by time, as far as from London to Moscow and back; and the baby arrived as happy and well as when the friends at "Moscow" sent her off with prayers and blessings and kindness. But the photograph was a shock. "Aiyo!" she said, quite upset to see her delight so misrepresented, "that is not Suseela! There is no smile, no pleasure in her face!" We comforted her by the assurance that any one who understood babies and their ways would consider the camera responsible for the expression. And at least the baby was obedient. Had she not told her to make a salaam, and had not the little hand gone up in serious salute? A perfectly obedient baby is Sellamuttu's ideal, and she was satisfied.

THE RIGHT, SUHINIE, AND HER BABY SUNUNDA

Both these sisters came to us at some loss to themselves, for both could have lived at home at ease if they had been so inclined. Ponnamal lost all her little fortune by joining us. She could, perhaps, have recovered it by going to law, but she did not feel it right to do so, and she suffered herself to be defrauded. "How could I teach others to be unworldly if I myself did what to them would appear worldly-minded?" That was all she ever said by way of explanation.

Next to Ponnamal and Sellamuttu come the motherly-hearted Gnanamal and Annamai. They came to us when we were in circumstances of peculiar difficulty. The work was just beginning, and we had not enough trustworthy helpers; so, wearied with disturbed nights, we were almost at the end of our strength. "Send us help!" we prayed, and went on each trying to do the work of three. It was one hot, tiring afternoon, when we longed to forget everything and rest for half an hour, but could not, because there was so much to do, that a bright, capable face appeared at the door of our room, and Annamai, Lulla's beloved, came in and said: "God sent me, and my relative" (naming a mission catechist) "brought me. And so I have come!"

And Gnanamal—we were in dire straits, for a dear little babe had suffered at the hands of one who thought first of herself and second of her charge, and the most careful tending was needed if the baby was to survive—it was then Gnanamal came and took charge of the delicate child, and became the comfort and help she has ever continued to be. When there is serious illness, and night-nursing is required, Gnanamal is always ready to volunteer; though to her, as to most of us in India, night work is not what the flesh would choose. Then in the morning, when we go to relieve her, we find her bright as ever, as if she had slept comfortably all the time. We think this sort of help worth gratitude.

Whose Names are in the Book of Life

The convert-workers, dear as dear children, but, thank God, dependable as comrades, come next in age to the head Accals. Arulai Tara (known to some as "Star") is what her name suggests, something steadfast, something shining, something burning with a pure devotion which kindles other fires. We cannot imagine our children without their beloved Arulai. Then there is Sundoshie (Joy), to the left next Suhinie in the photo, a young wife for whom poison was prepared three times, and whose escape from death at the hand of husband and mother-in-law was one of those quiet miracles which God is ever working in this land of cruelty in dark places. And Suhinie (Gladness), whose story of deliverance has been told before; and Esli, the gift of a fellow-missionary, a most faithful girl; and others younger, but developing in character and trustworthiness. All these young converts need much care, but the care of genuine converts is very fruitful work; and one interesting part of it is the fitting of each to her niche, or of fitting the niche to her. Discernment of spirit is needed for this, for misfits means waste energy and great discomfort; and energy is too good a thing to waste, and comfort too pleasant a thing to spoil. So those who are responsible for this part of the work would be grateful for the remembrance of any who know how much depends upon it.

Among the recognised "fits" in our family is "the Accal who loves the unlovable babies." This is Suhinie. We tried her once with the Taraha children; but the terrible activity of these young people was altogether too much for the slowly moving machinery of poor Suhinie's brain, and she was perfectly overwhelmed and very miserable. For Suhinie hates hurry and sudden shocks of any sort, and the babies of maturer years discovered this immediately; and Suhinie, waddling forlornly after the babies, looked like a highly respectable duck in charge of a flock of impertinent robins.

THREE CONVERT WORKERS.

It was quite a misfit, and Suhinie's worst came to the top, and we speedily moved her back again to the Prémalia nursery.

For there you see Suhinie in her true sphere. Give her a poor, puny babe, who will never, if she can help it, let her Accal have an undisturbed hour; give her the most impossible, most troublesome baby in the nursery, and then you will see Suhinie's best. We discovered this when Ponnamal was in charge of the Neyoor nursery. Ponnamal had one small infant so cross that nobody wanted her. She would cry half the night, a snarly, snappy cry, that would not stop unless she was rocked, and began again as soon as the rocking was stopped. Ponnamal gave her to Suhinie.

"Night after night till two in the morning she would sing to that fractious child"—this was Ponnamal's story to me when next I went to Neyoor. "She never seemed to tire; hymn after hymn she would sing, on and on and on. I never saw her impatient with it; she just loved it from the first." And a curious thing began to happen: the baby grew like her Accal. This likeness was not caught in the photograph, but is nevertheless so observable that visitors have often asked if the little one were her own child.

Sinners

This baby, Sununda by name, is greatly attached to Suhinie. As she is over two years old now, she has been promoted to the Taraha, and being an extremely wilful little person, she sometimes gets into trouble. One day I was called to remonstrate, and a little "morning glory" was required, and I put her in a corner to think about it. Another sinner had to be dealt with, and when I returned Sununda was nowhere to be found. I searched all over the Taraha and in the garden, and finally found her in the Prémalia cuddled close to Suhinie. "She has told me all about it," said Suhinie, who was nursing another edition of difficult infancy; and she looked down on the curly head with eyes of brooding affection, like a tender turtle-dove upon her nestling. Then the roguish brown eyes smiled up at me with an expression of perfect confidence that I would understand and sympathise with the desire to share the troubles of this strange, sad life with so beloved an Accal.

The question of discipline is sometimes rather difficult with so many dispositions, each requiring different dealing. We try, of course, to fit the penalty to the crime, so that the child's sense of justice will work on our side; and in this we always find there is a wonderful unconscious co-operation on the part of the merest baby. But the older children used to be rather a problem. Some had come to us after their wills had become developed and their characters partly formed. Most of them were with us of their own free will, and could have walked off any day, for they knew where they would be welcome. Discipline under these circumstances is not entirely easy. But three years ago something of Revival Power swept through all our family. It was not the Great Revival for which we wait, but it was something most blessed in effect and abiding in result; and ever since then the tone has been higher and the life deeper, so that there is something to which we can appeal confident of a quick response. But children will be scampish; and once their earnestness of desire to be good was put to unexpected and somewhat drastic proof.

At that time the mild Esli had charge of the sewing-class, and the class had got into bad ways; carelessness and chattering prevailed, so Esli came in despair to me, and I talked to the erring children. They were sorry, made no excuses, and promised to be different in future. I left them repentant and thoroughly ashamed of themselves, and went to other duties.

SEWING-CLASS IN THE COURTYARD.

The Mark

Shortly afterwards Arulai found them in a state of great depression. They told her they had promised to be good at the sewing-class, but were afraid they would forget. Arulai's ideas are usually most original, and she sympathised with the children, but told them there was no need for them ever to forget. They asked eagerly what could be done to help them to remember. They had prayed, but even so had doubts. Was there anything to be done besides praying? Arulai said there was, and she expounded certain verses from the Book of Proverbs. "Sometimes the best way to make a mark upon the mind is to make a mark upon the body," she suggested, and asked the children if they would like this done. The children hesitated. They were aware that Arulai's "marks" were likely to be emphatic, for Arulai never does things by halves. But their devotion to her and belief in her overcame all fears; and being genuinely anxious to reform, they one and all consented. So she sent a small girl off to look for a cane; and presently one was produced, "thin and nice and suitable," as I was afterwards informed. The younger children were invited to take the cane and look at it, and consider well how it would feel. This they did obediently, but still stuck undauntedly to their determination, in fact, were keen to go through with it. Then Arulai explained that when the King said, "Chasten thy son while there is hope, and let not thy soul spare for his crying," he must have been thinking of a very little boy who had not the sense to know what was good for him. They had sense. The mark on the body would be waste punishment if it were not received willingly and gratefully; so if any child cried or pulled her hand away, she would stop. Then the children all stood up and held out their hands—what a moment for a photograph! Arulai's "mark upon the body" was a genuine affair, but the class received it with fortitude and gratitude.

When I heard this history, an hour or so after its occurrence, I rather demurred. The children had appeared to be sincerely sorry when I spoke to them, and if so, why proceed to extremities? But Arulai answered with wisdom and much assurance: "They have been talked to before and have been sorry, but they forgot and did it again. This time they will not forget." And neither did they. As long as that class continued, its behaviour was exemplary; and "the mark upon the mind," to judge by their demeanour, remained as fresh as it must have been on that memorable day when the "mark" upon the body effected its creation. The story ought to end here; but most stories have a sequel, and this has two.

The first occurred a few weeks later. A little girl, one of the sewing-class, had slipped into the habit of careless disobedience, followed too often by sulks. If we happened to come across her just when the thunder-clouds were gathering, we could usually divert her attention and avert the threatened trouble; but if we did not happen to meet her just at the right moment, she would plunge straight into the most outrageous naughtiness with a sort of purposeful directness that was difficult to deal with. Knowing the child well, we often let her choose her own punishments; and she did this so conscientiously that at last, as she herself mournfully remarked, "they were all used up," and there was nothing left but the most ancient—and perhaps in some cases most efficacious, which, the circumstances being what they were, I was naturally reluctant to try. But the child, trained to be perfectly honest with herself, apparently thought the thing over, and calmly made up her mind to accept the inevitable; for when, anxious she should not misunderstand, I began to explain matters to her, I was met by this somewhat astonishing response: "Yes, Amma, I know. I know you have tried everything else" (she said this almost sympathetically, as if appreciating my dilemma), "and so you have to do it. I do not like it at all, but Arulai Accal says it is no use unless I take it willingly, so Amma, please give me a good caning." (The idiom is the same in Tamil as in English, but there is a stronger word which she now proceeded to use with great deliberation.) "Yes, Amma, a *hot* caning—with my full mind I am willing. And I will not cry. Or if I do cry" (this was added in a serious, reflecting sort of way), "let not your soul spare for my crying!"

The second is less abnormal. Esli, whose placid soul had been sadly stirred at the time of the infliction of the "mark," was so impressed by its salutary effect that she conceived a new respect for the methods of King Solomon. The application of "morning glory" is a privilege reserved, as a rule, for ourselves; but one day, being doubtless hard pressed, Esli produced a stick—a very feeble one—and calling up the leader of all rebels, addressed herself to her. Chellalu, as might have been expected, was taken by surprise; and for one short moment Esli was permitted to follow the ways of the King. But only for a moment: for, suddenly apprehending the gravity of the situation, and realising that such precedent should not pass unchallenged, Chellalu, with a quick wriggle, stood forth free, seized the stick with a joyous shout, snapped it in two, and flourished round the room: then stopping before her afflicted Accal, she solemnly handed her one of the pieces, and with a bound and a scamper like a triumphant puppy, was off to the very end of her world with the other half of that stick.

"Not Lukewarm, Selfish, Slack Souls"

When the Elf came to us on March 6, 1901, and we began to know some of the secrets of the Temple, we tried to save several little children, but we failed. The thought of those first children with whom we came into touch, but for whom all our efforts were unavailing, is unforgettable. We see them still, little children—lost. But we partly understand why we had to wait so long; we had not the workers then to help us to take care of them. We had only some of the older Accals, who could not have done it alone. These convert-girls, who now help us so much, were in Hindu homes; some of them had not even heard of Christ, whose love alone makes this work possible. For India is not England in its view of such work. There is absolutely nothing attractive about it. It is not "honourable work," like preaching and teaching. No money would have drawn these workers to us. Work which has no clear ending, but drifts on into the night if babies are young or troublesome—such work makes demands upon devotion and practical unselfishness which appeal to none but those who are prepared to love with the tireless love of the mother. "I do not want people who come to me under certain reservations. In battle you need soldiers who fear nothing." So wrote the heroic Père Didon; and, though it may sound presumptuous to do so, we say the same. We want as comrades those who come to us without reservations. But such workers have to be prepared, and such preparation takes time. "Tarry ye the Lord's leisure," is a word that unfolds as we go on.

Yet we find that the work, though so demanding, is full of compensations. The convert in her loneliness is welcomed into a family where little children need her and will soon love her dearly. The uncomforted places in her heart become healed, for the touch of a little child is very healing. If she is willing to forget herself and live for that little child, something new springs up within her; she does not understand it, but those who watch her know that all is well. Sometimes long afterwards she reads her own heart's story and opens it to us. "I was torn with longing for my home. I dreamed night after night about it, and I used to waken just wild to run back. And yet I knew if I had, it would have been destruction to my soul. And then the baby came, and you put her into my arms, and she grew into my heart, and she took away all that feeling, till I forgot I ever had it." This was the story of one, a young wife, for whom the natural joys of home can never be. But if there is selfishness or slackness or a weak desire to drift along in easiness, taking all and giving nothing, things are otherwise. For such the nurseries hold nothing but noise and interruptions. We ask to be spared from such as these. Or if they come, may they be inspired by the constraining love of Christ and "The Glory of the Usual."

FOOTNOTES:

Overweights of Joy, ch. xxiii. Suhinie left the nursery for a few hours' rest at noon on February 2, 1910. She fell asleep, to awaken in heaven.

CHAPTER XXV

The Little Accals

But Thou didst reckon, when at first
Thy word our hearts and hands did crave,
What it would come to at the worst
To save.
Perpetual knockings at Thy door,
Tears sullying Thy transparent rooms.

THREE LITTLE ACCALS.

THESE lines come with insistence as I look at the little Accals, who follow in order after the Accals, convert children, most of them, now growing up to helpfulness. If part of the story of one such young girl is told, it may help those to whom such tales are unfamiliar to understand and to care.

December 16, 1903, was spent by three of us in a rest-house on the outskirts of a Hindu town. We were on our way to Dohnavur from Madras, where we had seen Mr. and Mrs. Walker off for England. The two days' journey had left us somewhat weary; and yet we were strong in hope that day, for we knew there was special thought for us on board ship and at home, and something special was being asked as a birthday gift of joy. Arulai (Star) and Preena (the Elf), the two who were with me, were full of expectation. The day had often been marked by that joy of joys, a lost sheep found; and as we looked out at the heathen town with its many people so unconscious of our thoughts about them, we wondered where we should find the one our thoughts had singled from among the crowd, and we went out to look for her.

PREENA AND PREEYA
(To left and right) getting ready for a Coming-Day Feast.

Up and down the long white streets we looked for her; on the little narrow verandahs, in the courtyards of the houses, in their dark inner rooms when we were invited within, out again into the sunshine—but we could not find her. That evening I remember, though we did not say so to each other, we felt a little disappointed. We had not met one who even remotely cared for the things we had come to bring.

No one had responded. There was not, so far as we knew it, even a little blade to point to, much less a sheaf to lay at His feet. After nightfall a woman came to see us. But she was a Christian, and beyond trying to cheer her to more earnest service among the heathen, there was nothing to be done for her. She left us, she told us afterwards, warmed to hope; and she talked to a child next morning, a little relative of her own, whose heart the Lord opened.

For three months we heard nothing; then unexpectedly a letter came. "The child is much in earnest, and she has made up her mind to join your Starry Cluster" (a name given by the people to our band, which at that time was itinerating in the district), "so I purpose sending her at once." The parents, for reasons of their own, agreed to the arrangement, and the little girl came to Dohnavur. It was wonderful to watch her learning. She is not intellectually brilliant, but the soul awakened at once, and there was that tenderness of response which refreshes the heart of the teacher. She seemed to come straight to our Lord Jesus and know Him as her Saviour, child though she was; and soon the longing to win others possessed her, and a younger child, who was her special charge among the nursery children, was influenced so gently and so willingly, that we do not know the time when, led by her little Accal, she too came to the Lover of children.

"Across the Will of Nature"

But one day, suddenly, trouble came. The parents appeared in the Dohnavur compound and claimed their daughter; and we had no legal right to refuse her, for she was under age. We shall never forget the hour they came. They had haunted the neighbourhood, as we afterwards heard, and prowled about outside the compound, watching for an opportunity to carry the child off without our knowledge. But she was always with the other children, so that plan failed. When first she heard they had come, she fled to the bungalow. "My parents have come! My father is strong! Oh, hide me! hide me!" she besought us. "I cannot resist him! I cannot!" and she cried and clung to us. But when we went out to meet them, she was perfectly quiet; and no one would have known from her manner as she stood before them, and answered their questions, without a tremble in her voice, how frightened she had been before.

"What is this talk about being a Christian?" the father demanded stormily. "What can an infant know about such matters? Are you wiser than your fathers, that their religion is not good enough for you?" And scathing mockery followed, harder to bear than abuse. "Come! Say salaam to the Missie Ammal, and bring your jewels" (she had taken them off), "and let us go home together." The child stood absolutely still, looking up with brave eyes; and to our astonishment said, as though it were the only thing to be said: "But I am a Christian. I cannot go home."

We had not thought of her saying this. We had, indeed, encouraged her as we had encouraged ourselves, to rest in our God, who is unto us a God of deliverances; but we had not suggested any line of resistance, and were not prepared for the calm refusal which so quietly took it for granted that she had no power to refuse.

The father was evidently nonplussed. He knew his little daughter, a timid child, whose translated name, Fawn, seems to express her exactly, and he gazed down upon her in silence for one surprised moment, then burst out in wrath and indignant revilings. "Snake! nurtured in the bosom only to turn and sting! Vile, filthy, disgusting insect, born to disgrace her caste!" And they cursed her as she stood.

Then their mood changed, and they tried pleadings, much more difficult to resist. The father reminded her of his pilgrimage to a famous Temple at her birth: "He had named her before the gods." Her mother touched on tenderer memories, till we could feel the quiver of soul, and feared for the little Fawn. Then they promised her liberty at home. She should read her Bible, pray to the true God, "for all gods are one." I saw Fawn shut her eyes for a moment. What she saw in that moment she told me afterwards: a fire lighted on the floor, a Bible tossed into it, two schoolboy brothers (whose leanings towards Christianity had been discovered) pushed into an inner room, the sound of blows and cries. "And after that my brothers did not want to be Christians any more." Poor little timid Fawn! We hardly wonder as we look at her that she shrank and shut her eyes. I have seen a child of twelve held down by a powerful arm and beaten across the bare shoulders with a cocoa-nut shell fastened to the end of a stick; I have seen her wrists twisted almost to dislocation—seen it, and been unable to help. I think of the child, now our happy Gladness, lover of the unlovable babies; and I for one cannot wonder at the little Fawn's fear. But aloud she only said: "Forgive me, I cannot go home."

Not Peace, but a Sword

The father grew impatient. "Get your jewels and let us be gone!" Fawn ran into the house, brought her jewels, and handed them to her father. He counted them over—pretty little chains and bangles, and then he eyed her curiously. A child to give up her jewels like this—he found it unaccountable. And then he began to argue, but Fawn answered him with clearness and simplicity, and he could not perplex her. She knew Whom she believed.

At last they rose to go, cursing the day she was born with a curse that sounded horrible. But their younger daughter, whom they had brought with them, threw herself upon the ground, tearing her hair, beating her breast, shrieking and rolling and flinging the dust about like a mad thing. "I will not go without my sister! I will not go! I will not go!" And she clung to Fawn, and wept and bewailed till we hardly dared to hope the child would be able to withstand her. For a moment the parents stood and waited. We, too, stood in tension of spirit. "They have told her to do it," whispered Fawn, and stood firm. Then the father stooped, snatched up the younger child, and departed, followed by the mother.

All this time two of our number had been waiting upon God in a quiet place out of sight. One of the two went after the parents, hoping for a chance to explain matters to the mother. As she drew near she heard the wife say in an undertone to her husband: "Leave them for to-day. Wait till to-night. You have carried off the younger in your arms against her will. What hinders you doing the same to the elder?" And that night we prayed that the Wall of Fire might be round us, and slept in peace.

As a dream when one awaketh, so was the memory of that afternoon when we awoke next morning. And as a dream so the parents passed out of sight, for they left before the dawn. But weeks afterwards we heard what had happened that night. They had lodged in the Hindu village outside our gate. There has never been a Christian there, and the people have never responded in any way. It is a little shut-in place of darkness on the borders of the light. But when the parents proposed a raid upon the bungalow that night they would not rise to it. "No, we have no feud with the bungalow. We will not do it." The nearest white face was a day's journey distant, and a woman alone, white or brown, does not count for much in Hindu eyes. But the Wall of Fire was around us, and so we were safe.

If the story could stop here, how easy life would be! One fight, one fling to the lions, and then the palm and crown. But it is not so. The perils of reaction are greater for the convert than the first great strain of facing the alternative, "Diana or Christ." Home-sickness comes, wave upon wave, and all but sweeps the soul away; feelings and longings asleep in the child awake in the girl, and draw her and woo her, and blind her too often to all that yielding means. She forgets the under-side of the life she has forsaken; she remembers only the alluring; and all that is natural pleads within her, and will not let her rest. "Across the will of Nature leads on the path of God," is sternly true for the convert in a Hindu or Moslem land.

And so we write this unfinished story in faith that some one reading it will remember the young girl-converts as well as the little children. Fawn has been kept steadfast, but she still needs prayer. These last five years have held anxious hours for those who love her, and to us, as to all who have to do with converts. "Perpetual knockings at Thy door, tears sullying Thy transparent rooms," are words that go deep and touch the heart of things.

CHAPTER XXVI

The Glory of the Usual

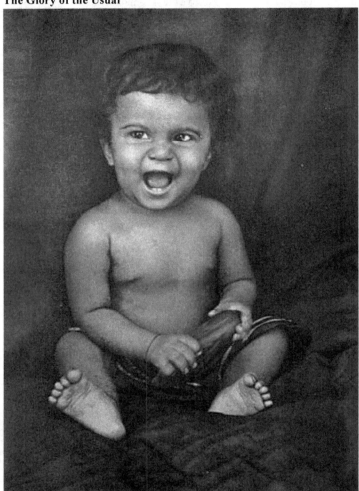

AFTER HER BOTTLE.

"AND all things were done in such excellent methods, and I cannot tell how, but things in the doing of them seemed to cast a smile"—is a beautiful sentence <u>from</u> Bunyan's *Holy War*, which has been with us ever since we began the Nursery work. Lately we found its complement in a modern book of sermons, *The Unlighted Lustre*, by <u>G. H.</u> Morrison. "No matter how stirring your life be, it will be a failure if you have never been wakened to the glory of the usual. There is no happiness like the old and common happiness, sunshine and love and duty and the laughter of children. . . . There are no duties that so enrich as dull duties."

The ancient voice and the new voice sing to the same sweet tune; and we in our little measure are learning to sing it too.

As we have said, India is a land where the secular does not appeal. When we were an Itinerating Band, we had many offers from Christian girls and women to join us, as many in one month as we now have in five years. Sometimes it has seemed to us that we were set to learn and to teach a new and difficult lesson, the sacredness of the commonplace. Day by day we learn to rub out a little more of the clear chalked line that someone has ruled on life's black-board; the Secular and the Spiritual may not be divided now. The enlightening of a dark soul or the lighting of a kitchen fire, it matters not which it is, if only we are obedient to the heavenly vision, and work with a pure intention to the glory of our God.

NORTH LAKE AND HILLS.

The nursery kitchen is a pleasant little place. We hardly ever enter it without remembering and appreciating John Bunyan's pretty thought, for there things in the doing of them seem to cast a smile. Ponnamal, who, as we said, superintends the more delicate food-making work, has trained two of her helpers to carefulness; and these two—one a motherly older woman with a most comfortable face, the other the convert, Joy—look up with such a welcome that you feel it good to be there. Scrubbing away at endless pots and pans and milk vessels is a younger convent-girl, who, when she first came to us, disapproved of such exertion. She liked to sit on the floor with her Bible on her lap and a far-away look of content on her face until the dinner-bell rang. Now she scrubs with a sense of responsibility.

All the younger converts have regular teaching, for they have much to learn, and all, older and younger, have daily classes and meetings; above all, it is planned that each has her quiet time undisturbed. But it is early understood that to be happy each must contribute her share to the happiness of the family; and one of the first lessons the young convert has to learn is to honour the "Grey Angel," Drudgery, and not to call her bad names.

The Story of a Raven

The kitchen has an outlook dear to the Tamil heart. A trellis covered with pink antigone surrounds it, but a window is cut in the trellis so that the kitchen may command the bungalow. "While I stirred the milk I saw everything you did on your verandah," remarked one of the workers lately, in tones of appreciation. The opposite outlook is the mountain shown in the photograph; only instead of water we have the kitchen-garden with its tropical-looking plantains and creeping marrows. "And the warm melon lay like a little sun on the tawny sand," is a line for an Eastern garden when the great marrows ripen suddenly.

The kitchen thus favoured without, is adorned within, according to the taste of its owners, with those very interesting pictures published by the makers of infant foods. "How do you choose them?" we asked one day. "The truest and the prettiest," was the satisfactory answer. Our Dohnavur text, which hangs in every nursery, looks down upon the workers, and, as they put it, "keeps them sweet in heart": "Love never faileth."

When first we began to cultivate babies we were very ignorant, and we asked advice of all who seemed competent to give it. The advice was most perplexing. Each mother was sure the food that had suited her baby was the best of all foods, and regarded all others as doubtful, if not bad. One whom we greatly respected told us Indian babies would be sure to get on anyhow, as it was their own land. And one seriously suggested rice-water as a suitable nourishment. Naturally we began with the time-honoured milk and barley-water, and some throve upon it. But we found each baby had to be studied separately. There was no universal (artificial) food. We could write a tractlet on foods, and if we did we would call it "Don't," for the first sentence in it would be, "Don't change the food if you can help it." This tractlet would certainly close with a word of thanks to those kind people, the milk-food manufacturers, who have helped us to build up healthy children; for feelings of personal gratitude come when help of this kind is given.

The nursery kitchen is a room full of reminders of help. "I have commanded the ravens," is a word of strength to us. Once we were very low. A little child had died under trying circumstances. One of the milk-sellers, instead of using the vessel sent him, poured his milk into an unclean copper vessel, and it was poisoned. He remembered that it would not be taken unless brought in the proper vessel, so at the last moment he corrected his mistake, but the correction was fatal, for there was no warning. The milk was sterilized as usual and given to the child. She was a healthy baby, and her nurse remembers how she smiled and welcomed her bottle, taking it in her little hands in her happy eagerness. A few hours later she was dead.

At such times the heart seems foolishly weak, and things which would not trouble it otherwise have power to make it sore. We were four days' journey from the nursery at the time, and had the added anxiety about the other babies, to whom we feared the poisoned milk might have been given, and we dreaded what the next post might bring. Just at that moment it was suggested, with kindest intentions, that perhaps we were on the wrong track, the work seemed so difficult and wasteful.

It was mail-day. The mail as usual brought a pile of letters, and the top envelope contained a bill for foods ordered from England some weeks before. It came to more than I had expected, in spite of the kindness of several firms in giving a liberal discount; and for a moment the rice-water talk (to give it a name which covers all that type of talk) came back to me with hurt in it: "To what purpose is this waste?" But with it came another word: "Take this child away (away from the terrible Temple) and nurse it for Me." And with the pile of letters before me, and the bill for food in my hand, I asked that enough might be found in those letters to pay it. It did not occur to me at the moment that the prayer was rather illogical. I only knew it would be comforting, and like a little word of peace, if such an assurance might even then come that we were not off the lines.

Because He hath Heard

Letter after letter was empty. Not empty of kindness, but quite empty of cheques. The last envelope looked thin and not at all hopeful. Cheques are usually inside reliable-looking covers. I opened it. There was nothing but a piece of unknown writing. But the writing was to ask if we happened to have a need which a sum named in the letter would meet. This sum exactly covered the bill for the foods. When the cheque eventually reached me it was for more than the letter had mentioned, and covered all carriage and duty expenses, which were unknown to me at the time the first letter came, and to which of course I had not referred in my reply. Thus almost visibly and audibly has the Lord, from whose hands we received this charge to keep, confirmed His word to us, strengthening us when we were weak, and comforting us when we were sad with that innermost sense of His tenderness which braces while it soothes.

Surely we who know Him thus should love the Lord because He hath heard our voice and our supplication. Every advertisement on the walls of the little nursery kitchen is like an illuminated text with a story hidden away in it:—

When Thou dost favour any action,
It runs, it flies;
All things concur to give it a perfection.

The nursery kitchen, we were amused to discover, has a sphere of influence all its own. Our discovery was on this wise:—

One wet evening we were caught in a downpour as we were crossing from the Taraha nursery to the bungalow, and we took shelter in the kindergarten room, which reverts to the Lola-and-Leela tribe when the kindergarten babies depart. The tribe do not often possess their Sittie and their Ammal both together and all to themselves, now that the juniors are so numerous, and they welcomed us with acclamations. "Finish spreading your mats," we said to them, as they seemed inclined to let our advent interrupt the order of the evening; and we watched them unroll their mats, which hung round the wall in neat rolls swung by cords from the roof, and spread them in rows along the wall. Beside each mat was what looked like a mummy, and beside each mummy was a matchbox and a small bundle of rags.

Presently the mummies were unswathed, and proved to be dolls in more or less good condition. Each was carefully laid upon a morsel of sheet, and covered with another sheet folded over in the neatest fashion. "If we teach them to be particular when they are young, they will be tidy when they are old," we were informed. It was pleasant to hear our own remarks so accurately repeated.

The matchboxes were next unpacked; each contained a bit of match, a small pointed shell, a pebble (preferably black), and a couple of minute cockles. "I suppose you don't know what all these are?" said Lola, affably. "That," pointing to the match, "is a spoon; and this," taking the pointed shell up carefully, "is a bottle. This is the 'rubber,' of course," and the black pebble was indicated; "and these" (setting the cockle-shells on a piece of white paper on the floor) "are bowls of water, one for the bottle and the other for the rubber." We suggested one bowl of water would hold both bottle and rubber; but Lola's entirely mischievous eyes looked quite shocked and reproving. "Two bowls are better," was the serious reply; "it is very important to be clean." "What does your child have?" we inquired respectfully. "Barley-water and milk, two-and-a-half ounces every two hours— that's five tablespoonfuls, you know." "And Leela's?" "Oh, Leela's child is delicate. She has to have Benger. Two ounces every two hours; and it has to be a long time digested." "Do all your children have their food every two hours?" Lola looked surprised, and Leela giggled: how very ignorant we seemed to be! "No, only the tiny ones; our babies are very young. After they get older they have more at a time and not so often. That child there," pointing to another mat, "has Condensed, as we haven't enough cow's milk for them all. It suits her very well. She has six ounces at a time; once before she goes to sleep, and then none till she wakens in the morning. She's a very healthy child." "How do you know the time?" we asked, prepared for anything now. "Oh, we have watches. This is mine," and a toy from a Christmas cracker was produced; "Leela's watch is different" (it was indeed different—a mere figment of the imagination), "but she can look at mine when she wants to." "Why does your child sleep with Leela's?" (All the other infants had separate sleeping arrangements.) Lola looked shy, and Leela looked shyer. These little matters of affection were not intended for public discussion.

The Usual

By this time the rain had cleared, so we prepared to depart, and the further entertainments provided for us by the cheerful tribe that evening do not belong to this story. We escaped finally, damp with much laughter in a humid atmosphere. "Come every evening!" shouted the tribe, as at last we disappeared, and we felt much inclined to accept the invitation.

The kitchen is a busy place in the morning, and again in the evening, when the fresh milk is carried to it in shining aluminium vessels to be sterilized or otherwise dealt with. But even in the busiest hours there is almost sure to be a baby set in an upturned stool, in which she sits holding on to the front legs in proud consciousness of being able to sit up. Or an older one will be clinging to the garments of the busy workers, or perched beside them on a stool. Once we found Tara and Evu seated on the window-sill. Ponnamal was making foods at the table under the window, and the little bare feet were tucked in between bowls and jugs of milk. "But, indeed, they are quite clean," explained Ponnamal, without waiting for remark from us, for she knew what we were thinking of her table decorations. "We dusted the sand off their little feet before we lifted them up." The babies said nothing, but looked doubtfully up at us, as if not very sure of our intentions. But Ponnamal's eyes were so appealing, and the little buff things in blue with a trellis of pink flowers for background made such a pretty picture, that we had not the heart to spoil it. Then the little faces smiled gratefully upon us, and everybody smiled. The kitchen is a happy place of innocent surprises.

CHAPTER XXVII

The Secret Traffic

"Sir, to leave things out of a book because they will not be believed, is meanness."—Dr. Johnson.

WHEN first, upon March 7, 1901, we heard from the lips of a little child the story of her life in a Temple house, we were startled and distressed, and penetrated with the conviction that such a story ought to be impossible in a land ruled by a Christian Power. The subject was new to us; we knew nothing of the magnitude of what may be called "The Secret Traffic of India"—a traffic in little children, mere infants oftentimes, for wrong purposes; and we did not appreciate, as we do now, the delicacy and difficulty of the position from a Government point of view, or the quiet might of the forces upon the other side. And though with added knowledge comes an added sense of responsibility, and a fear of all careless appeal to those whose burden is already so heavy, yet with every fresh discovery the conviction deepens that something should be done—and done, if possible, soon—to save at least this generation of children, or some of them, from destruction.

"It is useless to move without a body of evidence at your back," said a friend in the Civil Service to us at the close of a long conversation. "If you can get the children, of course they themselves will furnish the best evidence; but, anyhow, collect facts." And this was the beginning of a Note-book, into which we entered whatever we could learn about the Temple children, and in which we kept letters relating to them.

By Temple children throughout this book we mean children dedicated to gods, or in danger of being so dedicated. Dedication to gods implies a form of marriage which makes ordinary marriage impossible. The child is regarded as belonging to the gods. In Southern India, where religious feeling runs strong, and the great Temples are the centres of Hindu influence, this that I have called "The Traffic" is worked upon religious lines; and so in trying to save the children we have to contend with the perverted religious sense. Something of the same kind exists in other parts of India, and the traffic under another name is common in provinces where Temple service as we have it in the South is unknown. Again, in areas where, owing to the action of the native Government, Temple service, as such, is not recognised, so that children in danger of wrong cannot, strictly speaking, be called Temple children, there is yet need of legislation which shall touch all houses where little children are being brought up for the same purpose; so that the subject is immense and involved, and the thought of it suggests a net thrown over millions of square miles of territory, so finely woven as to be almost invisible, but so strong in its mesh that in no place yet has it ever given way. And the net is alive: it can feel and it can hold.

But all through this book we have kept to the South—to the area where the evil is distinctly and recognisably religious. Others elsewhere have told their own story; ours, though in touch with theirs (in that its whole motive is to save the little children), is yet different in manner, in that it is avowedly Christian. India is a land where generalisations are deceptive. So we have kept to the South.

We ourselves became only very gradually aware of what was happening about us. As fact after fact came to light, we were forced to certain conclusions which we could not doubt were correct. But at first we were almost alone in these conclusions, because it was impossible to take others with us in our tedious underground hunt after facts. So the question was often asked: "But do the children really exist?"

"If"

I have said we were almost alone, not quite. Members of the Indian Civil Service, who are much among the people, knew something of the custom of child-dedication, but found themselves unable to touch it. Hindu Reformers, of course, knew; and two or three veteran missionaries had come into contact with it and had grieved over their helplessness to do anything. One of these had written a pamphlet on the subject twenty years before our Nursery work began. He sent it to me with a sorrowful word written across it, "Result? Nil." But we do not often meet our civilian friends, for they are busy, and so are we; and the few missionaries whose inspiring sympathy helped us through those earlier years were in places far from us, and so were all the Reformers. So perhaps it was not wonderful that, beset by doubting letters from home and a certain amount of not unnatural incredulity in India, we sometimes almost wondered if we ourselves were dreaming. "Well, if they do exist, I hope you will be able to find them!"—varied by, "Well, if you do find them, they will be a proof of their own existence!"—were two of the most encouraging remarks of those early days.

From the beginning of this work, as stated before, we have tried to collect facts about the traffic and the customs connected with it. Notes were kept of conversations with Hindus and others, and these notes were compared with what evidence we were able to gather from trustworthy sources. These brief notes of various kinds we offer in their simplicity. We have made no attempt to tabulate or put into shape the information thus acquired, believing that the notes of conversations taken down at the time, and the quotations from letters copied as they stand, will do their work more directly than anything more elaborate would. Where there is a difference of detail it is because the customs differ slightly in different places. No names are given, for obvious reasons; but the letters were written by men of standing, living in widely scattered districts in the

South. The evidence contained in them was carefully sifted, and in many cases corroborated by personal investigation, before being considered evidence: so that we believe these chapters may be accepted as fact. Dated quotations from the *Madras Mail* are sufficient to prove that we are not writing ancient history:—

January 2, 1909.—"The following resolution was put from the chair and carried unanimously: 'The Conference (consisting of Hindu Social Reformers) cordially supports the movement started to better the condition of unprotected children in general, and appreciates particularly the agitation started to protect girls and young women from being dedicated to Temples.'"

Mysore

May 8, 1909.—"Once more we have an illustration from Mysore of the fact that the Government of a Native State are able to tread boldly on ground which the British Government in India are unable to approach. At various times, in these columns and elsewhere, has the cry raised against the employment of servants of the gods in Hindu Temples been uttered; but, as far as the Government are concerned, it has fallen, if not on deaf ears, on ears stopped to appeals of this kind, which demand action that can be interpreted as a breach of that religious neutrality which is one of the cardinal principles of British rule in India. The agitation against it is not the agitation of the European whose susceptibility is offended at a state of things that he finds hard to reconcile with the reverence and purity of Divine worship; but it is the outcry of the reverent Hindu against one of the corrupt and degrading practices that, in the course of centuries, have crept into his religion. In this particular instance the Mysore Government cannot be accused of acting hastily. As long ago as February, 1892, they issued a circular order describing the legitimate services to be performed in Temples by Temple women. In 1899, the Muzrai Superintendent, Rai Bahadur A. Sreenivasa Charlu, directed that the Temple women borne on the Nanjangud Temple establishment should not be allowed to perform *tafe* (or dancing) service in the Temple; but that the allowances payable to them should be continued for their lifetime, and that at their death the vacancies should not be filled up. Against this order the Temple women concerned memorialised H.H. the Maharajah as long ago as 1905, and the order disposing of it has only just been issued. In the course of the latter the Government say:—

"'From the Shastraic authorities quoted by the two Agamiks employed in the Muzrai Secretariat, it is observed that the services to be performed by Temple women form part and parcel of the worship of the god in Hindu Temples, and that singing and dancing in the presence of the deity are also prescribed. It is, however, observed that in the case of Temple women personal purity and rectitude of conduct and a vow of celibacy were considered essential. But the high ideals entertained in ancient days have now degenerated. . . . The Government now observe that whatever may have been the original object of the institution of Temple women in Temples, the state in which these Temple servants are now found fully justifies the action taken by them in excluding the Temple women from every kind of service in sacred institutions like Temples. Further, the absence of the services of these women in certain important Temples in the State has become established for nearly fifteen years past, and the public have become accustomed to the idea of doing without such services.'

"The exclusion of Temple women from Temple services obtains in Mysore in the case of a few large Temples whose *Tasdik Pattis* have been revised. But the time has come, the Government think, for its general application, and they therefore direct that the policy enunciated in the abstract given above should be extended to all Muzrai Temples in the State. It is to be hoped that the good example thus set will bear fruit elsewhere, where the Temple women evil is more notorious than it was in Temples of Mysore."

A copy of the Government document to which this cutting relates lies before me. It is bravely and clearly worded, and its intention is evident. The high-minded Hindu—and there are such, let it not be forgotten—revolts from the degradation and pollution of this travesty of religion, and will abolish it where he can. *But let it be remembered that, good as this law is, it does not and it cannot touch the great Secret Traffic itself. That will go on behind the law, and behind the next that is made, and the next, unless measures are devised to ensure its being thoroughly enforced.*

Cuttings from newspapers, quotations, evidence—it is not interesting reading, and yet we look to our friends to go through to the end with us. Let us pause for a moment here and remember the purpose of it all; and may the thought of some little, loved child make an atmosphere for these chapters!

CHAPTER XXVIII

Blue Book Evidence

"The precipitous sides of difficult questions."—E. B. B.

OUR first evidence consists of abridged extracts from the Census Report for 1901. After explaining the different names by which Temple women are known in different parts of the Madras Presidency, the Report continues: "The servants of the gods, who subsist by dancing and music and the practice of 'the oldest profession in the world,' are partly recruited by admissions and even purchases from other classes. . . . The rise of the Caste and its euphemistic name seem to date from the ninth and tenth centuries, during which much activity prevailed in South India in the matter of building Temples and elaborating the services held in them. . . . The duties then, as now, were to fan the idol with Tibetan ox-tails, to carry the sacred light, and to sing and dance before the god when he is carried in procession. Inscriptions show that in a.d. 1004 the great Temple of the Chola king at Tanjore had attached to it four hundred women of the Temple, who lived in free quarters in the four streets round it, and were allowed tax-free land out of its endowments. Other Temples had similar arrangements. . . . At the present day they form a regular Caste, having its own laws of inheritance, its own customs and rules of etiquette, and its own councils to see that all these are followed, and they hold a position which is perhaps without a parallel in any other country. . . .

"The daughters of the Caste who are brought up to follow the Caste profession are carefully taught dancing and singing, the art of dressing well, ;. . . and their success in keeping up their clientele is largely due to the contrast which they thus present to the ordinary Hindu housewife, whose ideas are bounded by the day's dinners and babies."

Closely allied to this Caste is that formed by the Temple musicians, who with the Temple woman are "now practically the sole repository of Indian music, the system of which is probably one of the oldest in the world." In certain districts the Report states that a custom obtains among certain castes, under which a family which has no sons must dedicate one of its daughters to Temple service. The daughter selected is taken to a Temple and married there to a god, the marriage symbol being put on her as in a real marriage. Henceforth she belongs to the god.

Writing in 1904, a member of the Indian Civil Service says: "I heard of a case of dedication (three girls) at A. at the beginning of this year, but I could not get any evidence. The cases very rarely indeed come up officially, as nearly every Hindu is interested in keeping them dark." We, too, have had the same difficulty, and the evidence we now submit is doubly valuable because of its source. It is very rarely that we have found it possible to get behind the scenes sufficiently to obtain reliable information from those most concerned in this traffic.

The head priest of one of our Temples admitted to a friend who was watching for opportunities to get information for us that the "marriage to the god is effected privately by the Temple priest at the Temple woman's house, with the usual marriage-symbol ceremony. To avoid the Penal Code (which forbids the marriage of children to gods) a nominal bridegroom is sometimes brought for the wedding day to become the nominal husband. This Caste is recruited by secret adoption."

A Temple woman's son, now living the ordinary life apart from his clan, explains the very early marriage thus: "If not married, they will not be considered worthy of honour. Before the children reach the age of ten they must be married. . . . They become the property of the Temple priests and worshippers who go to the Temple to chant the sacred songs."

"The Child should be about Eight"

A Temple woman herself told a friend of ours: "The child is dressed like a bride, and taken with another girl of the same community, dressed like a boy in the garb of a bridegroom. They both go to the Temple and worship the idol. This ceremony is common, and performed openly in the streets." In a later letter from the same friend further details are given: "The child, who should be about eight or nine years old, goes as if to worship the idol in the Temple. There the marriage symbol is hidden in a garland, and the garland is put over the idol, after which it is taken to the child's home and put round her neck." After this she is considered married to the god.

A young Temple woman in a town near Dohnavur told us she had been given to the Temple when she was five years old. Her home was in the north country, but she did not remember it. She had, of course, understood nothing of the meaning of the ceremony of marriage. She only remembered the pretty flowers and general rejoicing and pleasure. Afterwards, when she began to understand, she was not happy, but she gradually got accustomed to it. Her adopted relations were all the friends she had. She was fond of them and they of her. Her "husband" was one of the Temple priests.

A Hindu woman known to us left home with her little daughter and wandered about as an ascetic. She went to a famous Temple, where it is the custom for such as desire to become ascetics to enter the life by conforming to certain ceremonies ordained by the priests. She shaved her head, took off her jewels, wore a Saivite necklet of berries, and was known as a devotee. She had little knowledge of the life before she entered it, and only gradually became aware of the character borne by most of her fellow-devotees. When she knew, she fled from them and returned to her own village and the secular life, finding it better than the religious.

How she is Trained

In telling us about it she said: "I expected whiteness, I found blackness." She told us that she constantly came into contact with Temple women, none of whom had chosen the life as she and her fellow-ascetics had chosen theirs. "Always the one who is to dance before the gods is given to the life when she is very young. Otherwise she could not be properly trained. Many babies are brought by their parents and given to Temple women for the sake of merit. It is very meritorious to give a child to the gods. Often the parents are poor but of good Caste. Always suitable compensation and a 'joy gift' is given by the Temple women to the parents. It is an understood custom, and ensures that the child is a gift, not a loan. The amount depends upon the age and beauty of the child. If the child is old enough to miss her mother, she is very carefully watched until she has forgotten her. Sometimes she is shut up in the back part of the house, and punished if she runs out into the street. The punishment is severe enough to frighten the child. Sometimes it is branding with a hot iron upon a place which does not show, as under the arm; sometimes nipping with the nail till the skin breaks; sometimes a whipping. After the child is reconciled to her new life, occasionally her people are allowed to come if they wish; and in special circumstances she pays a visit to her old home. But this is rare. If she has been adopted as an infant, she knows nothing of her own relations, but thinks of her adopted mother as her own mother. As soon as she can understand she is taught all evil and trained to think it is good."

As to her education, the movements of the dance are taught very early, and the flexible little limbs are rendered more flexible by a system of massage. In all ways the natural grace of the child is cultivated and developed, but always along lines which lead far away from the freedom and innocence of childhood. As it is important she should learn a great deal of poetry, she is taught to read (and with this object in view she is sometimes sent to the mission school, if there is one near her home). The poetry is almost entirely of a debased character; and so most insidiously, by story and allusion, the child's mind is familiarised with sin; and before she knows how to refuse the evil and choose the good, the instinct which would have been her guide is tampered with and perverted, till the poor little mind, thus bewildered and deceived, is incapable of choice.

CHAPTER XXIX

"Very Common in those Parts"

"The dark enigma of permitted wrong."—F. R. H.

THE mixture of secrecy and openness described by the Temple woman is confirmed by Hindus well acquainted with Temple affairs. "All the Temple women are married to the gods. In former times the marriages were conducted upon a grand scale, but now they are clandestinely performed in the Temple, with the connivance of the priest, and with freedom to deny it if questioned. Some ceremonies are performed in the Temple, the rest at home. Sometimes the marriage symbol is blessed by the priest, and taken home to the child to be worn by her. In all these cases the priest himself has to tie it round her neck. The previous arrangements for the marriage are made by the priests with the guardians of the child who is to be initiated into the order of Temple women.

"The ceremony of tying on the marriage symbol is never in our district performed in public. None but intimate friends know about it. There is a secret understanding between the priests and the Temple women concerned. When the time arrives for the marriage symbol to be tied on, after the usual ceremonies the priest hands over the symbol hidden in a garland of flowers.

"Of course, there is music on the occasion. When outsiders ask what all the noise is about, the people who know do not say the real thing. They say it is a birthday or other festival day. The symbol is tied on when the child is between five and eleven, after which it is considered unholy to perform the marriage ceremony. The symbol is at first hidden from the gaze of the public. Later it is shown publicly, but not while the girl is still young."

This tallies exactly with our own experience. More than once an eager child in her simplicity has shown me the marriage symbol, a small gold ornament tied round her neck, or hanging on a fine gold chain; but the Temple woman in whose charge she was has always reproved her sharply, and made her cover it up under her other jewels, or under the folds of her dress.

The reason for this secrecy, which, however, is not universal, is, as is inferred in the evidence of the head priest, because it is known to the Temple authorities that what they are doing is illegal; though, as a matter of fact, as will be seen later, prosecutions are rare, and convictions rarer still.

The Caste is recruited, as the Blue Book states, by "admissions and even purchases from other classes." On this point a Brahman says: "When the Temple woman has no child, she adopts a girl or girls, and the children become servants of the gods. Sometimes children are found who, on account of a vow made by their parents, become devotees of the gods." Another Brahman, an orthodox Hindu, writes: "In some districts people vow that they will dedicate one of their children to the Temple if they are blessed with a family. Temple women often adopt orphans, to whom they bequeath their possessions. In most cases the orphans are bought."

Convictions are Rare

The position of the Temple woman has been a perplexity to many. The Census Report touches the question: "It is one of the many inconsistencies of the Hindu religion, that though their profession is repeatedly vehemently condemned in the Shastras (sacred books), it has always received the countenance of the Church." Their duties are all religious. A well-informed Hindu correspondent thus enumerates them: "First they are to be one of the twenty-one persons who are in charge of the key of the outer door of the Temple; second, to open the outer door daily; third, to burn camphor, and go round the idol when worship is being performed; fourth, to honour public meetings with their presence; fifth, to mount the car and stand near the god during car-festivals." The orthodox Hindu quoted before remarks on the "high honour," as the Temple child is taught to consider it, the marriage to the god confers upon her.

We have purposely confined ourselves almost entirely to official and Hindu evidence so far, but cannot forbear to add to this last word the confirmatory experience of our own Temple children worker: "When I try to persuade the Hindus to let us have their little ones instead of giving them to the Temples they say: 'But to give them to Temples is honour and glory and merit to us for ever; to give them to you is dishonour and shame and demerit. So why should we give them to you?'"

We have said that convictions are rare. This is because of the great difficulty in obtaining such evidence as is required by the law as it stands at present. One case may be quoted as typical. A few years ago, in one of our country towns, a father gave his child in marriage to the idol "with some pomp," as the report before us says. He was prosecuted, but the prosecution failed, for the priest and the parents united in denying the fact of the marriage; and the evidence for the defence was so skilfully cooked that it was found impossible to prove an offence against the Penal Code.

Once, deeply stirred over the case of a little girl of six who was about to be married to a god as her elder sisters had been a few months previously, we wrote to a magistrate of wide experience and proved sympathy with the work. His letter speaks for itself:—

"I have been waiting some little time before answering your letter, because I wanted time to think over your problem. As far as I can make out, there is no way in the world of preventing a woman marrying her own daughter to the gods at any age; but you can prosecute her if she does. If you could get her into prison for marrying the elder girls, the younger might be safe; but I don't think you can do anything directly for her. She is not being 'unlawfully detained'; and even if she were, all you could do would be to get her returned to her parents and guardians, which would be worse than useless.

"The question is whether you can hope to get a conviction in the other case.

"I don't see how you can. You can say in court that you saw the little girls with their marriage symbol on, and that they said they had been married to the god. The little girls will deny it all, and say they never set eyes on you before. Moreover, I don't think the ordinary Court would be satisfied without some other evidence of the fact of dedication; and considering how everyone would work against you, I think you would find it extraordinarily hard. The local police would be worse than useless."

To every man his work: it appears to us that expert knowledge is required, and ample means and leisure, if the expenditure involved is to result in anything worth while; and a careful study of all available information regarding prosecutions, convictions, and, I may add, sentences, has convinced us, at least, of the futility of such attempts from a missionary point of view: for even if convictions were certain, *as long as the law hands the child back to its guardians after their unfitness to guard it from the worst that can befall it has been proved*, so long do we feel unable to rejoice exceedingly over even the six months' rigorous imprisonment, which in more than one case has been the legal interpretation of the phrase "up to a term of ten years," which is the penalty attached to this offence in the Indian Penal Code.

In this connection it may be well to quote a paragraph from the *Indian Social Reformer:*—

"The Public Prosecutor at Madras applied for admission of a revision petition against the order of the Sessions Judge, made in the following circumstances:—

Ten years—Six Months

"One, S., a priest, was convicted by the first-class subdivisional magistrate of having performed the ceremony of dedicating a young girl in the Temple of N., and thereby committing an offence punishable under Section 372 of the Penal Code. He accordingly sentenced him to six months' rigorous imprisonment. On appeal, the Sessions Judge reduced the sentence to two months, on the ground that the rite complained against was a very common one in those parts. The Public Prosecutor based his petition on the ground that it had been held in a previous case 'that such a dedication was an offence, and that it was highly desirable that the interests of minors should be properly protected.' This protection, it was submitted, could only be vouchsafed by making offending people understand that they would render themselves liable to heavy punishment. The present sentence would not have a deterrent effect, and he accordingly applied for an enhancement of the same. His lordship admitted the petition, and directed notice to the accused."

It is something to know the six months' sentence was confirmed. But is not the fact that a Sessions Judge should commute such a sentence, on the ground that the offence was "very common," enough to suggest a doubt as to the deterrent effect of even this punishment?

NOTE

During the last few months the Secretary of State for India has addressed official inquiries to the Government of India regarding the dedication of children to Hindu gods, and the measures necessary for the protection of such children.

If the anticipated change in the law is to result in more than a Bill on paper—a blind, behind which things will go on as before only more out of sight—it is, we believe, needful to ensure:

1st. Protection for all children found to be in moral danger, whether or not they are or may be dedicated to gods.

2nd. That, irrespective of nationality or religion, whoever has worked for and won the deliverance of the child should be allowed to act as guardian to it.

3rd. That such a Bill shall be most thoroughly enforced.

February, 1912.
To face p. 268.

CHAPTER XXX

On the Side of the Oppressors there was Power

I HAVE been looking over my note-book, in which there are some hundreds of letters, clippings from newspapers, and records of conversations bearing upon the Temple children. It is difficult to know which to choose to complete the picture already outlined in the preceding chapters. A mere case record would be wearisome; and indeed the very word "case" sounds curiously inappropriate when one thinks of the nurseries and their little inhabitants; or looks up to see mischievous eyes watching a chance to stop the uninteresting writing; or feels, suddenly, soft arms round one's neck, as a baby, strayed from her own domain, climbs unexpectedly up from behind and makes dashes at the typewriter keyboard. Such little living interruptions are too frequent to allow of these chapters being anything but human.

The newspaper clippings are usually concerned with public movements, resolutions, petitions, and the like. There is one startling little paragraph from a London paper, dated July 7, 1906; the ignorance of the subject so flippantly dealt with is its only apology. No one could have written so had he understood. The occasion was the memorial addressed to the Governor in Council by workers for the children in the Bombay Presidency:—

"Society must be very select in Poona. There has been a custom there for young ladies to be married to selected gods. You would have thought that to be the bride of a god was a good enough marriage for anyone. But it is not good enough for Poona." It is time that such writing became impossible for any Englishman.

In India the feeling of the best men, whether Hindu or Christian, is strongly against the dedication of little children to Temples, and some of the newspapers of the land speak out and say so in unmistakable language. The *Indian Times* speaks of the little ones being "steeped deep from their childhood" in all that is most wrong. A Hindu, writing in the *Epiphany*, puts the matter clearly when he says: "Finally, one can hardly conceive of anything more debasing than to dedicate innocent little girls to gods in the name of religion, and then leave them with the Temple priests"; and another writer in the same paper asks a question which those who say that Hinduism is good enough for India might do well to ponder: "If this is not a Hindu practice, how can it take place in a Temple and no priest stop it, though all know? . . . In London religion makes wickedness go away; but in Bombay religion brings wickedness, and Government has to try to make it go away." This immense contrast of fact and of ideal contains our answer to all who would put sin in India on a level with sin in England.

Christian writers naturally, whether in the *Christian Patriot* of the South or the *Bombay Guardian* of the West, have no doubt about the existence of the evil or the need for its removal. They, too, connect it distinctly with religion, and recognise its tremendous influence.

But we turn from the printed page, and go straight to the houses where the little children live. The witnesses now are missionaries or trusted Indian workers.

"She Belongs to the god"

"There were thirteen little children in the houses connected with the Temple last time I visited them. I saw the little baby—such a dear, fat, laughing little thing. It was impossible to get it, and I see no hope of getting any of the other children."

"When I was visiting in S. a woman came to talk to me with her three little children. Two of them were girls, very pretty, 'fair' little children. 'What work does your husband do?' I asked; and she answered, 'I am married to the god.' Then I knew who she was, and that her children were in danger. I have tried since to get them, but in vain. Everyone says that Temple women never give up their little girls. These two were dedicated at their birth. This is only one instance. We have many Temple women reading with us, and many of the little children attend our schools."

"There are not scores but hundreds of these children in the villages of this district. Here certain families, living ordinary lives in their own villages, dedicate one of their children as a matter of course to the gods. They always choose the prettiest. It is a recognised custom, and no one thinks anything of it. The child so dedicated lives with her parents afterwards as if nothing had happened, only she may not be married in the real way. She belongs to the god and his priests and worshippers."

"The house was very orderly and nice. I sat on the verandah and talked to the women, who were all well educated and so attractive with their pretty dress and jewels. They seemed bright, but, of course, would not show me their real feelings, and I could only hold surface conversation with them."

We are often asked if the Temple houses are inside the walls which surround all the great Temples in this part of the country. They are usually in the streets outside. Most of the Brahman Temples are surrounded by a square of streets, and the houses are in the square or near it. There is nothing to distinguish them from other houses in the street. It is only when you go inside that you feel the difference. An hour on the shady verandah of one of these houses is very revealing. You see the children run up to welcome a tall, fine-looking man, who pats their heads in the kindest way, and as he passes you recognise him. Next time you see him in the glory of his office, you wish you could forget where you saw him last.

Sometimes we are asked who the children are. How do the Temple women get them in the first instance?

We have already answered this question by quotations from the Census Report, and by statements of Hindus well acquainted with the subject. It should be added that often the Temple woman having daughters of her own dedicates them, and as a rule it is only when she has none that she adopts other little ones. A few extracts from letters and notes from conversations are subjoined, as they show how the system of adoption works:—

"We are in trouble over a little girl, the daughter of wealthy parents, who have dedicated her to the gods and refuse to change their mind. The child was ill some time ago, and they vowed then that if she recovered they would dedicate her."

"The poor woman's husband was very ill, and the mother vowed her little girl as an offering if he recovered. He did recover, and so the child has been given."

"It is the custom of the Caste to dedicate the eldest girl of a certain chosen family, and nothing will turn them from it. One child must be given in each generation."

"She is of good caste, but very poor. Her husband died two months before the baby was born, and as it was a girl she was much troubled as to its future, for she knew she would never have enough money to marry it suitably. A Temple woman heard of the baby, and at once offered to adopt it. She persuaded the mother by saying: 'You see, if it is married to the gods, it will never be a widow like you. It will always be well cared for and have honour, and be a sign of good fortune to our people—unlike you!' (It is considered a sign of good omen to see a Temple woman the first thing in the morning; but the sight of a widow at any time is a thing to be avoided.) The poor mother could not resist this, and she has been persuaded."

"Not Wrong because Religious"

"The mother is a poor, delicate widow, with several boys as well as this baby girl. She cannot support them all properly, and her relatives do not seem inclined to help her. The Temple women have heard of her, and they sent a woman to negotiate. The mother knew that we would take the little one rather than that she should be forced to give it up to Temple women; but she said when we talked with her: 'It cannot be wrong to give it to the holy gods! This is our religion; and it may be wrong to you, but it is not wrong to us.' So she refused to give us the baby, and seems inclined to go away with it. It is like that constantly. The thing cannot be wrong because it is religious!"

"I heard of two little orphan girls whose guardian, an uncle, had married again, and did not want to have the marriage expenses of his two little nieces to see to. So at the last great festival he brought the children and dedicated them to the Saivite Temple, and the Temple women heard about it before I did, and at once secured them. I went as soon as I could to see if we could not get them, but she would not listen to us. She said they were her sister's children, and that she had adopted them out of love for her dead sister."

A lawyer was consulted as to this case, but it was impossible to trace the uncle or to prove that the children were not related to the Temple woman. Above all, it was impossible to prove that she meant to do anything illegal. So nothing could be done.

As a rule the Temple woman receives little beyond bare sustenance from the Temple itself. In some Temples when the little child is formally dedicated, she (or her guardian) receives two pounds, and her funeral expenses are promised. But though there is little stated remuneration, the Temple woman is not poor. Poverty may come. If she breaks the law of her caste, or offends against the etiquette of that caste, she is immediately excommunicated, and then she may become very poor. Or if she has spent her money freely, or not invested it wisely, her old age may be cheerless enough. But we have not found any lack of money among the Sisterhood. No offer of compensation for all expenses connected with a child has ever drawn them to part with her. They offer large sums for little ones who will be useful to them. We have several times known as much as an offer of one hundred rupees made and accepted in cases where the little child (in each case a mere infant) was one of special promise. A letter, which incidentally mentions the easy circumstances in which many are, may be of interest:—

"K. is a little girl in our mission school. Her mother is a favourite Temple woman high up in the profession. She dances while the other women sing, and sometimes she gets as much as three or four hundred rupees for her dancing. She is well educated, can recite the 'Ramayana' (Indian epic), and knows a little English. She spends some time in her own house, but is often away visiting other Temples. Just now she is away, and little K. is with her. . . . Humanly speaking, she will never let her go."

The Pressure Tells

The education of the mission school is appreciated because it makes the bright little child still brighter; and we, who know the home life of these children, are glad when they are given one brief opportunity to learn what may help them in the difficult days to come. We have known of some little ones who, influenced by outside teaching, tried to escape the life they began to feel was wrong, but in each case they were overborne, for on the side of the oppressors there was power. I was in a Temple house lately, and noticed the doors—the massive iron-bossed doors are a feature of all well-built Hindu houses of the South. How could a little child shut up in such a room, with its door shut, if need be, to the outside inquisitive world—how could she resist the strength that would force the garland round her neck? She might tear it off if she dared, but the little golden symbol had been hidden under the flowers, and the priest had blessed it; the deed was done—she was married to the god. And only those who have seen the effect of a few weeks of such a life upon a child, who has struggled in vain against it, can understand how cowed she may become, how completely every particle of courage and independence of spirit may be caused to disappear; and how what we had known as a bright, sparkling child, full of the fearless, confiding ways of a child, may become distrustful and constrained, quite incapable of taking a stand on her own account, or of responding to any effort we might be able to make from outside. It is as if the child's spirit were broken, and those who know what she has gone through cannot wonder if it is.

And then comes something we dread more: the life begins to attract. The sense of revolt passes as the will weakens; the persistent, steady pressure tells. And when we see her next, perhaps only three months later, the child has passed the boundary, and belongs to us no more.

CHAPTER XXXI

And there was None to Save

Thou canst conceive our highest and our lowest
Pulses of nobleness and aches of shame.

Frederic W. H. Myers.

IN speaking of these matters I have tried to keep far from that which is only sentiment, and have resolutely banished all imagination. I would that the writing could be as cold in tone as the criticism of those who consider everything other than polished ice almost amusing—to judge by the way they handle it, dismissing it with an airy grace and a hurting adjective. Would they be quite so cool, we wonder, if the little wronged girl were their own? But we do not write for such as these. The thought of the cold eyes would freeze the thoughts before they formed. We write for the earnest-hearted, who are not ashamed to confess they care. And yet we write with reserve even though we write for them, because nothing else is possible. And this crushing back of the full tide makes its fulness almost oppressive. It is as though a flame leaped from the page and scorched the brain that searched for words quite commonplace and quiet.

The finished product of the Temple system of education is something so distorted that it cannot be described. But it should never be forgotten that the thing from which we recoil did not choose to be fashioned so. It was as wax—a little, tender, innocent child—in the hands of a wicked power when the fashioning process began. Let us deal gently with those who least deserve our blame, and reserve our condemnation for those responsible for the creation of the Temple woman. Is it fair that a helpless child, who has never once been given the choice of any other life, should be held responsible afterwards for living the life to which alone she has been trained? Is it fair to call her by a name which belongs by right to one who is different, in that her life is self-chosen? No word can cut too keenly at the root of this iniquity; but let us deal gently with the mishandled flower. Let hard words be restrained where the woman is concerned. Let it be remembered she is not responsible for being what she is.

In a Canadian book of songs there is a powerful little poem about an artist who painted one who was beautiful but not good. He hid all trace of what was; he painted a babe at her breast.

I painted her as she might have been
If the Worst had been the Best.

And a connoisseur came and looked at the picture. To him it spoke of holiest things; he thought it a Madonna:—

So I painted a halo round her hair,
And I sold her and took my fee;
And she hangs in the church of St. Hilaire,
Where you and all may see.

"It Crowns with the Golden Crown"

Sometimes as we have looked at the face of one whose training was not complete we have seen as the artist saw: we have seen her "as she might have been if the worst had been the best." There was no halo round her hair, only its travesty—something that told of crowned and glorified sin; and yet we could catch more than a glimpse of the perfect "might have been." So we say, let blame fall lightly on the one who least deserves it. Perhaps if our ears were not so full of the sounds of the world, we should hear a tenderer judgment pronounced than man's is likely to be: "Unto the damsel thou shalt do nothing. . . . For there was none to save her."

Our work at Dohnavur is entirely among the little children who are innocent of wrong. We rarely touch these lives which have been stained and spoiled; but we could not forbear to write a word of clear explanation about them, lest any should mistake the matter and confuse things that differ.

We leave the subject with relief. Few who have followed us so far know how much it has cost to lead the way into these polluted places. Not that we would make much of any personal cost; but that we would have it known that nothing save a pressure which could not be resisted could force us to touch pitch. And yet why should we shrink from it when the purpose which compels is the saving of the children? Brave words written by a brave woman come and help us to do it:—

"This I say emphatically, that the evil which we have grappled with to save one of our own dear ones does not sully. It is the evil that we read about in novels and newspapers for our own amusement; it is the evil we weakly give way to in our lives; above all, it is the destroying evil that we have refused so much as to know about in our absorbing care for our own alabaster skin; it is that evil which defiles a woman. But the evil that we have grappled with in a life and death struggle to save a soul for whom Christ died does not sully; it clothes from head to foot with the white robe, it crowns with the golden crown."

There remains only one thing more to show. It was evening in an Indian town at a time of festival. The great pillared courts of the Temple were filled with worshippers and pilgrims from all over the Tamil country and from as far north as Benares. Men who eagerly grasped at anything printed in Sanscrit and knew nothing of our vernacular were scattered in little groups among the crowd, and we had freedom to go to them and give them what we could, and talk to the many others who would listen. Outside the moonlight was shining on the dark pile of the Temple tower, and upon the palms planted along the wall, which rises in its solid strength 30 feet high and encloses the whole Temple precincts. There were very few people out in the moonlight. It was too quiet there for them, too pure in its silvery whiteness. Inside the hall, with its great-doored rooms and recesses, there were earth-lights in abundance, flaring torches, smoking lamps and lanterns. And there was noise—the noise of words and of wailing Indian music. For up near the closed doors which open on the shrine within which the idol sat surrounded by a thousand lights, there was a band of musicians playing upon stringed instruments; sometimes they broke out excitedly and banged their drums and made their conch-shells blare.

Suddenly there was a tumultuous rush of every produceable sound; tom-tom, conch-shell, cymbal, flute, stringed instruments and bells burst into chorus together. The idol was going to be carried out from his innermost shrine behind the lights; and as the great doors moved slowly, the excitement became intense, the thrill of it quivered through all the hall and sent a tremor through the crowd out to the street. But we passed out and away, and turned into a quiet courtyard known to us and talked to the women there.

The Harebell Child

There were three, one the grandmother of the house, one her daughter, and another a friend. The grandmother and her daughter were Temple women, the eldest grandchild had been dedicated only a few months before. There were three more children, one Mungie, a lovable child of six, one a pretty three-year-old with a mop of beautiful curls, the youngest a baby just then asleep in its hammock; a little foot dangled out of the hammock, which was hung from a rafter in the verandah roof. We had come to talk to the grandmother and mother about the dear little six-year-old child, and hoped to find their heart.

But we seemed to talk to stone, hard as the stone of the Temple tower that rose above the roofs, black against the purity of the moonlit sky. It was a bitter half-hour. Some hours are like stabs to remember, or like the pitiless pressing down of an iron on living flesh. At last we could bear it no longer, and rose to go. As we left we heard the grandmother turn to her daughter's friend and say: "Though she heap gold on the floor as high as Mungie's neck, I would never let her go to those degraded Christians!"

Once again it was festival in the white light of the full moon, and once again we went to the same old Hindu town; for moonlight nights are times of opportunity, and the cool of evening brings strength for more than can be attempted in the heat of the day. And this time an adopted mother spoke words that ate like acid into steel as we listened.

Her adopted child is a slip of a girl, slim and light, with the ways of a shy thing of the woods. She made me think of a harebell growing all by itself in a rocky place, with stubbly grass about and a wide sky overhead. She was small and very sweet, and she slid on to my knee and whispered her lessons in my ear in the softest of little voices. She had gone to school for nearly a year, and liked to tell me all she knew. "Do you go to school now?" I asked her. She hung her head and did not answer. "Don't you go?" I repeated. She just breathed "No," and the little head dropped lower. "Why not?" I whispered as softly. The child hesitated. Some dim apprehension that the reason would not seem good to me troubled her, perhaps, for she would not answer. "Tell the Ammal, silly child!" said her foster-mother, who was standing near. "Tell her you are learning to dance and sing and get ready for the gods!" "I am learning to dance and sing and get ready for the gods," repeated the child obediently, lifting large, clear eyes to my face for a moment as if to read what was written there. A group of men stood near us. I turned to them. "Is it right to give this little child to a life like that?" I asked them then. They smiled a tolerant, kindly smile. "Certainly no one would call it right, but it is our custom," and they passed on. There was no sense of the pity of it:—

Poor little life that toddles half an hour,
Crowned with a flower or two, and then an end!

We had come to the town an hour or two earlier, and had seen, walking through the throng round the Temple, two bright young girls in white. No girls of their age, except Temple girls, would have been out at that hour of the evening, and we followed them home. They stopped when they reached the house where little Mungie lived, and then,

127

turning, saw us and salaamed. One of the two was Mungie's elder sister. Little Mungie ran out to meet her sister, and, seeing us, eagerly asked for a book. So we stood in the open moonlight, and the little one tried to spell out the words of a text to show us she had not forgotten all she had learned, even though she, too, had been taken from school, and had to learn pages of poetry and the Temple dances and songs.

The girls were jewelled and crowned with flowers, and they looked like flowers themselves; flowers in moonlight have a mystery about them not perceived in common day, but the mystery here was something wholly sorrowful. Everything about the children—they were hardly more than children—showed care and refinement of taste. There was no violent clash of colour; the only vivid colour note was the rich red of a silk underskirt that showed where the clinging folds of the white gold-embroidered *sari* were draped a little at the side. The effect was very dainty, and the girls' manners were modest and gentle. No one who did not know what the pretty dress meant that night would have dreamed it was but the mesh of a net made of white and gold.

But with all their pleasant manners it was evident the two girls looked upon us with a distinct aloofness. They glanced at us much as a brilliant bird of the air might be supposed to regard poultry, fowls of the cooped-up yard. Then they melted into the shadow of an archway behind the moonlit space, and we went on to another street and came upon little Sellamal, the harebell child; and, sitting down on the verandah which opens off the street, we heard her lessons as we have told, and got into conversation with her adopted mother.

We found her interested in listening to what we had to say about dedicating children to the service of the gods. She was extremely intelligent, and spoke Tamil such as one reads in books set for examination. It was easy to talk with her, for she saw the point of everything at once, and did not need to have truth broken up small and crumbled down and illustrated in half a dozen different ways before it could be understood. But the half-amused smile on the clever face told us how she regarded all we were saying. What was life and death earnestness to us was a game of words to her; a play the more to be enjoyed because, drawn by the sight of two Missie Ammals sitting together on the verandah, quite a little crowd had gathered, and were listening appreciatively.

"Now Listen to my Way"

"That is your way of looking at it; now listen to my way. Each land in all the world has its own customs and religion. Each has that which is best for it. Change, and you invite confusion and much unpleasantness. Also by changing you express your ignorance and pride. Why should the child presume to greater wisdom than its father? And now listen to me! I will show you the matter from our side!" ("Yes, venerable mother, continue!" interposed the crowd encouragingly.) "You seem to feel it a sad thing that little Sellamal should be trained as we are training her. You seem to feel it wrong, and almost, perhaps, disgrace. But if you could see my eldest daughter the centre of a thousand Brahmans and high-caste Hindus! If you could see every eye in that ring fixed upon her, upon her alone! If you could see the absorption—hardly do they dare to breathe lest they should miss a point of her beauty! Ah, you would know, could you see it all, upon whose side the glory lies and upon whose the shame! Compare that moment of exaltation with the grovelling life of your Christians! Low-minded, flesh-devouring, Christians, discerning not the difference between clean and unclean! Bah! And you would have my little Sellamal leave all this for that!"

"But afterwards? What comes afterwards?"

"What know I? What care I? That is a matter for the gods."

The child Sellamal listened to this, glancing from face to face with wistful, wondering eyes; and as I looked down upon her she looked up at me, and I looked deep into those eyes—such innocent eyes. Then something seemed to move the child, and she held up her face for a kiss.

This is only one Temple town. There are many such in the South. These things are not easy to look at for long. We turn away with burning eyes, and only for the children's sake could we ever look again. For their sake look again.

The World turned Black

It was early evening in a home of rest on the hills. A medical missionary, a woman of wide experience, was talking to a younger woman about the Temple children. She had lived for some time, unknowingly, next door to a Temple house in an Indian city. Night after night she said she was wakened by the cries of children—frightened cries, indignant cries, sometimes sharp cries as of pain. She inquired in the morning, but was always told the children had been punished for some naughtiness. "They were only being beaten." She was not satisfied, and tried to find out more through the police. But she feared the police were bribed to tell nothing, for she found out nothing through them. Later, by means of her medical work, she came full upon the truth. . . . "Why leave spaces with dotted lines? Why not write the whole fact?" wrote one who did not know what she asked. Once more we repeat it, to write the whole fact is impossible.

It is true this is not universal; in our part of the country it is not general, for the Temple child is considered of too much value to be lightly injured. But it is true beyond a doubt that inhumanity which may not be described is possible at any time in any Temple house.

Out in the garden little groups of missionaries walked together and talked. From a room near came the sound of a hymn. It was peaceful and beautiful everywhere, and the gold of sunset filled the air, and made the garden a glory land of radiant wonderful colour. But for one woman at least the world turned black. Only the thought of the children nerved her to go on.

CHAPTER XXXII

The Power behind the Work

"To Him difficulties are as nothing, and improbabilities of less than no account."— *Story of the China Inland Mission.*

THE Power behind the work is the interposition of God in answer to prayer.

Recently—so recently that it would be unwise to go into detail—we were in trouble about a little girl of ten or eleven, who, though not a Temple child, was exposed to imminent danger, and sorely needed deliverance. I happened to be alone at Dohnavur at the time, and did not know what to answer to the child's urgent message: "If I can escape to you" (this meant if she braved capture and its consequences, and fled across the fields alone at night), "can you protect me from my people?" To say "Yes" might have had fatal results. To say "No" seemed too impossible. The circumstances were such that great care was needed to avoid being entangled in legal complications; and as the Collector (Chief Magistrate) for our part of the district happened just then to be in our neighbourhood, I wrote asking for an appointment. Early next morning we met by the roadside. I had been up most of the night, and was tired and anxious; and I shall never forget the comfort that came through the quiet sympathy with which one who was quite a stranger to us all listened to the story, not as if it were a mere missionary trifle, but something worthy his attention. But nothing could be done. It was not a case where we had any ground for appeal to the law; and any attempt upon our part to help the child could only have resulted in more trouble afterwards, for we should certainly have had to give her up if she came to us.

As the inevitableness of this conclusion became more and more evident to me, it seemed as if a great strong wall were rising foot by foot between me and that little girl—a wall like the walls that enclose the Temples here, very high, very massive. But even Temple walls have doors, and I could not see any door in this wall. Nothing could bring that child to us but a Power enthroned above the wall, which could stoop and lift her over it. I do not remember what led to the question about what we expected would happen; but I remember that with that wall full in view I could only answer, "The interposition of God." Nothing else, nothing less, could do anything for that child.

Voices Blown on the Winds

Her case was complicated, if I may express it so, by the fact that though she knew very little—she had only had a few weeks' teaching and could not read—she had believed all we told her most simply and literally, and witnessed to her own people, whose reply to her had been: "You will see who is stronger, your God or ours! Do you think your Lord Jesus can deliver you from our hand, or prevent us from doing as we choose with you? We shall see!" And the case of an older girl who had been, as those who knew her best believed, drugged and then bent to her people's will, was quoted: "Did your Lord Jesus deliver her? Where is she to-day? And you think He will deliver you!" "But He will not let you hurt me," the child had answered fearlessly, though her strength was weakened even then by thirty hours without food; and, remembering one of the Bible stories she had heard during those weeks, she added, "I am Daniel, and you are the lions"—and she told them how the angel was sent to shut the lions' mouths. But she knew so little after all, and the bravest can be overborne, and she was only a little girl; so our hearts ached for her as we sent her the message: "You must not try to come to us. We cannot protect you. But Jesus is with you. He will not fail you. He says, 'Fear thou not, for I am with thee.'" That night they shut her up with a demon-possessed woman, that the terror of it might shake her faith in Christ. Next day they hinted that worse would happen soon. Our fear was lest her faith should fail before deliverance came.

Three and a half months of such tension as we have rarely known passed over us. Often during that time, when one thing after another happened contrariwise, as it appeared, and each event as it occurred seemed to add another foot to the wall that still grew higher, help to faith came to us through unexpected sources like voices blown on the winds.

Once it was something Lieut. Shackleton is reported to have said to Reuter's correspondent concerning his expedition to the South Pole: "Over and over again there were times when no mortal leadership could have availed us. It was during those times that we learned that some Power beyond our own guided our footsteps." And the illustrations which followed of Divine interposition were such that one at least who read, took courage; for the God of the great Ice-fields is the God of the Tropics.

Once it was a passage opened by chance in a friend's book—Pastor Agnorum. The subject of the paragraph is the schoolboy's attitude towards games: "Glimpses of his mind are sometimes given us, as on that day at Risingham when you refused to play in your boys' house-match, unless the other house excluded from their team a half-back who was under attainder through a recent row. They declined, and you stood out of it. The hush in the field when your orphaned team, in defiance of the odds, scored and again scored! Their supporters, in chaste awe at the marvel, could hardly shout: it was more like a sob: a judgment had so manifestly defended the right. The cricket professional, a man naturally devout, looked at me with eyes that confessed an interposition, and all came away quiet as a crowd from a cemetery. It was not a game of football we had looked at, it was a Mystery Play: we had been edified, and we hid it in our hearts."

And once, on the darkest day of all, it was the brave old family motto, on a letter which came by post: "Dieu défend le droit." It was something to be reminded that, in spite of appearances to the contrary, the kingdom is the Lord's, and He is Governor among the people.

"Eyes that confessed an interposition." The phrase was illuminated for us when God in very truth interposed in such fashion that every one saw it was His Hand, for no other hand could have done it. Then we, too, looked at each other with eyes that confessed an interposition. We had seen that which we should never forget; and until the time comes when it may be more fully told to the glory of our God, we have hid it in our hearts.

The reason we have outlined the story is to lead to a word we want to write very earnestly; it is this: Friends who care for the children, and believe this work on their behalf is something God intends should be done, "pray as if on that alone hung the issue of the day." More than we know depends upon our holding on in prayer.

All through those months there was prayer for that child in India and in England. The matter was so urgent that we made it widely known, and some at least of those who heard gave themselves up to prayer; not to the mere easy prayer which costs little and does less, but to that waiting upon God which does not rest till it knows it has obtained access, knows that it has the petition that it desires of Him. This sort of prayer costs.

"I Should utterly have fainted but—"

But to us down in the thick of the battle, it was strength to think of that prayer. We were very weary with hope deferred; for it was as if all the human hope in us were torn out of us, and tossed and buffeted every way till there was nothing left of it but an aching place where it had been. God works by means, as we all admit; and so every fresh development in a Court case in which the child was involved, every turn of affairs, where her relatives were concerned (and these turns were frequent), every little movement which seemed to promise something, was eagerly watched in the expectation that in it lay the interposition for which we waited. But it seemed as if our hopes were raised only to be dashed lower than ever, till we were cast upon the bare word of our God. It was given to us then as perhaps never before to penetrate to the innermost spring of consolation contained in those very old words: "I should utterly have fainted, but that I believe verily to see the goodness of the Lord in the land of the living. Oh, tarry thou the Lord's leisure: be strong, and He shall comfort thine heart; and put thou thy trust in the Lord."

This Divine Interposition has been very inspiring. We feel afresh the force of the question: "Is anything too hard for the Lord?" And we ask those whose hearts are with us to pray for more such manifestations of the Power that has not passed with the ages. Lord, teach us to pray!

For it has never been with us, "Come, see, and conquer," as if victory were an easy thing and a common. We have known what it is to toil for the salvation of some little life, and we have known the bitterness of defeat. We have had to stand on the shore of a dark and boundless sea, and watch that little white life swept off as by a great black wave. We have watched it drift further and further out on those desolate waters, till suddenly something from underneath caught it and sucked it down. And our very soul has gone out in the cry, "Would God I had died for thee!" and we too have gone "to the chamber over the gate" where we could be alone with our grief and our God—O little child, loved and lost, would God I had died for thee!

Should we forget these things? Should we bury them away lest they hurt some sensitive soul? Rather, could we forget them if we would, and dare we hide away the knowledge lest somewhere someone should be hurt? For it is not as if that black wave's work were a thing of the past: it has gone on for centuries unchecked: it is going on to-day.

Several months have passed since the chapters which precede this were written. We are now, with some of our converts who needed rest and change, in a place under the mountains a day's journey from Dohnavur. It is one of the holy places of the South; for the northern tributary of the chief river of this district falls over the cliffs at this point in a double leap of one hundred and eighty feet, and the waters are so disposed over a great rounded shoulder of rock that many people can bathe below in a long single file. To this fall thousands of pilgrims come from all parts of India, believing that such bathing is meritorious and cleanses away all sin. And as they are far from their own homes, and in measure out on holiday, we find them more than usually accessible and friendly. This morning I was on my way home after talk with the women, and was turning for a moment to look back upon the beautiful sorrowful scene—the flashing waterfall, the passing crowd of pilgrims, the radiance of sunshine on water, wood, and rock, when a Brahman, fresh from bathing, followed my look, and glancing at the New Testament and bag of Gospels in my hand, smiled indulgently and asked if we seriously thought these books and their teaching would ever materially influence India. "Look at that crowd," and he pointed to the people, his own caste people chiefly. "Have we been influenced?"

Deep Calleth unto Deep

Then he told me the story of the Falls, how ages ago a god, pitying the sins and the sufferings of the people, bathed on the ledge where the waters leap, and thereafter those waters were efficacious to the cleansing of sin from the one who believingly bathes. To the one who believes not, nothing happens beyond the cleansing of his body and its invigoration. "Even to you," he added, in his friendliness, "virtue of a sort is allowed; for do you not experience a certain exhilaration and a buoyancy of spirit and a pleasure beyond anything obtainable elsewhere ? This is due to the benevolence of our god, whose merits extend even to you."

He was an educated man; he had studied in a mission school, and afterwards in a Government college. He had read English books, and parts of our Bible were familiar to him. He assured me he found no more difficulty in accepting this legend than we did in accepting the story of our Saviour's incarnation. And then, standing in the Temple porch with its carved stone pillars, almost within touch of the great door that opens behind into the shrine, he led the way into the Higher Hinduism—that mysterious land which lies all around us in India, but is so seldom shown to us. And I listened till in turn he was persuaded to listen, and we read together from the Gospel which transcends in its simplicity the profoundest reach of Hindu thought: "In the beginning was the Word, and the Word was with God, and the Word was God." We did not pause till we came to the end of the paragraph. I could see how it appealed, for deep calleth unto deep; but he rose again up and up, and that unknown part of one's being which is more akin to the East than to the West, followed him and understood—when the door behind us creaked, and a sudden blast of turbulent music sprang out upon us, deafening us for a moment, and he said, "It is the morning worship. The priests and the Servants of the gods are worshipping within." It was like a fall from far-away heights to the very floor of things.

Then he told me how in the town three miles distant, the Benares of the South, the service of the gods was conducted with more elaborate ceremonial. "I could arrange for you to see it if you wished." I explained why I could not wish to see it, and asked him about the Servants of the gods, and about the little children. "Certainly there are little children. The Servants of the gods adopt them to continue the succession. How else could it be continued?"

CHAPTER XXXIII

If this were All

AN hour earlier three of us had stood together by the pool at the foot of the Falls, and watched the people bathe. At the edge of the rock an old grandmother had dealt valiantly with an indignant baby of two, whom, despite its struggles, she bathed after prolonged preparation of divers anointings, by holding it grimly, kicking and slippery though it was, under what must have seemed to it a terrible hurrying horror. When at last that baby emerged, it was too crushed in spirit to cry.

Beyond this little domestic scene was a group of half-reluctant women, longing and yet fearing to venture under the plunging waters; and beyond them again were the bathers, crowding but never jostling each other, on the narrow ledge upon and over which the Falls descend. Some were standing upright, with bowed heads, under the strong chastisement of the nearer heavier fall; some bent under it, as if overwhelmed with the thundering thud of its waters. Some were further on, where the white furies lash like living whips, and scourge and sting and scurry; and there the pilgrims were hardly visible, for the waters swept over them like a veil, and they looked in their weirdness and muteness like martyr ghosts. Further still some were carefully climbing the steps cut into the cliff, or standing as high as they could go upon an unguarded projection of rock, with eyes shut and folded hands, entirely oblivious apparently to the fact that showers of spray enveloped them, and the deep pool lay below.

I had never seen anything quite like this: it was such a strange commingling of the beautiful and sorrowful. The women—"fair"-skinned Brahman women they chanced to be—were in their usual graceful raiment of silk or cotton, all shades of soft reds, crimson, purple, blue, lightened with yellow and orange, which in the water looked like dull fire. Their golden and silver jewels gleamed in the sunlight, and their long black hair hung round faces like the faces one sees in pictures. The men wore their ordinary white, and the ascetics the salmon-tinted saffron of their profession.

Under the Waterfall

Then, as if to add an ethereal touch to it all, a rainbow spanned the Falls at that moment, and we saw the pilgrims through it or arched by it as they stood, some at either end of the bow where the colours painted the rock and the spray, and some in the space between. The sun struck the forest hanging on the steeps above, and it became a vivid thing in quick delight of greenness. It was something which, once seen, could hardly be forgotten. The triumphant stream of white set deep in the heart of a great horseshoe of rock and woods; the delicate, exquisite pleasure of colour; and the people in their un-self-consciousness, bathing and worshipping just as they wished, with for background rock and spray, and for a halo rainbow. To one who looked with sympathy the picture was a parable. You could not but see visions: you could not but dream dreams.

Then from the quiet heights crept a colony of monkeys, their chatter drowned in the roar of the Falls. On they came, wise and quaint, like the half-heard whispers of old-time jokes. And they bathed in the mimic pools above, as it seemed in imitation of the pilgrims, holding comical little heads under the light trickles.

And below the scene changed as a company of widows came and entered the Falls. They were all Brahmans and all old, and they shivered in their poor scanty garments of coarse white. Most of them were frail with long fasting and penance, and they prayed as they stood in the water or crouched under its weight. Such a one had sat on the stone under the special fall which, as the friend who had taken me observed with more forcefulness than sentiment, "comes down like a sack of potatoes." I had tried to stand it for a minute, but it pelted and pounded me so that less than a minute was enough, and I moved to make room for a Brahman widow who was bathing with me. And then she sat down on the stone, and the waters beat very heavily on the old grey head; but she sat on in her patience, her hands covering her face, and she prayed without one moment's intermission. How little she knew of the other prayer that rose beside hers through the rushing water—it was the first time I at least had ever prayed in a waterfall—"Oh, send forth Thy light and Thy truth; let them lead her!" She struggled up at last and caught my hand; then, steadying herself with an effort, she felt for the iron rod that protects the ledge, and blinded by the driving spray and benumbed by the beat of the water, she stumbled slowly out. But the wistful face had a look of content upon it, and her only concern was to finish the ceremonial out in the sunshine—she had brought her little offerings of a few flowers with her—and so, much as I longed to follow her and tell her of the cleansing of which this was only a type, it could not have been then. Oh, the rest it is at such a time to remember that the Lord is good to all, and His tender mercies are over all His works.

Below the pool, in the broad bed of the stream and on its banks, all was animation and happy simple life. Here the women were drying their garments, without taking them off, in a clever fashion of their own. There some were washing them in the stream. Children played about as they willed. But in and among the throng, anywhere, everywhere, we saw worshippers, standing or sitting facing the east, alone or in company, chanting names for the deity, or adoring and meditating in silence. Doubtless some were formal enough, but some were certainly sincere; and we felt if this were all there is to know in Hinduism, the time must soon come when a people so prepared would recognise in the Saviour and Lover of their souls, Him for whom they had been seeking so long, "if haply they might feel after Him and find Him."

But this is not all there is to know. Back out of sight behind the simple joyousness of life, to which the wholesome waters and the sparkling air and the beauty everywhere so graciously ministered, behind that wonderful wealth of thought as revealed in the Higher Hinduism which is born surely of nothing less than a longing after God—behind all this what do we find? Glory of mountain and waterfall, charm and delight of rainbow in spray; but what lies behind the coloured veil? What symbols are carved into the cliff? Whose name and power do they represent?

This book touches one of the hidden things; would that we could forget it! Sometimes, through these days as we sat on the rocks by the waterside, in the unobtrusive fashion of the Indian religious teacher, who makes no noise but waits for those who care to come, we have almost forgotten in the happiness of human touch with the people, the lovable women and children more especially, that anything dark and wicked and sad lay so very near. And then, suddenly as we have told, we have been reminded of it. We may not forgot it if we would. It is true that the thing we mean is disowned by the spiritual few, but to the multitude it is part of their religion. "Of course, Temple women must adopt young children; and they must be carefully trained, or they will not be meet for the service of the gods." So said the Brahman who only a moment before had led me into the mystic land, deep within which he loves to dwell: what does the training mean?

To-morrow, How will it Be?

A fortnight ago the friend to whom the child is dear took me to see the little girl described in a letter from an Indian sister as "a little dove in a cage." I did not find that she minded her cage. The bars have been gilded, the golden glitter has dazzled the child. She thinks her cage a pretty place, and she does not beat against its bars as she did in the earlier days of her captivity. As we talked with her we understood the change. When first she was taken from school the woman to whose training her mother has committed her gave her polluting poetry to read and learn, and she shrank from it, and would slip her Bible over the open page and read it instead. But gradually the poetry seemed less impossible; the atmosphere in which those vile stories grew and flourished was all about her; as she breathed it day by day she became accustomed to it; the sense of being stifled passed. The process of mental acclimatisation is not yet completed, the lovely little face

134

is still pure and strangely innocent in its expression; but there is a change, and it breaks the heart of the friend who loves her to see it. "I must learn my poetry. They will be angry if I do not learn it. What can I do?" And again, "Oh, the stories do not mean anything," said with a downward glance, as if the child-conscience still protested. But this was a fortnight ago. It is worse with that little girl to-day; there is less inward revolt; and to-morrow how will it be with her?

CHAPTER XXXIV

"To Continue the Succession"

FOR to-morrow holds no hope for these children so far as our power to save them to-day is concerned. It will be remembered that we felt we could do more for them by working quietly on our own lines than by appealing to the law; but lately, fearing lest we were possibly doing the law an injustice by taking it for granted that it was powerless to help us, we carefully gathered all the evidence we could about three typical children: one a child in moral danger, though not in actual Temple danger; another the adopted child of a Temple woman; the third a Temple woman's own child: and we submitted this evidence to a keen Indian Christian barrister, and asked for his advice.

L., the first child he deals with, the little "dove in the cage," is in charge of a woman of bad character, by the consent and arrangement of her mother. The mother speaks English as well as an Englishwoman, and her eldest son is studying for his degree in a Government college. Although Temple service is not intended, the proposed life is such that a similar course of training as that to which the Temple child is subjected, is now being carried on. This is the barrister's reply to my letter:—

"I have carefully perused the statements of the probable witnesses. L.'s mother is not a Temple woman, and the foster-mother also is not a Temple woman. The law of adoption relating to Temple women does not apply to them. The foster-mother, therefore, can have no legal claim to the child. But the mother has absolute control over the bringing-up of the child, and it would not be possible in the present state of the law to do anything for the child now."

S. This is the little one who whispered her texts to me in the moonlight, and whose foster-mother told her to tell me she was being trained for the Service of the gods. She is evidently destined to be a Temple woman. "The first question for consideration is how the old woman is related to her. If she is the adopted mother, or if she could successfully plead adoption of the child, the Civil Courts will be powerless to help. If we can get some reliable evidence that the child has not been adopted" (this is impossible) "we may be able to induce the British Courts to interfere on her behalf and say she shall not be devoted to Temple service until she attains her majority; but it would not be possible to induce the Courts to hand the child over to the Mission."

K., the little girl whose own mother is a Temple woman. She has been taught dancing, which to our mind was conclusive proof of her mother's intentions. To make sure we asked the question, to which the following is the reply: "No children of Hindu parents are taught dancing. Even the lowest caste woman thinks it beneath her dignity to dance, excepting professional devil-dancers, who are generally old women, mostly widows, of an hysterical temperament. When young children of women of doubtful character are taught dancing, it means they are going to be married to the idol. When children of Temple women are taught dancing the presumption is all the greater. But the difficulty in the case of K. is to get one who has higher claims to guardianship than the mother. In the case of a Temple woman's child there is no one.

"It is this which makes it impossible for the well-wishers of the children to interfere. . . . The law punishes only the offence committed and not the intent to commit, or even the preparation, unless it amounts to an attempt under the Penal Code."

.　.　.　.　.

"We have no Right to Interfere"

Bluebeards are not an institution in England; but if they were, and if one of the order were known to possess a cupboardful of pendent heads, would Englishmen sit quiet while he whetted his butcher's knife quite calmly on his doorstep? Would they say as he sat there in untroubled assurance of safety, feeling the edge of the blade with his thumb, and muttering almost audibly the name of his intended victim, "We have no right to interfere, he is only sharpening his knife; an intent to commit, or even the preparation for crime, is not punishable by law, unless it amounts to an attempt, and he has not 'attempted' yet." Surely, if such intent were not punishable it very soon would be. It would be found possible—who can doubt it?—to frame a new law, or amend the old one, so as to deal with Bluebeards. And a Committee of Vigilance would be appointed to ensure its effectual working.

Of course, the simile is absurdly inadequate, and breaks down at several important points, and the circumstances are vastly more difficult in India than they ever could be in England, just because India is India; but will it not at least be admitted that the law meant in kindness to the innocent is fatal to our purpose?—which is to save the children while they are still innocent.

.　.　.　.　.

We do not want to ask for anything unreasonable, but it seems to us that the law concerning adoption requires revision. In Mayne's *Hindu Law and Usage* it is stated that among Temple women it is customary in Madras and Pondicherry and in Western India to adopt girls to follow their adopted mother's profession: and the girls so adopted succeed to their property; no particular ceremonies are necessary, recognition alone being sufficient. In Calcutta and Bombay such adoptions have been held illegal, but in the Madras Presidency they are held to be legal. In a case where the validity of such adoption was questioned, the Madras High Court affirmed it, and it has now, "by a series of decisions, adopted the rule ;. . . which limits the illegality of adoption to cases where they involve the commission of an offence under the Criminal Code." This, as we have said, makes it entirely impossible to save the child through the law before her training is complete; and after it is complete it is too late to save her. Train a child from infancy to look upon a certain line of life as the one and only line for her, make the prospect attractive, and surround her with every possible unholy influence; in short, bend the twig and keep it bent for the greater part of sixteen years, or even only six—is there much room for doubt as to how it will grow? An heir to the property may be required; but with the facts of life before us, can we be content to allow the adoption of a child by a Temple woman to be so legalised that even if it can be proved to a moral certainty that her intention is to "continue the succession," nothing can be done?

What we Want

Then as to the guardianship: again we do not want to ask too much, but surely if it can be shown that no one else has moved to save the child (which argues that no one else has cared much about her salvation) we should not be disqualified for guardianship on the sole ground that we are not related? In such a case the relatives are the last people with whom she would be safe. An order may go forth from that nebulous and distant Impersonality, the British Government, to the effect that a certain child is not to be dedicated to gods during her minority. But far away in their villages the people smile at a simplicity which can imagine that commands can eventually affect purposes. They may delay the fulfilment of such purpose; but India can afford to wait.

We would have the law so amended, that whoever has been in earnest enough about the matter to try to save the child from destruction, should be given the right to protect her, if in spite of the odds against him he has honestly fought through a case and won.

"Is it not a sad thing," writes the Indian barrister—we quote his words because they seem to us worthy of notice at home—"that a Christian Government is unable to legislate to save the children of Temple women? I am sorry my opinion has made you sad. Giving my opinion as a lawyer, I could not take an optimistic view of the matter. *The law as it stands at present is against reform in matters of this kind.* Even should a good judge take a strong view of the matter, the High Court will stick to the very letter of the law."

So that, as things are, it comes to this: We must stand aside and watch the cup of poison being prepared—so openly prepared that everyone knows for which child it is being mixed. We must stand and wait and do nothing. We must see the little girl led up to the cup and persuaded to taste it. We must watch her gradually growing to like it, for it is flavoured and sweet. We must not beckon to her before she has drunk of it and say, "Come to us and we will tell you what is in that cup, and keep you safely from those who would make you drink it"; for "any attempt to induce the child to come to you, or any assistance given to help her to escape to you, would render you liable to prosecution for kidnapping—a criminal offence under the Penal Code." Any one of us would gladly go to prison if it would save the child; but the trouble is, it would not: for the law could only return her to her lawful guardians from whose hold we unlawfully detached her. We, not they, would be in the wrong; they did nothing unlawful in only preparing the cup. Does someone say that we put the case unfairly—that the law does not forbid us to warn the child, it only forbids us to snatch her away when the cup is merely being offered her? But remember, in our part of India at least, these cups are not given in public. The preparation is public enough, the bare tasting is public too; but the cup in its fulness is given in private, and once given, the poison works with stealthy but startling rapidity. Warn the child before she has drunk of it, and she does not understand you. Warn her after she has drunk, and the poison holds her from heeding.

Besides, to be very practical, what is the use of warning if we may only warn? Suppose our one isolated word weighs with the child against the word of mother or adopted mother, and all who stand for home to her; suppose she says (she would very rarely have the courage for any such proposal, but suppose she does say it): "May I come to you? and will you show me the way, for it is such a long way and I do not know how to find it? I should be so frightened, alone in the night" (the only time escape would be possible), "for I know they would run after me, and they can run faster than I!" What may we say to her? What may I say to the Harebell supposing she asks me this question? She is only six, and there are six long miles over broken country between her home and ours. We could not find it ourselves in the dark. But supposing she dared it all, and an angel were sent to guide her, have we any right to protect her? None whatever. If there are parents, or a parent, they or she have the right of parentage; if an adopted mother, the right of adoption.

We know that the law is framed to protect the good, and the rights of parentage cannot be too carefully guarded; but to one who has not a legal mind, but only sees a little girl in danger of her life, and has to stand with hands tied by a law intended to deal with totally different matters, it seems strange that things should be so. This is not the moment (if ever there is such a moment) to choose, for deliberate lawlessness; but there are times when the temptation is strong to break the law in the hope that, once broken, it may be amended. Only those who have had to go through it know what it is to stand and see that cup of poison being prepared for an unsuspicious child.

Then unto Thee we Turn

The last sentence in the barrister's letter begins with "I despair." The sentence is too pungent in its outspoken candour to copy into a book which may come back to India: "I despair": then unto Thee we turn, O Lord our God; for now, Lord, what is our hope? truly our hope is even in Thee: oh, help us against the enemy; for vain is the help of man. Hath God forgotten to be gracious? Will the Lord absent Himself for ever? O God, wherefore art Thou absent from us for so long? Look upon the Covenant, for all the earth is full of darkness and cruel habitations. Surely Thou hast seen it, for Thou beholdest ungodliness and wrong. The wicked boasteth of his heart's desire. He sitteth in the lurking-places of the villages: in the secret places doth he murder the innocent. He saith in his heart, "God hath forgotten: He hideth His face; He will never see it." Arise, O Lord God, lift up Thine hand! Up, Lord, disappoint him, and cast him down; deliver the children! Show Thy marvellous lovingkindness, Thou that art the Saviour of them which put their trust in Thee, from such as resist Thy right hand. Thy voice is mighty in operation: the voice of the Lord is a glorious voice. We wait for Thy lovingkindness, O God: be merciful unto the children: O God, be merciful unto the children, for our soul trusteth in Thee, and we call unto the Most High God, even unto the God that shall perform the cause which we have in hand. For Thou hast looked down from Thy sanctuary; out of heaven did the Lord behold the earth, that He might hear the mournings of such as are in captivity, and deliver the children appointed to death. Arise, O God, maintain Thine own cause! Our hope is in Thee, Who helpeth them to right that suffer wrong. The Lord looseth the prisoners. God is unto us a God of deliverances. Power belongeth unto Thee. Our soul hangeth upon Thee: Thou shalt show us wonderful things in Thy righteousness, O God of our salvation, Thou that art the hope of all the ends of the earth. And all men that see it shall say, This hath God done; for they shall perceive that it is His work. He shall deliver the children's souls from falsehood and wrong; for God is our King of old; the help that is done upon earth He doeth it Himself. Sure I am, the Lord will avenge the poor, and maintain the cause of the helpless. Why art thou so heavy, O my soul, and why art thou disquieted within me? Oh, put thy trust in God; for I will yet praise Him which is the help of my countenance and my God!

Are there any prayers like the old psalms in their intense sincerity? In the times when our heart is wounded within us we turn to these ancient human cries, and we find what we want in them.

Let us pray for the children of this generation being trained now "to continue the succession," whom nothing less than a Divine interposition can save. The hunters on these mountains dig pits to ensnare the poor wild beasts, and they cover them warily with leaves and grass: this sentence about the succession is just such a pit, with words for leaves and grass. Let us pray for miracles to happen where individual children are concerned, that the little feet in their ignorance may be hindered from running across those pits, for the fall is into miry clay, and the sides of the pit are slippery and very steep.

Let us Pray

More and more as we go on, and learn our utter inability to move a single pebble by ourselves, and the mighty power of God to upturn mountains with a touch, we realise how infinitely important it is to know how to pray. There is the restful prayer of committal to which the immediate answer is peace. We could not live without this sort of prayer; we should be crushed and overborne, and give up broken-hearted if it were not for that peace. But the Apostle speaks of another prayer that is wrestle, conflict, "agony." And if these little children are to be delivered and protected after their deliverance, and trained that if the Lord tarry and life's fierce battle has to be fought—and for them it may be very fierce—all that will be attempted against them shall fall harmless at their feet like arrows turned to feather-down; then some of us must be strong to meet the powers that will combat every inch of the field with us, and some of us must learn deeper things than we know yet about the solemn secret of prevailing prayer.

FOOTNOTES:

To-day (February 16, 1912) as I go through proofs of the second edition, I hear by post of a young girl in a distant city who lately escaped to a missionary, and asked for what he could not give her—protection. She had to return to her own home. In her despair, she drowned herself.

CHAPTER XXXV

What if she misses her Chance?

"Who would be planted chooseth not the soil
Or here or there, ;. . .
Lord even so
I ask one prayer,
The which if it be granted
It skills not where
Thou plantest me, only I would be planted."

T. E. Brown.

TWO pictures of two evenings rise as I write. One is of an English fireside in a country house. The lamps have been lighted, and the curtains drawn. The air is full of the undefined scent of chrysanthemums, and the stronger sweetness of hyacinths comes from a stand in the window. Curled up in a roomy arm-chair by the fire sits a girl with a kitten asleep on her lap. She is reading a missionary book.

The other this: a white carved cupola in the centre of a piece of water enclosed by white walls. People are sitting on the walls and pressing close about them in their thousands. A gorgeous barge is floating slowly round the shrine. There is very little moon, but the whole place is alight; sometimes the water is ablaze with ruby and amber; this fades, and a weird blue-green shimmers across the barge, and electric lamps at the corners of the square lend brilliancy to the scene. The barge is covered with crimson trappings, and hundreds of wreaths of white oleander hang curtain-wise round what is within—the god and goddess decked with jewels and smothered in flowers. Round and round the barge is poled, and in the coloured light all that is gaudy and tawdry is toned, and becomes only oriental and impressive; and the white shrine in the centre reflected in the calm coloured water appears in its alternating dimness, and shining more like a fairy creation than common handiwork.

We who were at the festival, three of us laden with packets of marked Gospels, met sometimes as we wandered about unobserved, losing ourselves in the crowd, that we might the more quietly continue that for which we were there; and in one such chance meeting we spoke of the English girl by the fireside, and longed to show her what we saw; and to show it with such earnestness that she would be drawn to inquire where her Master had most need of her. But no earnestness of writing can do much after all. It is true the eye affects the heart, and we would show what we have seen in the hope that even the second-hand sight might do something; but words are clumsy, and cannot discover to another that poignant thing the eye has power to transmit to the heart. And it is well that it is so, for something stronger and more consuming than human emotion can ever be must operate upon the heart if the life is to be moved to purpose. "A moving story" is worth little if it only moves the feelings. How far out of its selfish track does it move the life into ways of sacrifice? That is the question that matters. What if it cost? Did not Calvary cost? Away with the cold, calculating love that talks to itself about cost! God give us a pure passion of love that knows nothing of hesitation and grudging, and measuring, nothing of compromise! What if it seem impossible to face all that surrender may mean? Is there not provision for the impossible? "In the Old Testament we find that in almost every case of people being clothed with the Spirit it was for things which were impossible to them. To be filled with the Spirit means readiness for Him to take us out of our present sphere and put us anywhere away from our own choice into His choice for us." These words hold a message alike for us as we meet and pass in that Indian crowd, and for the girl by the fireside at home who wants to know her Lord's will that she may do it, and whose heart's prayer is: "May Thy grace, O Lord, make that possible to me which is impossible by nature."

"All the Way"

Let us have done with limitations, let us be simply sincere. How ashamed we shall be by and by of our insincerities:—

Thy vows are on me, oh to serve Thee truly,
Pants, pants my soul to perfectly obey!
Burn, burn, O Fire, O Wind, now winnow throughly!
Constrain, inspire to follow all the way!
Oh that in me
Thou, my Lord, may see
Of the travail of Thy soul,
And be satisfied.

We had only a few hours to spend in the town of the Floating Festival; and being anxious to discover how things were among the Temple community, I spent the first hour in their quarter, a block of substantial buildings each in its own compound, near the Temple. I saw the house from which two of our dearest children came, delivered by a miracle; it looked like a fortress with its wall all round, and upstairs balcony barred by a trellis. The street door was locked as the women were at the Festival. In another of less dignified appearance I saw a pretty woman of about twenty, dressed in pale blue and gold, evidently just ready to go out. One of those abandoned beings whose function it is to secure little children "to continue the succession" was in the house, and so nothing could be attempted but the most casual conversation. All the other houses in the block were locked as the women were out; but I saw a new house outside, built in best Indian style, and finely finished. It had been built for, and given as a free gift, to a noted Temple woman.

These houses would open, in the missionary sense of the word, but not in an afternoon. It would take time and careful endeavour to win an entrance. Such a worker would need to be one whom no disappointment could discourage, a woman to whom the word had been spoken, "Go, love, ;. . . according to the love of the Lord." When will such a worker come?

As I left the Temple quarter, I met my two companions who had been at work elsewhere, and we walked together to the place of festival. Tripping gaily along in front was a little maid with flowers in her hair. It was easy to know who she was, there was something in the very step that marked the light-footed Temple child. Poor little all-unconscious illustration of India's need of God!

Later on we saw the same illustration again, lighted up like a great transparency, the focus for a thousand eyes. For on the daïs of the barge, in the place of honour nearest the idols, stood three women and a child. The women were swathed in fold upon fold of rich violet silk, sprinkled all over with tinsel and gold; they were crowned with white flowers, wreathed round a golden ornament like a full moon set in their dark hair; and the effect of the whole, seen in the luminous flush of colour thrown upon them from the shore, was as if the night sky sparkling with stars had come down and robed them where they stood. Then when it paled, and sheet-lightning played, as it seemed, across water and barge and shrine, the effect was wholly mysterious. The three swaying forms—for they swayed keeping time to the music that never ceased—resembled one's idea of goddesses rather than familiar womenkind. To the Indian mind it was beautiful, bewilderingly beautiful; and the simple country-folk around drew deep breaths of admiration as they passed.

The little girl looked more human. She too was in violet silk and spangles and gold, and her little head was wreathed with flowers. It may have been her first Floating Festival, for she gazed about her with eyes full of guileless wonder, and the woman beside whom she stood laid a light, protecting hand upon her shoulder.

That Little Child!

That little child! How the sight of her held us in pity as the barge sailed slowly round. She was so near to us at times that we could almost have touched her when the barge came near the wall; and yet she was utterly remote, miles of space might have lain between; it was as if we and she belonged to different planets. And yet our little ones who might have been as she, were so close—we could almost feel their loving little arms round our necks at that moment—this child, how far away she was! Had one of us set foot on the place where she stood, the friendly thousands about us would have changed in a second into indignant furies, and so long as the memory of such impiety remained no white face would have been welcome at the Floating Festival.

We stood by the wall awhile and watched; the sorrow of it all sank into us. There in the holiest place of all, according to their thinking, close to the emblems of deity, they had set this grievous perversion of the holy and the pure. Right on the topmost pinnacle of everything known as religious there they had enthroned it, and robed it in starlight and crowned it as queens are crowned. "Oh, worship the Lord in the beauty of holiness!" "One thing have I desired of the Lord ;. . . to behold the fair beauty of the Lord"—such words open chasms of contrast. God pity them; like those of old, they know not what they do.

We came away, our books all sold and our strength of voice spent out, for everywhere people had listened; and as we came home, strong thanksgiving filled our hearts, thanks and praise unspeakable for the little lives safe in our nursery, for the two especially who but for God's interposition might have been on that barge—and oh, from the ground of our heart we were grateful that He had not let us miss His will concerning these little children. We thought of those special two with their dear little innocent ways. We could not think of them on the barge. We could not bear to think of it—again and again we thanked God, with humble adoring thanksgiving, that He kept us from missing our chance.

But the mere thinking of that intolerable thought brought us back upon another thought. What of that girl by the fireside? What if she misses her chance? We know, for letters confess it, that many a life has missed its chance. What of the woman, strong and keen, with pent-up energies waiting for she knows not what? What of the girl by the fireside crushing down the sense of an Under-call that will not let her rest? The work to which that Call would lead her will not be anything great: it will only mean little humble everyday doings wherever she is sent. But if the Call is a true Call from heaven, it will change to a song as she obeys; and through all the afterward of life, through all the loneliness that may come, through all the disillusions when her "dreams of fair romance which no day brings" slip away from her—and the usual and commonplace are all about her—then and for ever that song of the Lord will sing itself through the quiet places of her soul, and she will be sure—with the sureness that is just pure peace—that she is where her Master meant her to be.

"This I wish to do, this I Desire"

Not that we would write as if obedience must always mean service in the foreign field. We know it is not so: we know it may be quite the opposite; but shall we not be forgiven if we sometimes wonder how it is that with so much earnest Church life at home, with so many evangelistic campaigns, and conventions, there is so poor an output so far as these lands abroad are concerned? Can it be that so many are meant to stay at home? We would never urge any individual friend to come, far less would we plead for numbers, however great the need; we would only say this: Will the girl by the fireside, if such a one reads this book, lay the book aside, and spend an hour alone with her Lord? Will she, if she is in doubt about His will, wait upon Him to show it to her? Will she ask Him to fit her to obey? "And this I wish to do, this I desire; whatsoever is wanting in me, do Thou, I beseech Thee, vouchsafe to supply."

Forgive if we seem to intrude upon holy ground, but sometimes we see in imagination some great gathering of God's people, and we hear them singing hymns; and sometimes the beautiful words change into others not beautiful, but only insistent:—

The Lord our God arouse us! We are sleeping,
Dreaming we wake, while through the heavy night
Hardly perceived, the foe moves on unchallenged,
Glad of the dream that doth delay the fight.
O Christ our Captain, lead us out to battle!
Shame on the sloth of soldiers of the light!

.   .   .   .   .

Good Shepherd, Jesus, pitiful and tender,
To whom the least of straying lambs is known,
Grant us Thy love that wearieth not, nor faileth;
Grant us to seek Thy wayward sheep that roam
Far on the fell, until we find and fold them
Safe in the love of Thee, their own true home.

CHAPTER XXXVI

"Thy Sweet Original Joy"

Beacons of hope, ye appear!
Languor is not in your heart,
Weakness is not in your word,
Weariness not on your brow.

WITHIN the last few months a friend, a lover of books, sent me *The Trial and Death of Socrates*, translated into English by F. J. Church. Opening it for the first time, I came upon this passage:—

Socrates: "Does a man who is in training, and who is in earnest about it, attend to the praise and blame of all men, or of the one man who is doctor or trainer?"

Crito: "He attends only to the opinion of the one man."

Socrates: "Then he ought to fear the blame and welcome the praise of the one man, not the many?"

Crito: "Clearly."

And Socrates sums the argument thus: "To be brief; is it not the same in everything?"

Surely the wise man spoke the truth: it is the same in everything. The one thing that matters is the opinion of the One. If He is satisfied, all is well. If He is dissatisfied, the commendation of the many is as froth. "Blessed are the single-hearted, for they shall have much peace."

But Nature is full of pictures of bright companionship in service; the very stars shine in constellations. This book of the skies has been opening up to us of late. Who, to whom the experience is new, will forget the first evenings spent with even a small telescope, but powerful enough to distinguish double stars and unveil nebulæ? You look and see a single point of light, and you look again and twin suns float like globes of fire on a midnight sea; and sometimes one flashes golden yellow and the other blue, each the complement of the other, like two perfectly responsive friends. You look and see a little lonely cloud, a breath of transparent mist; you look and see spaces sprinkled with diamond dust, or something even more awesome, reaches of radiance that seem to lie on the borderland of Eternity.

And the shining glory lingers and lights up the common day, for the story of the sky is the story of life.

Far was the Call, and farther as I followed
Grew there a silence round my Lord and me—

is for ever the inner story, as for ever the stars must move alone, however close they are set in constellations or strewn in clusters; but in another sense is it not true that there is the joy of companionship and the pure inspiration of comradeship? God fits twin souls together like twin suns; and sometimes, with delicate thought for even the sensitive pleasure of colour, it is as if He arranged them so that the gold and the blue coalesce.

And we think of the places which were once blank, mere misty nothings to us. They sparkle now with friends. Some of them are familiar friends known through the wear and tear of life; some we shall never see till we meet above the stars. And there the nebula speaks its word of mystery beyond mystery, but all illuminated by the light from the other side.

Another Compelling Influence

In the work of which these chapters have told there has been the wonderful comfort of sympathy and help from fellow-missionaries of our own and sister missions; and, as all who have read, understand, nothing could have been done without the loyal co-operation of our Indian fellow-workers whose tenderness and patience can never be described. We think of the friends in the mission houses along the route of our long journeyings; we remember how no hour was too inconvenient to receive us and our tired baby travellers; we think of those who in weariness and painfulness have sought for the little children; and we think of those who have made the work possible by being God's good Ravens to us. We think of them all, and we wish their names could be written on the cover of this book instead of the name least worthy to be there. And now latest and nearest comfort and blessing, there are the two new "Sitties," whose first day with us made them one of us. What shall I render unto the Lord for all His benefits towards me?

The future is full of problems. Even now in these Nursery days questions are asked that are more easily asked than answered. We should be afraid if we looked too far ahead, so we do not look. We spend our strength on the day's work, the nearest "next thing" to our hands. But we would be blind and heedless if we made no provision for the future. We want to gather and lay up in store against that difficult time (should it ever come) a band of friends for the children, who will stand by them in prayer.

There has been another compelling influence. We recognise something in the Temple-children question which touches a wider issue than the personal or missionary. Those who have read *Queen Victoria's Letters* must have become conscious of a certain enlargement. Questions become great or dwindle into nothingness according as they affect the honour and the good of the Empire. We find ourselves instinctively "thinking Imperially," regarding things from the Throne side—from above instead of from below.

But

We fear exaggerated language. We would not exaggerate the importance of these little children or their cause. We have said that we realise, as we did not when first this work began, how very delicate and difficult a matter it would be for Government to take any really effective action, and less than effective action is useless. We recognise the value of our pledge of neutrality in religious matters, and we know what might happen if Government moved in a line which to India might appear to be contrary to the spirit of that pledge. It would be far better if India herself led the way and declared, as England declared when she passed the Industrial Schools Amendment Act of 1880, that she will not have her little children demoralised in either Temple houses recognised as such, or in any similar houses, such as those which abound in areas where the Temple child nominally is non-existent. But must we wait till India leads the way? Scattered all over the land there are men who are against this iniquity, and would surely be in favour of such legislation as would make for its destruction. But few would assert that the people as a whole are even nearly ready. A great wave of the Power of God, a great national turning towards Him, would, we know, sweep the iniquity out of the land as the waters of the Alpheus swept the stable-valley clean, in the old classic story. Oh for such a sudden flow of the River of God, which is full of water! But must we wait until it comes? Did we wait until India herself asked for the abolition of suttee? Surely what is needed is such legislation as has been found necessary at home, which empowers the magistrate to remove a child from a dangerous house, and deprives parents of all parental rights who are found responsible for its being forced into wrong. Surely such action would be Imperially right; and can a thing right in itself and carried out with a wise earnestness, ever eventually do harm? Must it not do good in the end, however agitating the immediate result may appear? Surely the one calm answer, "*It is Right*," will eventually silence all protest and still all turbulence!

Such a law, it is well to understand at the outset, will always be infinitely more difficult to enforce in India than in England, because of the immensely greater difficulty here in getting true evidence; and because—unless that River of God flow through the land—there will be for many a year the force of public opinion as a whole against us, or if not actively against, then inert and valueless. Caste feeling will come in and shield and circumvent and get behind the law. The Indian sensitiveness concerning Custom will be all awake and tingling with a hidden but intense vitality; and this, which is inevitable because natural, will have to be taken into account in every attempt made to enforce the law. The whole situation bristles with difficulties; but are difficulties an argument for doing nothing?

"Whoever buys hires or otherwise obtains possession of, whoever sells lets to hire or otherwise disposes of any minor under sixteen with the intent that such minor shall be employed or used for ;. . . any unlawful purpose or knowing it likely that such minor will be employed or used for any such purpose shall be liable to imprisonment up to a term of ten years and is also liable to a fine."

But where it appeared that certain minor girls were being taught singing and dancing and were being made to accompany their grandmother and Temple woman to the Temple with a view to qualify them as Temple women, it was held that this did not amount to a disposal of the minors within the meaning of the section.

Ought this interpretation of the Indian Penal Code to be possible? The proof the law requires at present, proof of the sale of the child or its definite dedication to the idol, is rarely obtainable. The fact that it is being taught singing and dancing (although it is well known, as the barrister's letter proves, that among orthodox Hindus such arts are never taught to little children except when the intention is bad) is not considered sufficient evidence upon which to base a conviction. To us it seems that the presence of the child in such a house, or in any house of known bad character, is sufficient proof that it is in danger of the worst wrong that can be inflicted upon a defenceless child—the demoralisation of its soul, the spoiling of its whole future life, before it has ever had a chance to know and choose the good.

From the Rock, Dohnavur.

And so we write it finally as our solemn conviction that there is need for a law like our own English law, and we add—and those who know India know how true this sentence is—*such legislation, however carefully framed, will be a delusion, a blind, a dead letter, unless men of no ordinary insight and courage and character are appointed to see that it is carried out.*

God grant that these chapters, written in weakness, may yet do something towards moving the Church to such prayer that the answer will be, as once before, that an angel will be sent to open the doors of the prison-house!

The frontispiece shows the rock to which we go sometimes when we feel the need of a climb and a blow. It is associated in our minds with a story:—"Between the passages by which Jonathan sought to go over unto the Philistines' garrison there was a sharp rock on the one side and a sharp rock on the other side. . . . And Jonathan said to the young man that bare his armour: 'Come and let us go over unto the garrison of these uncircumcised: it may be that the Lord will work for us: for there is no restraint to the Lord to save by many or by few.' And his armour-bearer said unto him: 'Do all that is in thine heart: turn thee, behold I am with thee according to thy heart.'"

We have a rock to climb, and there is nothing the least romantic about it. We shall have to climb it "upon our hands and upon our feet." It is all grim earnest. "We make our way wrapped in glamour to the Supreme Good, the summit," writes Guido Rey, the mountaineer, in the joy of his heart. But later it is: "One precipice fell away at my feet, and another rose above me. . . . It was no place for singing." Friends, we shall come to such places on the Matterhorn of life. As we follow the Gleam wherever it leads, may we count upon the upholding of those for whom we have written—the lovers of little children?

"So God maketh His Precious Opal"

And now, in conclusion, all I would say has already been so perfectly said, that I cannot do better than copy from the writings of two who fought a good fight and have been crowned—Miss Ellice Hopkins, brave, sensitive, soldier-soul on the hardest of life's battlefields; and George Herbert, courtier, poet, and saint. "Often in that nameless discouragement," wrote Miss Hopkins, as she lay slowly dying, "before unfinished tasks, unfulfilled aims and broken efforts, I have thought of how the creative Word has fashioned the opal, made it of the same stuff as desert sands, mere silica—not a crystallised stone like the diamond, but rather a stone with a broken heart, traversed by hundreds of small fissures which let in the air, the breath, as the Spirit is called in the Greek of our Testament; and through those two transparent mediums of such different density it is enabled to refract the light, and reflect every lovely hue of heaven, while at its heart burns a mysterious spot of fire. When we feel, therefore, as I have often done, nothing but cracks and desert dust, we can say: So God maketh His precious opal!"

We would never willingly disguise one fraction of the truth in our desire to win sympathy and true co-operation. There will be hours of nameless discouragement for all who climb the rock. For some there will be the "broken heart."

And yet there is a joy that is worth it all a thousand times—well worth it all. Who that has known it will doubt it? This reach of water recalls it. The palms, as we look at them, seem to lift their heads in solemn consciousness of it. For the water-side—where we stand with those for whom we have travailed in soul, when for the first time they publicly confess their faith in Christ—is a sacred place to us.

THE PLACE OF BAPTISM.

Has our story wandered sometimes into sorrowful ways? To be true it has to be sorrowful sometimes. We look back to the day of its beginning, the day that our first little Temple child came and opened a new door to us.

Since that time many a bitter storm
My soul hath felt, e'en able to destroy,
Had the malicious and ill-meaning harm
His swing and sway;
But still Thy sweet original joy
Sprung from Thine eye did work within my soul,
And surging griefs when they grew bold control,
And got the day.

It is true. Many a bitter storm has come; there have been the shock and the darkness of new knowledge of evil, and grief beside which all other pain pales, the grief of helplessness in the face of unspeakable wrong. But still, above and within, and around, like an atmosphere, like a fountain, there has been something bright, even that "sweet original joy" which nothing can darken or quench.

If Thy first glance so powerful be
A mirth but opened and sealed up again,
What wonders shall we feel when we shall see
Thy full-orbed love!
When Thou shalt look us out of pain,
And one aspect of Thine spend in delight,
More than a thousand worlds' disburse in light
In heaven above!

And not alone, oh, not alone, shall we see Him as He is! There will be the little children too.

CPSIA information can be obtained
at www.ICGtesting.com
Printed in the USA
LVHW010953030422
715184LV00010B/1115